REDEMPTION

Time to Stop

Tania Park

ISBN: 978-0-6455254-0-3 (Paperback)
ISBN: 978-0-6455254-2-7 (E-book)

A catalogue record for this book is available from the National Library of Australia

Tania Park Publishing
For all enquires contact the author at:
goldpark3@gmail.com

DEDICATION

Thank you to the members of the three writing groups I attend and help facilitate. Each one has had some sort of input into each chapter, be it by listening to me read it out, pointing out silly typos and offering suggestions to make a sentence, scene or chapter better.

Special thanks to Karen Woodward, Leonie Gorman and Ann Grylls who have been particularly picky with their red pens and even more important, endowing me with never-ending encouragement.

Thank you to those who read, Retribution, the pre-cursor to this book. So many asked – what happens next? At the time I had no idea. Now, the ideas have gelled.

Other Books by the Author

The Only Way I Know: 2011 - Biography

Mistaken: 2015 – Crime/mystery/romance
Retribution: 2015 – Crime/mystery
Blind Justice: 2016 – Crime/mystery
Commended 2016 Christina Stead National Literary Awards.
Road Trip: 2016 – Adventure/mystery
The Swan: 2018 - Crime/mystery/romance
Finalist 2020 The Wishing Shelf International Awards.
Stalked: 2019 - Psychological Thriller
Long listed 2020 Davitt Awards.
Double Cross: 2020 – White collar crime
Long listed 2021 Davitt Awards
The Chest: 2021 – Mystery/crime
Beloved Intruder: 2022 – Romance -*Third place – Romance Writers of Australia – Sapphire Award.*
Workshop Workings: 2023 – Collection of Winning short stories and poems created in writing workshops.
Jilted in Greece: 2024 – Romance
The Price of Freedom: 2024 - Romance

One

It was hard to maintain an act of normalcy each time the pain writhed through his gut. He would much rather roll onto his side and curl into a ball than make out he was fit and well. An underlying layer of hospital scent hovered while stronger antiseptic tickled his nose. Desperate to stifle the urge, Rico Giovannazzo squeezed his nostrils tight but the sneeze defeated his will. A long groan followed at the wave of agony. On a held breath to keep his body still, he eyed the lawyer. A serious frown marred James Ward's face while he took his time to study each page on the side table before he signed at the bottom. At last, he refolded the lot together and placed them in the pocket of his suit jacket.

'Is there anything else?' James stood, lifted the metal chair and *thunked* it against the wall. He winced as he took more care to move it away a fraction. 'Sorry.'

'Take care of Amanda for me.'

'I…'

'I know you care about her. I see it in your eyes whenever her name is mentioned. I also noticed the way you treated her at the barbecue. She deserves a good man like you.'

'I barely know her. We met little more than a week ago.'

'I fell in love with her the first day we met. She was my only love. I wish she had come today but tell her I understand. All I wanted was to see her one last time, to explain, apologise and beg her forgiveness. I appreciate your time - and apologise to your brother. My intention wasn't to harm him, but…'

'He fought back,' James interrupted. 'Said he walked into your knife. You didn't deliberately stab him.'

'Yes. I now realise he did what he did to protect Amanda. Thank you for coming but now I need to phone my mother and two sisters. I'd rather be the one to break the news to them. I don't think they are yet aware of my father's arrest. But then again maybe they do know since both my brothers-in-law work for the bastard.'

James nodded and left. The moment the door closed on the lawyer's back, Rico wriggled his hand under the pillow, patted around, grasped the rest of the pills and drew them out. No way would he go back to gaol. He'd served his time, paid for the worst moment of his life. Yet now he'd stuffed up again. Amanda had gone. Without her, life meant zilch. With a sip of water to wash each down, he took his time to swallow the pills one-by-one.

It had been easier than he'd thought to break into the pharmacy on this floor. To leave little indication he'd been there he took a single pill from as many packets he figured were strong enough to be lethal if taken in quantity. A mixture of chemicals had to be more effective than a handful of the same medication. Some names he recognised. Others he had a vague idea of their potency from the poison's rating printed on each box but didn't have a clue how they would react with each other. All he could do was pray they worked before any medical staff came to check on him. He studied the last pill, popped it on his tongue, added the last of the water, swallowed.

'Please let them take effect fast,' he said to himself as he settled back against the pile of pillows. The white linen puffed up around his head and shoulders. At least he would be comfortable while departing this world and he wouldn't be around to suffer the consequences of grassing on his father. It had to be done to end his evil regime.

To fill in time, he dialled dear, sweet Mama for a final chat. Darkness seemed appropriate for his mood so he switched off the bedside lamp but streaks of sunlight managed to thwart his desire and peek through cracks in the drawn blind. With a sigh, he turned from the intrusion and squirmed to get more comfortable on the firm mattress. 'Please, Mama, pick up.'

It was impossible to hold back a smile at her voice, the brightness a hint she didn't yet know of his father's arrest since she didn't mention it nor sound distraught. If she knew there would be wild rants between bouts of tears, although he couldn't figure out why she would be upset after thirty-five years of denigration, put-downs and bullying. It amazed him how she'd been such a faithful wife and great mother with so many years ruled by an autocrat. She was always biddable, with a smile, although often he noticed the smile was forced. Rico still wasn't sure if she understood, or even had knowledge of her husband's dark life. For the amount of money he spent, she must have a slight suspicion for District Court judges were paid well, but not to the extent of the luxuries she enjoyed.

Eager to enjoy the last moments of his life with the one person in his family he loved, he spoke at length until a heavy drowsiness dragged his eyes shut and an incredible pain gripped his innards. His breath caught. 'I love you, Mama,' he managed before a finger clicked off the connection and he dropped the phone in the open drawer of the bedside cabinet. The screech as he juggled the drawer shut, grated raw nerves and sent a shudder weaving down his spine. His last words to Mama. How many people never got the chance to say goodbye. Regret surged. She would be in a world of pain when she learned the truth and since he was on the other side of the country and about to die, he wouldn't be there to support her.

Desperate to not let his body eject the strong medication, he gulped down rising acid, closed his eyes and pictured Amanda. Memories flashed of the glorious months of their courtship. While he waited for the pills to take him from the life he hated an image of her in her wedding gown centred in his mind. So beautiful. So vibrant. So adorable. 'God knows how much I love you, Sweetheart,' he groaned as another jolt of agony ripped through him. To gain some relief he turned onto his side, hugged the end of a pillow and forced his mind to ignore the pain. Eyes open he took one last look at the world, one last vision of life. A pale grey wall with a metal chair at a slight angle. A closed door with a thin strip of light determined to sneak its way in underneath. Two printed posters pasted to the door, one a fire escape route, the other telling him to avoid falls by pressing the green button to ask for help. The faint hum of an air-conditioner is the only sound inside, the scrape of trolley wheels and a hushed murmur of voices in the distance outside.

It disconcerted him the way darkness descended in waves, accompanied by strong jabs of agony as though a blunt serrated knife tore away at innards which churned and boiled. He hadn't imagined death would be like this or take so long. He thought it might be peaceful and painless but then again he didn't deserve calm and serenity. He, Enrico Joseph Giovannazzo, had destroyed Amanda's life - or at least his bastard of a father had.

Heavy eyelids dropped of their own accord. Somewhere in the dark fuzziness, he thought someone shouted and alarms clanged but there was no heat or smoke from fire. An incredible agony settled in his gut followed by a painful thump on his chest and sear of heat in his throat. Ah, the fire was in his throat.

Voices.

Jerks.

Shouts.

Suffocation.

Darkness.

Two

*B*eep - beep - beep - beep.

Apart from regular beeps and swishes, the silence was profound. It was cold but he expected cold with death. Rico wanted to open his eyes but leaden lids wouldn't move. Some strange object ran over his face and his arms were paralysed despite willing them to move. It hurt to swallow. A rasp had been jammed down his throat.

'At last, you are awake.' The voice was high and sweet. An angel? He expected the devil.

A buzzer beeped near his ear. He tried to turn towards the sound to see what would beep in hell but like the rest of his body, neither his head nor neck would obey his mind.

'The doctor is on his way.'

Doctor? A doctor in hell?

A sudden bright red haze through closed lids was followed by pressure on one eye. The lid lifted. A bright light shocked his foggy brain to awareness.

'One of the drugs we gave to intubate you caused temporary paralysis.' A male voice this time. 'When it wears off you will feel as though a fully laden fifty-metre road-train is constantly running over you. I can't give you any painkillers. Your system can't handle any more chemicals. You're a lucky man. We almost lost you. Your stomach has been pumped and your throat probably feels like steel-wool has scoured away the lining.'

'Lucky?' he squeaked but it came out as a gurgle. How the hell was he lucky to be alive when he was desperate to get away from the fallout of grassing on one of the biggest crime gang bosses in the entire country.

'You won't be able to speak with a tube down your throat. You have fluids going in via a canula to dilute the poisons in your blood stream and a catheter to drain the fluid out. The best thing for you right now is to sleep.'

Isn't that what he wanted - to sleep? On a permanent basis.

'Ah, your finger moved. A good sign. Soon you will be able to move. Rest well.' A shuffle was followed by fading footsteps. The barely audible swish of a door and a soft snick. He was alone.

It took a moment to figure out the hisses came from a machine pumping oxygen into his lungs. The cold irritated his nasal passages. Well, at least his ears worked. And his lungs. He concentrated on fingers, forced a wriggle on the first finger of both hands. The thumb. It moved but felt weird. Not quite pins and needles but heavy as though weighted down with lead. He turned his thoughts to his toes, managed a movement - he thought, but wasn't sure. His entire body was a stranger.

'You should sleep a while longer. Let nature do the healing.' The same sweet voice startled him. A warm hand wrapped around his: one he could actually sense. It had been an eternity since he'd felt a woman's gentle touch. Too long. He opened his mouth to speak. A groan came out. Embarrassed, he did as the doctor suggested and quit the fight to move. Instead, he forced tense muscles to relax and centred his concentration on the cold spurts of oxygen as it hissed in and out.

A dull light came from the left but at least his eyes had opened with ease. Rico turned his head towards the sheen, surprised his neck now moved. A woman dressed in pink scrubs sat in a cushioned metal chair on the other side of a raft of medical machinery. An open book rested on her lap. Pretty, he thought. Light brown hair scraped back in a bun. A pen in the pocket of her top dangled – ready to fall. She glanced up, smiled, caught the pen and replaced it.

'Good morning.' She stood, adjusted a monitor, glanced at him and smiled again. 'You are out of danger but the doctor instructed me to call him when you roused.' She removed a pager from the pocket of her cotton pants, pressed and spoke before re-pocketing the pager. She straightened the sheet and blanket, placed a warm hand on his brow. 'How do you feel?'

'Like crap. Sorry,' he apologised at her startled eyes. 'The doctor was right. There's a road train running over me.' It was a surprise when he realised he could talk with no rasp down his throat although there was a kind of dryness in his mouth that wanted to suck his tongue to the roof.

'It won't last long and there's no need to apologise for expressing how you feel.' Cool fingers spread the lids of each eye apart before a flash of light centred into each. 'You must be thirsty, here.' A paper cup with a bent straw poked over the edge, appeared before his eyes. When he struggled to lift his head high enough to sip, the nurse eased one arm behind his shoulders and supported him a tad higher. Icy water ran over his parched tongue. He swished and swallowed the welcome moisture, took another long suck. So darn good.

'Not too much.' The nurse placed the cup on the side cupboard and eased him back down onto the soft mound of pillows. 'Too much at one time might cause you to vomit.'

'Thank you, I needed that but even more I need to talk to the lawyer who was in here before… hell, how long have I been out to it?'

'About twelve hours.' Her soft hand went back to his, covered his wrist for a second before she went back to study the monitors.

'You been here all twelve hours?' Rico asked.

'No, I've not long come back on duty. Another nurse kept watch during the night. What's this about a lawyer?'

'James Ward. He was here before…' He had no idea what to say. 'We spoke. I need to see him again. It's important.' It sure was. What the hell was he supposed to do now? If word got out he was alive, in a hospital bed, vulnerable... damn, what a mess. His father had long tentacles in places most people would never even think of. A shiver wound through him and managed to wake up every one of those wheels of the road-train. His lungs stalled until the pain subsided a fraction but enough to be game to ease the breath out to avoid too much movement.

Rico now recalled the old bastard had been arrested. Even so, there were men on his payroll from every state police force and the legal fraternity as well as a whole host of low life who would do anything to earn enough for the next fix, or grasp at a cash payment. Payment to pay Rico a visit, with a gun, or a knife and evil intent. Was the bastard even still in gaol? Given his position he must be able wangle his way out. Rico swore under his breath, glanced at the nurse who looked way too young to be in her position.

'Sorry, but I must speak with James Ward. His card is with my things, in the drawer I think, but am not sure. I can't remember.' He pointed to the bedside cabinet but grimaced at the stab of pain. 'You can use my phone to call him. Tell him it's urgent.'

A frown creased her face. 'I'm not...'

'Please. The man knows me, knows the danger I'm in.'

'Danger?'

'It's complicated and to tell you any details could put you in danger as well.'

Her gasp was quiet while all colour drained from her face. Before he could say more, the door to the room swished open, heavy footsteps approached.

His body went taut. Could be anyone here, even his father's cohorts. It didn't take long for messages to pass along the razor-sharp wire of his father's network. Eyes hooded, lips thin with an odd twist, the man who entered wore scrubs, blue this time but why did Rico even notice the colour of scrubs?

'Ah, you are with us again.' When Rico recognised the voice he forced the tension in his muscles to ease off. Same doctor – not an assassin. 'How's he doing?' The doctor stood next to the monitor and studied the images.

'BP and pulse back to normal, as is the temp. Patient is lucid but doesn't appreciate the road train.' The nurse grinned at Rico before she turned to the doctor.

The doctor smiled. 'All are back to normal. Good, very good.' He came to Rico's side. 'No solid food for a while. You'll need to stay in for at least another twenty-four hours. Now let me check your wound.' The doctor lifted the bed covers and probed Rico's genitals.

The wound he'd forgotten about. Events crowded into his brain in an almighty rush. God, when was it? How many days had he been here?

Amanda, the lawyer's brother – Jonathan, the fight. Hell, where did Amanda learn to fight like that?

'Looks good, no infection. Stitches need to be removed in six days but no sex for a while.'

Rico snorted. He hadn't had sex for so long he'd forgotten what it felt like. The last time? He swept a hand across his eyes at the memory. Amanda. Their wedding night. The night his life went to hell. All thanks to his bastard of a father.

'When can I get out of here?'

'At least twenty-four hours. There could be residual effects from some of the pills you took even though I think we got most out in time. You need to thank your lawyer for saving your life.'

'My lawyer? What do you mean?'

'He suspected something wasn't right. Gave us the heads up to check on you. Lucky for you we did.'

'I'm better off dead.'

'I'm sure that can't be true.' The doctor patted Rico's hand. 'Every problem has a solution, even dire problems. We can put you onto suitable resources.'

'Shrinks? No thanks. I'm far from psycho.'

'You want to talk about it?'

Rico laughed, winced at the trident stab into abdominal organs. 'The one person who can help me now is the man I want to curse for giving you the heads up – the lawyer. Can you get all these tubes and wires out of me?' He swept his hand over spaghetti junction. They hadn't been there when… hell, what day is it?

'Not yet.'

'When?'

'Give it another four hours or so. It's best to keep the fluids up to flush out your system. I'll call back, see how much you have improved. Best thing for you is to rest.'

Rico laughed again but regretted it when every atom in his body rebelled. 'What choice do I have? Before you go, can you hand me my phone and the card from the lawyer?' He pointed to the drawer. 'In there, I hope, but my brain is still a bit hazy.'

This time it was the doctor who laughed but he opened the drawer, searched around, drew out a card and phone.

Rico waited until the doctor left before he dared dial the number. When he glanced down at the phone he noticed the battery was low. Damn, he didn't have a charger with him. It was in the hotel along with all of his gear. It took too many rings before James Ward gave his name.

'You're a bastard,' Rico said. 'But I need to see you. Now. It's imperative.'

Three

*T*hwack. Every muscle in Rico's body tensed at the slap on the door. Every atom stood to attention as the door *swished*. When he recognised the huge frame of James Ward, the air whooshed from his lungs as he slumped back against the pillows. At this rate nervous tension would achieve what pills hadn't.

'You wanted to see me?' James strode across the polished linoleum, each footfall echoed in the silence. Even though he wore a dark suit, the knot of the yellow tie hung loose and the top two shirt buttons were undone.

'Why?' Rico stuttered with edgy nerves not yet settled.

'Why what?'

'Why did you speak to the staff? And how did you know?'

James quirked up one eyebrow along with one corner of his mouth, which soon turned into a grin. 'I'm a lawyer. I'm trained to read people. It's what I'm good at. The signs were obvious, especially when you handed me your will. The message was lit up in bright iridescent lights. As to why? I didn't see you to be a coward and suicide is a cowardly act. You're a much stronger person than a coward. You stood up to your father.' A nerve-stretching racket ensued as James dragged the chair from the far wall and eased down as though he was afraid his massive build would break the chair. 'And we might want more information from you. Details you alone can give.'

'I'm a dead man in any case. The minute the old bastard figures out it was me who gave him up, he'll have someone here to finish me off.'

'He's your father. Fathers don't have their own child assassinated.'

'He's a bastard. The so-called family is his law, his world. Nothing and no-one else matters if it gets in way of the family. Not even real family members. You have no idea.'

'It's unlikely he'll be able to get any messages out. He won't be given bail and will be kept in isolation. What's so urgent? I'm a busy man with a new court case to prepare. I'm supposed to be on my way to interview a witness.'

'You have to get me out of here.'

'You know I can't. I have no influence.'

'Sure you do. What about the fact I gave so many details about the entire organisation?'

'You will be protected. The top brass have ensured your information will carry a huge weight to keep you out of gaol. There's an armed officer outside your door. You have twenty-four hour protection. When you are released from hospital you'll be taken into protective custody. You did skip parole, amongst other indiscretions. You kidnapped and injured my brother although he hasn't pressed any charges and won't, plus there's the terror you caused Amy.'

'Amanda.'

'Her name was changed by deed poll five years ago. Amanda no longer exists in the legal sense.'

'She'll always be Amanda to me. Where is she?'

James laughed. 'Even if I knew where she is right now, I wouldn't tell you. Amy was given the opportunity to meet with you but she declined. Give her a break. Her life has been pure hell since the day you beat the crap out of her. On your wedding night. Who beats up their new wife on the first night?' James rubbed a hand through his hair as he shook his head. 'Even when you first landed in gaol, your father tormented her until the Feds gave her a new identity. Poor girl never broke any law or committed any sins, yet she is the one who suffered horrific injuries and has lived on tenterhooks for the past five years. If you love her, let her be. Her happiness must be worth more to you than a chat.'

Rico cringed. 'What you say makes sense but I still love her, always will. I just want to talk to her, apologise, make peace.'

'I think there's more to it. I'm sure you want to get back with her, but she is adamant she never wants to see you again. Can't say I blame her. What you did was abhorrent, to say the least.'

Rico winced as he hunched further into the pillows. The guilt and shame bit hard. 'You don't think I'm horrified? I still don't remember the incident. It was detailed in court but even after all this time my mind is still blank about those minutes. One second I was kissing my beautiful wife. The next second it was as though a bolt of lightning hit me in the head and I went crazy. When... oh God, when I came to, Amanda... the mess. She was naked, her dress torn to shreds. She just lay there, unmoving, a stream of tears and smudged make-up down her face, smears of blood. I didn't know what had happened, didn't know what to do. I ran to get my car close to the hotel front door to take her to hospital. Came back. She was gone. I searched the hotel, inside and out but couldn't find any trace of her. It was those damn steroids, thanks to the old bastard.'

'You're the one who put them in your mouth. Your responsibility.'

A snort escaped Rico's nose. 'Yeah, on my father's insistence. Nobody says no to my father, not even Mama.' He shook his head. 'You have no idea what he's like.'

'I'm sorry. No-one deserves to be brought up in such a way but at the time you lived in your own home, independent of your parents. You popped the pills even when you knew they were illegal and stupid.'

'I know, I know – now. But I had no idea about the libido loss nor what would happen when the steroids reacted with the damn Viagra.' He raised one hand in the air in a dismissive sweep.

'But now you do. I trust you learnt a valuable lesson.'

'And some.'

'I must go.' James rose and swept the chair back to where it stood before, this time with more care so it didn't hit the wall.

'Before you go, I want you to be my lawyer when this all gets to court.'

James spun around. His stunned face told a story. 'You can't be serious.'

'Sure, I'm serious.'

'Even if I wanted to, I can't. I'm tied up with cases until May when I take annual leave. I have a date with my daughter in Paris.' He smiled. 'I've booked a table at the highest restaurant of the Eiffel Tower as a surprise for her. No way will I let work prevent me from catching up with my daughter.' The moment the words were out, he grimaced. 'I can give you names of good lawyers but I can't represent you.'

'Can't or won't?'

'Probably both but right now I don't have the time to take on new cases. I'll be snowed under until I go on leave. I have current cases due to be heard in court. I've got your mobile number. I'll message you with a couple of names. Good lawyers – not on the take.'

'You might want to give me the names so I can check.'

'Names not on the list you've already given me.' He shook his head. 'I still find it hard to believe quite a few of those names. Others, I'm not so surprised, which is a damn shame. But I guess like all professions, there is always someone who is less scrupulous than we'd hope for.'

'How many were arrested?'

'A lot. Not all. No more than they could research in a hurry to get reasonable grounds to obtain warrants to arrest. And believe me, they had an awful lot of staff in every state who worked hours of overtime to do in-depth investigations, based on your information. None of those arrested will be released on bail. What usually takes months to investigate, had to be done in hours but the detail of your information was vital. The authorities won't forget what you did.'

'Dad's a judge - knows all the loopholes. He'll get out.'

'Not a chance. He's the one man who doesn't have a hope in hell of being granted bail. I doubt he'll even be able to have any visitors.'

'Not even Mama? I'm almost certain she doesn't have a clue about Dad's extra-curricular activities.' Rico put air quotation marks around the last three words.

James laughed. 'Experience tells me women know a darn sight more about their men's secrets than they ever let on unless crunch time occurs. In particular, wives who are denied justice in the marriage. They tend to explode with all the details they've stored away if it means they can give some form of pay-back.'

Rico quirked up one eyebrow. 'Speaking from personal experience?'

'I was never stupid enough to keep secrets from my wife and I'd appreciate it if you didn't malign her. She was one in a million.'

'Was?'

'Yes, she died.'

'Sorry, I apologise.'

James turned to leave but paused and swung back. 'I don't believe you're all bad. Stupid, maybe. Especially the way you approached my brother, and Amy. The way you terrified Amy made her more determined to escape and never see you again, not even to talk. If you wanted to talk why in God's name did you wave such a wicked knife in front of her? You must have known it would put her on the defensive.'

'I thought it would show I was serious. Thought she would be too scared to not stay. I had no idea she had gained a black belt.' Rico grinned. 'Impressive. I'm proud of her. But I also protected her. Called the cops when Zappacosta tried to break into your house. He's a real mean bugger, a paid assassin. It's how he earns his money. And I led those other two local idiots away from her. I also told my father she was dead so he would give up. Not sure he believed me though.'

'You broke into her house.'

'I was sent to find the files. My father was certain she had them. I wasn't. Pure logic says if she did she would have used the info five years ago.' He choked on a snort. 'To find out she had them but didn't know is kind of funny. But the way my father acted, some of the awful comments he made over the phone while I was here in Perth, well, it put a different slant on my view of him. I realised I could never trust him, or his word. So maybe I am stupid. After all it's taken me almost thirty-five years to figure out he's one cruel, mean bastard. I discovered there are a lot of key details he kept from me, and I worked for him. Not the dirty stuff. I was the bookkeeper when I wasn't on police duty.' He stared at James. 'I swear I've never hurt anyone in the physical sense, well, apart from what happened to Amanda. I never could and I'm certain the old bastard knew I didn't have it in me, which is why I doubt he believed I'd disposed of Amanda.' He brushed a hand through his hair. 'God, just the thought sends my nerves into panic mode.'

'Good to know. I believe you but you may find it difficult to convince others. The information you gave up is incredible. Even I, who prosecutes scum from the bottom of the pond, had no idea how deep the tentacles of filth had reached into the mire. Sure, law enforcement had inklings and suspicions but could never reach far enough in to scour the pond clean. But now, dear Lord, now they have electrically charged bombs which have already sent shock waves through both the underworld and the entire country's law enforcement. All thanks to you and Amy, who took refuge behind my rubbish bin. But it was your presence that had her in my backyard, terrified for her life. I'll send through those names but I must go.' As he backed towards the door, James did up the final two buttons on his shirt and tugged the tie into place.

Paris, Rico thought as he snuggled back against the pillows after the door hissed shut. He hadn't missed the way James winced after he'd mentioned the Eiffel Tower. Bet it wasn't his daughter the man intended to wine and dine in such an expensive restaurant. Bet it was Amanda. So she had gone overseas or maybe not yet. She could still be here, hidden away. Maybe she'll fly out with Ward. God, she'd better not get in a relationship with the guy. Hmm, her sister. More likely she's gone to visit her sister.

At the sound of his phone, he reached over, lifted it to his ear to be greeted by a deep sob. 'Hello.'

'Rico...' More sobs mixed with a few wails caused him to wince.

'Mama, what is it?' Stupid question because he knew.

'Your father.' The two words were a drawn out wail.

'I…' he paused. Discretion was needed. 'What about him? There hasn't been an accident has there? Is he okay?

'No, no. He's in… in... gaol.'

'Why?'

'I don't know. The police - they asked so many questions.'

'They asked you? What has he done?'

'I don't know. They asked about secret accounts, my role, about you, and Guido, and Peter, and Tony and names I've never heard of. You must come home.'

'Mama, calm down. My battery is low so we might get cut off.'

'Well, charge it.' Now she sounded more like his Mama. Determined.

'I can't, not at the moment and I can't come home.'

'Why not? I need you. You must help Matteo.'

Never, he thought but he needed to give some sort of excuse. 'Look Mama, I'm in hospital right now.'

When she screeched, he moved the phone at arm's length, waited three seconds and moved it back to his ear.

'I'm okay, just a few stitches. A slight accident.' He snorted at the memory of the accident. Amanda had gained her revenge. She'd done to him what he'd been told he'd meted out to her but he'd almost killed her when she'd been much kinder. All he lost was one testicle and a good dose of humiliation. If he hadn't hurt Jonathan Ward, she wouldn't have given him the last vicious kick which turned one side of his groin into mush. The pain had been so intense he'd almost passed out but it was own stupid fault. Again. Where she learned to fight, he had no idea but she sure surprised him. If he were honest, he admired her gumption and her impressive ability. He deserved the retribution.

'Rico!' Mama yelled.

'Sorry, Mama. I'm fine; just can't get home. You've got the girls and their husbands are there.'

'No. Peter and Tony have also been arrested. You must come home.'

'Impossible.'

'Which hospital?'

'Sorry, Mama, can't hear you. No battery.' He pressed the off button and swore. He shouldn't have revealed where he was. Now he had to get out. She would talk. It would take his father's men mere minutes to find out where he was. Damn, damn, damn. The pillow puffed around his head when he flopped back, closed his eyes and forced a still marshmallow brain to think with more clarity. How could he escape with an armed police officer outside the only exit? And he still had tubes galore attached to various parts of his body. The tubes he could deal with, the officer would be more difficult. There were essential items in the hotel room. The hire car was – goodness knows where. With a bit of luck, it was still parked a block from Jonathan Ward's place. He needed to change identity but to do so required one of his other passports. And of course, they were hidden on his property, back in Sydney. Money wasn't a problem, he had oodles stashed away in various accounts under various names: accounts nobody else knew about. At least he'd learnt something of value from the old man. But first he needed a few minutes to rest: to find enough energy. A click on the hand gadget. Lights went out except for a dim light that filtered through the drawn blind and the strip under the door still shone as bright. Eyes shut, he willed his body to relax, evened out each breath.

Four

Matteo Giovannazzo scowled as he took his eyes on a journey around the tiny room he'd been ensconced in for way too long. Floor, ceiling and walls, all painted cold grey, all solid concrete and steel, the same as the ledge on which he sat, legs hung over the side, bare feet on the icy floor. The poor excuse for a mattress was so thin, the cold of the metal seeped through the foam and thick plastic cover as well as the fabric of the ridiculous garment he'd been forced to don. It was either put it on or go naked. They hadn't even let him have his underwear after he'd been strip-searched, photographed and fingerprinted. Sleep had been scanty due to the continuous hum from the air-conditioner, which in turn kept him cold. He was used to a large bed, really comfy mattress and thick warm quilt, not one inadequate blanket and the hard, skinny steel bunk. It had been impossible to get comfortable, or warm.

The stench of bleach was strong. It didn't hide the sour smell of stale urine and a deeper unpleasant mustiness. In the corner, a stainless steel commode jutted from the wall. No seat. No damn privacy. A sparse basin and tap meant he could at least wash his hands and slake his thirst but there was no chair, no bench, no nothing.

'Bloody Rico lied,' he muttered under his breath. 'The bitch had the file. Must have. There's no other way.' He punched the mattress but recoiled when a shaft of pain shot up his arm. As he let loose with a raft of curses, he stood, paced the few steps to the wall, spun around and paced back – wall-to-wall-to-wall. He had to get out, get this mess sorted and find the bitch. No way did Rico get rid of her, he didn't have the balls.

'Where the hell is my lawyer?' To make sure he was heard, he yelled with his face against the barred doorway, both hands gripped around cold steel rods.

'Keep your voice down,' came back a bark.

'I know my rights, I'm a freak'n judge.'

Footsteps echoed, scraped closer. 'One who is in a gaol cell. One who might know his rights but sure doesn't know right from wrong.' The police officer wore a smirk on his face and three stripes on the shoulder of his blue shirt. The face was unfamiliar, the accent British. One of them imports. Not one of his men but there had to be one here. This was the bloody central station. Although with three shifts a day his own men weren't always on roster. Maybe they didn't know yet, but he'd been here more than a day so at least one had to have been on duty.

'Where's my lawyer? Have you called him yet?' Matteo figured he needed to play Mr Innocent Nice Guy here so kept the tone meek even though it rankled. He was used to giving the orders, not asking the questions.

'We rang but he's unavailable.'

No way. Guido was always available. It was the reason he was paid an exorbitant figure - to come at the click of Matteo's fingers. He ran his eyes up and down the huge officer with shoulders as wide as his height. Hmm, he'd be a good man to have on board.

'I don't believe you. Are you sure you rang the right number?' Matteo wanted to say more; to demand but figured if he let loose with the aggression that simmered under the surface, it would get him nowhere fast. Subservience didn't sit well with him. It wasn't in his make-up to ever kowtow to another. He was the damn boss.

'We dialled the numbers you wrote. Asked to speak with one Mr Guido Bianchi. A female voice informed us the man was unavailable for any legal advice.'

'Excuse me?' Guido was paid to always be available.

'If you would let me finish.' The officer stiffened his stance, held up one hand in the stop position but there was a sly look on his face; one Matteo was certain he didn't like.

'Sorry, I'm just surprised.'

'Probably about as surprised as he is. You see, a lawyer is unable to do any lawyering if his current residence is a gaol cell and he's in about as much trouble as you.'

Matteo reeled backwards. 'In gaol? Why?' But he knew why, which meant this entire shemozzle was far more serious than he'd first thought.

Although, Guido's details weren't in the missing file. So how? Shit. Someone else must have blabbed. Who would damn well dare? The two cops in the west? Verteramo and Lo Presti? No way. They hadn't been arrested so had no reason to blab and besides, he had too much info on them for them to dare open their mouths. Both owed him a small fortune in gambling debts. And they knew it. If they were the snitches, they were dead men. Damn, he should have had them taken out when they failed to nail Amanda. Had they grassed on him as payback? Nah, they knew the rules. If you talk, you die. Salvatore Zappacosta? Nah, he was in too deep. He'd assassinated too many people and the detailed paperwork Matteo kept on every assassination meant Salvatore would never snitch. Not that he knew the details Matteo kept. None of them did.

'Why? You need to ask?' The sergeant turned away. 'You have a law degree so you can represent yourself or we can find you a court lawyer. One who isn't on your payroll.' He strode away.

'Holy…' Matteo staggered back to the bench, plonked down and buried his face in his hands. What the hell happened? How could they know about Guido or lawyers on his payroll? No-one knew. All payments went through dozens of hidden channels. Off-shore accounts to other off-shore accounts. Well, maybe not all. Yes, the main men, not the small fry.

The thick plastic cover of the mattress crinkled as he stretched out, placed his head on the thin pillow with his hands gripped under his head. To gain some sort of comfort, he drew up his knees, wriggled his toes on the cold slippery plastic. Time to think. He hadn't even had a chance to make a phone call before the bloody cops snaffled his phone from the desk and shoved it into a plastic bag. As if he was stupid enough to store secret details of family business on his work phone. Handcuffs went on so quick he hadn't been able to reach the panic button under the desk top. Not that it would have done any good since everyone in the building had ignored his calls for help. Not one person came forward. They all stood there and gawped as he was frog-marched through the back rooms of the courthouse. Bastards, the lot of them. They'll all pay.

He twisted his head to glance through the bars. A plain grey wall stretched along the other side of a narrow passage. Shadows crept upwards. Not even a bloody window. The end of a dust-laden air-conditioner hummed to the right, way up high. He quirked the corners of his mouth up. Out of reach of any feisty prisoner eager to make a run for it but also out of reach of the cleaning staff, hence the tendrils of grime crawling over the top edges. Real healthy. And God, how he hated grime or to wear the same clothes for more than a few hours. And here he was in the same ridiculous jumpsuit he'd been wearing since they threw him into this hell hole.

To the left, he could make out the edge of a doorframe. A flicker of memory about the layout of this place shot through. The door led to the front foyer where there was a long counter behind which sat several officers to deal with the public and they were always busy which meant it would be possible to sneak out. If he could escape this cell.

How could he get a message out to get some help? Sylvie. They had to let her know sooner or later. Rico? Nah, he wouldn't dare show his face back here in Sydney. Not only would he be put in gaol because he'd skipped parole but Matteo would have him beaten to within an inch of his damn life. He'd failed his task. The boys would soon come. He sure made good choices for his sons-in-law. Peter and Tony were solid, true to the cause, not like his own yellow-livered boy. Takes too much after Sylvie. Where is she? She should be here by now?

He sat up, swung his legs over the edge. 'Hey, officer.'

The man returned, hefted his hands to his hips on an exaggerated sigh. 'Yes?'

'My wife. She needs to know what has happened. Can you call her? Ask her to come in. Please.' He teeth ground together at the need to beg and utter the word, please.

'Your wife knows but we haven't finished with her.'

'Finished? What the…'

'She's being questioned again now.'

'Why? Again?'

The sergeant laughed. 'Because she is your wife. We questioned her yesterday, needed a follow-up today to clarify a few details.'

A wife who wouldn't be able to answer any of the questions the police would be interested in. Somehow, she never suspected where their money came from, never questioned his gifts or how they could afford the luxuries he had provided to keep her sweet and meek. Mind you, he never disclosed their true value, always quoted a price way under what he paid. Sometimes so low, the price was ridiculous. Many times no price at all. But it was what a man did to keep his wife submissive, especially after the one time he almost lost her when she discovered his indiscretion with another woman. It took him an entire month to find out she had flown all the way back to Italy and another two weeks to convince her to return. But the passion in bed after she agreed had resulted in their first child. A son – his only son. It was a good job she was a traditionalist with strong family values, for the birth of their son tied her to him. Damn pity Rico took after his mother in nature. He loved the two daughters who followed but they weren't boys. A man needed strong sons to carry on the family business: a son who gave him grandsons. Bloody Rico stuffed up his marriage on the first night. And now? He would have to depend on his daughter's sons. At least their husbands would steer their lads into the cause. Pity the grandies were still too young. But first he had to get out of here.

With a flick of two fingers in the bird salute aimed at the sergeant who had already disappeared, Matteo lay back down and swore. Plans need to made.

Five

'Giovannazzo, if you promise to stay seated on the bed, I'll allow five minutes with your wife.' The sergeant appeared and stood, feet apart, arms folded, slap bang in the middle of the doorway to give the impression of authority. 'If you come anywhere near her, she goes.'

Shocked by the suddenness, Matteo shot upright, swung his legs over the side of the bed and stood. It was difficult to hold back a grin. Now he could begin to sort this mess. Sylvie would do whatever he demanded. 'Sure.'

'You're not seated.' The sergeant cocked one eye with the eyebrow raised higher than it should be possible to do.

Matteo sat. 'Sorry, bit of a surprise.'

'Do not come closer.'

'I can't even kiss my own wife?'

'No. Orders from above. No touches, kisses or sly whispers. Five minutes to talk, with me on guard.'

'I want privacy.'

The sergeant laughed. 'Seems you don't want to see her. Obey orders or I ask an officer to drive her home. Your choice.' He glanced at his watch. 'Time starts from,' he paused with eyes on the dial, 'now.' The other hand cut downwards through the air as though to start a foot race.

'Okay, bring her in.'

The sergeant twisted his head, gave a nod. Hurried footsteps scraped on the heavy-duty vinyl floor of indistinct colour. More beige than grey, Matteo decided. The only change of colour to the morose grey décor but it wasn't a pleasant change. The colours clashed – maybe on purpose as a subtle psychological method to bring disharmony to frazzled minds.

'Oh, Matteo.'

He winced at the distraught cry. It was a shock to see her pallid face with red-rimmed eyes. The fine wrinkles of age had deepened into chasms. Wisps of uncombed hair sprang in every direction yet she never left home without immaculate hair. Never would he allow her to appear in public wearing such shabby clothes and her feet... The reason for the scrapes became evident. Garden scuffs were on her feet. The oldest, tattiest pair of shoes she owned: shoes designated for the dirty work in the garden. It was apparent she'd been dragged from the house and not given a chance to change into more suitable clothes.

'Sylvie, so glad you're here.' Desperation urged him to go to the door but a sense of self-preservation kept his backside glued to the bed. He wasn't stupid. To make a good impression and go some way to prove he was innocent he needed to play it safe.

She planted her body against the bars, wrapped her fingers around one on each side of her head and glared at him. 'What have you done?' The tone was far more fierce than he'd ever heard from her before. Never would she dare speak to him in such a tone. He wanted to chastise her, bring her into line but didn't dare.

'I... nothing. This is all a huge mistake.'

'A mistake?' He winced at the high-pitched squeal.

'I've been dragged here dressed in my garden gear, questioned for hours about ridiculous subjects I've never even heard of before and it's because of a mistake? Do not lie to me, Matteo Giovannazzo. I've seen the evidence. Proof of your lies, your dishonesty, your... I don't know what to say. This is all so unbelievable.'

Oh, hell, what have they told her? 'You are wrong. They are wrong. Get Rico here. He'll tell you otherwise.'

'Rico is in hospital. Says he can't come home.'

'In what? Why? Where? I don't believe you. He's just too much of a coward. Doesn't have any balls. That bitch he married caused all this.' Matteo swept one hand around in a dismissive circle and pointed one figure at Sylvie.

'Don't blame others for your own evil misdemeanours. Amanda was the best thing that ever happened to Rico. They loved each other. She was so gentle, kind and soft hearted. You,' she stabbed one finger in Matteo's direction, with her arm reaching through the bars. 'You caused the annulment of their marriage with your stupid demands. Called your son a poofter because he wasn't musclebound like a heavyweight boxer. You supplied him with illegal drugs, insisted he take them. Oh, look at your face, all shocked as if you figured I didn't have a clue what went on in my own home. You are so stupid, so bossy, such a bully. If you are such an honest, goody two-shoes how come the diamond bracelet you gave me for our anniversary is stolen property? Hmm? Want to explain that?' As she withdrew her arm and re-gripped the bars, her face screwed into a fierce scowl.

Matteo had to fight back a wince. How the hell did she find out?

'And the necklace for my birthday, also stolen. They,' she waved one hand in the direction of the door, 'went through our house – *my home*.' She paused. Her chest heaved. In and out. Shoulders rose. Up and down. Mouth opened and closed several times as though she couldn't find the right words. Squinted eyes stared at him. 'They searched through every single cupboard and drawer, even went through my underwear. Took all of my jewellery, all our electronic gear, even my phone, which they returned when they found nothing improper. I don't do improper. And you dare sit there and say your arrest is nothing more than a simple mistake. I've seen the pictures of the stolen jewellery.' She punched each word on the bars as if she wanted to do the same to him. Good job he had the sense to remain seated.

'The pictures are identical in every aspect to the pieces you gave me. A mistake!' A snort escaped while she fought for either her breath or to calm, he couldn't tell which.

'Add on the millions of dollars hidden away in secret offshore accounts I have never heard of. I've seen the statements. Your name on every single one. Millions. Far beyond what you could ever earn in three lifetimes.' Sylvie paused, shook her head and huffed hard. In and out as though building up steam. When she raised her head, she stared straight at him. 'Since when did we own property in Forestville?'

Matteo's lungs forgot how to work. How on earth did they find out about that place? The bodies. Had they been found? Dear God. Please, no.

'I never signed any papers for such a property yet *my* name is on the title deed.' Sylvie pressed her face into the bars. It straightened out the wrinkles but distorted her features into a scary image. 'Would you like to explain how my name got onto such a legal document without my knowledge?'

Matteo scowled at the sergeant who stood leant against the far wall with a smarmy snigger spread across his face. Asshole. He turned back to Sylvie, desperate to get her to see reason, despite not having a clue as to what he could say to convince her.

'Sweetheart, I can explain. Rico did all the accounts. Get him here. He can tell you all the details about our worldwide investments.'

'Don't lie.'

'I'm not.'

'Sure you are, for how can Rico be responsible when he's been locked up for the past five years, thanks to you.'

Damn it, when did she become so smart? 'Honey, you never went without. Lived a good life. Had the best of everything you wanted. We could afford those luxuries because I made such sound investments. First we need to get Rico back. He's the mastermind of our investments. Rico will explain it all to you and to these bastards.' He sent another glare in the sergeant's direction. 'Look, all you need to do is speak to Johnny. Tell him Rico is in hospital and to get Rico back. Use those words. Get Rico back. Johnny will understand. He'll know what they mean. Once Johnny speaks with him, Rico will come.'

'Johnny? As in the gardener? Are you crazy?'

'Yes, Johnny Thomas. He'll... look, I'll explain later. After we sort out all this misunderstanding. Please, speak to Johnny.'

'Time's up.' The sergeant straightened and neared. 'Come on Mrs Giovannazzo, we have to leave.' He held out a hand.

Sylvie seemed uncertain as she released her firm grip on the rails. An obvious wave of shivers ran from her head down as far as Matteo could see. She glanced at the sergeant, paused, turned back to Matteo. 'I'll speak to Johnny but I'll also phone Rico and talk to him. If what the police have shown me is true – we're done. I'll have divorce papers served to you within days. I have no faith in you, don't trust you and I can do without you always trying to control me with your demands.' She turned, slid one hand into the crook of the sergeant's arm and shuffled away, the scuffs making a racket as she disappeared.

Matteo swore under his breath, lay back on the bed and frowned. Forestville. Bloody hell. How many bodies were buried there? Too damn many. But they were well hidden. Nobody knew. Well, except for Salvatore, and Tony, and Peter. It couldn't have been one of them who blabbed. But how did the coppers know about the property? Damn. The title deeds. They would have done a search for all properties in any of their names. A groan wound its way up from deep down but he bit it off, shut his eyes and swept one arm over his face. His eyelids sprang apart when an answer came. A search of title deeds didn't mean they would search the property. Phew. With a grin he closed his eyes again. The grin widened. Johnny knew what the words meant. Get Rico back was the code to take him out, not bring him home. Rico was a dead man.

Six

A t the soft squeak, Rico's eyes jerked open. A fist came from nowhere. At the split-second movement, Rico turned his head away. Knuckles crunched on the side of his jaw, knocked him sideways. To lessen the impact, he curled and kept going with the impetus, over the side of the mattress. A loud clatter, tubes tugged and tightened. Despite the tape holding it in place, the canula tore from the back of his hand with a harsh sting. He landed on his feet and pranced upright, arms bent, hands bunched, ready to defend himself.

In the dim light it was almost impossible to make out any features of the looming shadow. It had to be a man. No woman had such powerful shoulders.

'Who the hell are you? What do you want?' Rico growled as he parried his fists.

The man's hand reached for the steel stand holding the fluid bag. Wheels scraped as it was flung out of the way. A loud metallic rattle and bang echoed as it hit the far wall. The plastic tube whipped through the air, arched up and spun around. Since he was on the other side of the bed, the stranger paused, glanced at Rico, swore, turned and ran.

Rico shot around the end of the bed. The catheter still attached to him must have torn free from whatever it was attached to for it slapped against his legs and spat cold fluids. He ignored the hot searing pain, lunged and grabbed the man by the scruff of the neck. A spurt of anger gave him the strength to spin the man around. Rico let go with a fist, aimed for the nose. A satisfactory crunch was followed by a loud grunt. Blood spurted, the sudden warmth splashed against his arm and face. A second punch to the soft area just below the rib cage. The man folded over with a *whoosh*. With one raised leg, Rico hooked his toes around the knee and tugged as he shoved hard at the shoulders. The man hit the ground. The thud echoed. Locked bed wheels scraped as the bed was shoved aside. The intruder groaned as he struggled over onto his stomach and rose to a crouch position, ready to flee. Rico planted one knee in the small of the back and jumped to press hard until the man lay prone. Rico had to grapple to get a hold of both hands. He yanked them back and upwards. The man screeched when his shoulder joints twisted at the awkward angle but thank goodness, he couldn't move.

Everything happened so fast, Rico had to fight for breath. When he managed to focus his eyes he reached for the remote gadget, pressed the first button his finger landed on. The bedside light flared. He stared at the side of the face smeared in blood. 'I know you. Mark Johansson. What the hell do you want?'

The man groaned. 'I was ordered to kill you.'

'By my father?' Rico shook the man hard, pressed his knee in further, twisted the shoulder joint tighter until Johansson yelped.

'Someone else gave the order,' Johansson squealed as though terrified.

'Who?'

When there was no answer, Rico yanked the body up and slammed the head onto the floor.

Johansson squealed. 'No more. I'll talk. Johnny Thomas.'

The family gardener, who was also a bodyguard, messenger boy, patsy and general dogsbody for the bastard. The best paid gardener to ever exist.

'Why?' Rico asked even though the answer was obvious.

'I wasn't told why.'

Rico believed him. The henchmen like Johnny were employed to obey orders, not question them. They all knew better than to ask questions. 'If you want to live you'd better report back that you succeeded, not that it'll make any difference. The old man is in gaol and won't get out.'

'He's what?'

'You heard and since he's been arrested don't expect to get paid for this job. I imagine all accounts have been frozen by the coppers. What was your fee?'

'Shit. Ten thousand.'

'Ten grand? To kill the bosses son? Too cheap my man.'

'It's what they offered. I didn't know it was you. I would never have agreed. I like you. You're not anything like the others. I was just given the hospital, room number and your phone number for Find My Phone tracking device.'

'Tracking device? What the hell?' Rico got off his knees, planted his feet on the ground and hauled the man over onto his back. With one foot on a wrist to hold it on the floor, he held the other arm in a tight grip. With his free hand he searched for a weapon. Pockets were empty but a bulge under the shirt revealed a strange shape. Rico wriggled his fingers inside the shirt, grasped a piece of wood and tugged it free. A second piece of thin dowel attached to wires dropped down. Teeth bit into his tongue at the grim picture of what the crude object could do. It made sense. A gun made too much noise. He flung the garotte across the room. Even such a small object made too much noise.

'What tracking device? If you don't tell me I will re-arrange your wife's pretty face and as for your daughter, it's been five years since I've been with a woman. She will be a good one to start with.'

'You wouldn't.'

'Try me. I'm so pissed off at the moment I am capable of almost anything.' He kicked the man the same place he had punched.

The man wheezed in agony. 'Your phone,' Mark stuttered before refilling his lungs on a long gasp.

'It's new. Has one of those trackers so you can find it if someone steals it. I was given the number.'

Flabbergasted, Rico stared at the man. The old bastard had given Rico the phone when he'd been picked up after being released from gaol. The same time he'd been ordered to go to Perth within a week which gave him no time to settle in his home. It had been long enough to open up the house, have the services turned on, deal with financial institutions and pack a bag.

'I should kill you,' Rico growled as he hauled the man to his feet. 'But I'm not my father. I don't kill a man because I don't agree with him. My advice to you is to go home, pack up your gear and family and get the hell out of Sydney. The entire organisation is in turmoil, most have already been arrested. I'm surprised you are still free but you couldn't have come from Sydney this quick. You were already over here - why?'

'Back-up.'

'For what?'

'To make sure you got some files and got rid of Amanda.'

Rico shook his head in disbelief. 'You won't find her. She's gone for good.'

'Dead?'

'As dead as you will be if you come anywhere near me again. But what the hell does it matter anymore? The organisation is kaput. There will be no more jobs, no money, no drugs, no brothels, no standovers, no blackmail, tat parlours or protection. No anything. Somebody snitched. The cops know every last detail. I presume you have a flight ticket to get you home?'

'Yeah, sure.'

'Then, my man, I suggest you get on the first available plane and take my prior advice. Get the hell out of Sydney, as far away as you can. Even leave the country if you don't want to be arrested. I have no doubt your name is on the list.' He released the man and gave him a shove towards the door. 'There was a cop out there so how did you get in?'

'I dealt with him.' Mark sneered over his shoulder as he stepped through the doorway.

Rico swore, turned around and staggered back to the bed on legs which threatened to buckle. Never had he experienced such weakness. Perched on the side of the mattress, he paused long enough for his head to cease spinning and his churned stomach to settle. Every part of his body hurt. 'First…' He grasped the catheter threaded into his bladder, tugged, swore under his breath and eased the tube out with a little more care but no finesse for it stung like blazes. Both eyes flooded with the wash of tears at the pain. Eyes screwed tight; he swore over and over until the tube sprang free. He flung it across the room to join the garotte.

Clothes, he needed clothes. Dizziness returned when he bent at the bedside cupboard and tugged it open. Despite his spinning head, he grinned at the clothes folded in a neat pile next to his leather sneakers. It took less than two minutes in the bathroom to pull off the undignified hospital gown, drag on clothes, drown his face under a basin of water to rid it of blood spatters. Back in the room, he pocketed his gear, scanned the room for any other item he might own and crept to the door.

With utmost care he inched the door open, winced at the bright light and had to take a second to focus. When his pupils had adjusted themselves he peered both ways along the passage. Normal hospital noises, wheeled trolleys, a hum of voices sat in the background. Neither the officer nor Mark were there but it didn't mean neither lay in wait, although he doubted it. An olive green painted dado strip about a third of the way up the wall, led him past closed room doors, along the passage to silver metal doors of an elevator. Next to it was a stairwell. To avoid being seen, he chose the stairs instead of waiting for the elevator to arrive. The numbers told him he was on the second floor. Luck was with him so far. Stuffiness filled his nasal passages as he clattered down. When a woman dressed in civvies joined him at the first level he slowed to a more sedate pace. Had to be a visitor who wouldn't recognise him. Hand in pocket he smiled and hurried past.

Ground floor. He shoved the door open to find himself in a vast reception area not unlike any hospital he'd visited before. They all seemed to have the same architect. Vast and echoing, with a glassed-in reception desk and three rows of chairs for patients and visitors to wait interminable hours. The air was fresher to the extent it chilled his skin in an instant. To make himself less noticeable, he tagged on behind a family of three and kept pace until he was outside where he grimaced at the brightness when the sun pierced his pupils. It hung on a downward arc in the west giving him a rough indication of the time. It had to be mid-afternoon. The air was hot but fresh and a pleasant change after the continual air-conditioning and distinct hospital aromas.

Unfamiliar with the city, he had no idea where he was but tall buildings to his right gave an indication the city centre wasn't far away. Perth wasn't big. He'd already trawled the streets over the past two weeks. His hotel wasn't far. A taxi would be quicker if he managed to find one straight away but with a phone needing to be charged he figured to walk would be as fast.

Down the slight incline for two blocks, turn right. Along the next block, turn left, cut through the shops to his right. When he exited the shop, one street over, he knew where he was. The railway station across the road held a police station at one end. This he knew because when he had come across it, he turned tail and hiked away to avoid the place. An arcade a few metres ahead was more than handy and if he kept going south for two entire blocks he should, if he was in the right spot, find his hotel.

As he increased his pace, he searched his wallet to ensure the room key card was still there. Yes, but he would need to check out and find somewhere else to stay until he could figure out how to get back to Sydney without being discovered. It might be too risky to fly. A disguise of some description sounded good. Hell, Amanda had changed her hairstyle so many times in a mere week, she'd fooled everyone.

Sweat soaked his shirt, underwear and socks by the time he reached the hotel. A headache had turned to dizziness and the road train had returned with a vengeance. He understood why the doctor recommended another twenty-four hours in bed: time he didn't have. Ten metres from the hotel entry, he paused. Did the police know which hotel he was booked into? Not that he'd spent much time in residence and it had been booked in his father's name. Oh, terrific. A sure red flag to have police officers on his door. Unsure, he took a detour around to the back entrance: a short cut for patrons to reach the Swan River. An entrance he'd used several times. It was fortunate two men in gaudy shirts approached the back entry at the same time. He tagged on behind the obvious tourists, peeked over their shoulders to see if anyone who gave even the remotest hint they were men in authority or another familiar face from the less savoury side of his life, lurked in the corridor.

Nerves were twitched to high alert by the time he reached his hotel room. Mark Johansson had been sent to do the dirty work. It was unlikely anyone else was on his tail, at least anyone from his father's gang, but it wasn't impossible. Cops were another matter. Chances were, he hadn't yet been missed from the hospital although he didn't have a clue how long he'd been asleep. Not the four hours the doc had mentioned because the tubes hadn't been removed. He figured he had time to at least get cleaned up and download vital files from phone to computer so he could dump the phone. Which meant he needed ten minutes minimum to charge the battery enough to download. Confident it was safe he slid the key card into the slot and used a shoulder to push the door open.

All was quiet. The room was spotless apart from his few bits still where he'd left them. The normal mustiness of a glassed in hotel room greeted him, along with the faint aroma of cleaning chemicals. Gut instinct told him he was alone and he always trusted his gut.

He strode across the carpet, lifted the receiver on the landline, took out James Ward's card and dialled.

'Ward here.'

'I was attacked in the hospital room.'

'You what? Rico?'

'Let me talk. You need to jot down the details.'

'Hang on a sec, I need paper. Okay, go ahead.'

'One of my father's men. Mark Johansson. Blond curly hair on top at the front, shaved sides and back. Just under six feet. Blue eyes, thin build but powerful shoulders as in chemically enhanced. He's headed to the airport. His name is on the list but I didn't know he was here in the west. Originally sent to double check I obeyed orders, but today was given the kill order for me. He took out the guard. I don't know how or what he did or where the guard is. Johansson had a garotte stuffed in his shirt. I'm not sure if he used it before he found me. I hope not. I got the hell out of there, not game to wait around or search for the officer. You might want to let them know. My phone had a tracker set up by the old bastard. I'm about to dump the phone. You also need to get the family gardener arrested. Johnny Thomas. Somehow my father got word to him. He's not just a gardener and will be armed.'

'Where are you?'

'Not saying. I'll SMS new contact details when I get a new phone. No names attached. Just a single phone number. Please don't use my name for any messages. You can use the letters J.R. It's an alias but as from now Rico Giovannazzo doesn't exist.' He hung up, pulled out the cord from the wall.

Exhausted, he had to sit for a moment to regain at least a smidgen of strength. Nourishment was needed and so was a shower. Perched on the side of the bed, he sorted through a tangle of cables, set the mobile phone on charge and wound the others into neat bundles, ready to be packed. In the bar fridge he found a couple of chocolate bars, two bottles of water and four mini wines. Alcohol he didn't need. The one time in the past five years he'd indulged, in Amanda's home, had been an unmitigated disaster. He'd been too drunk to notice Amanda sneak in during the night. The thick furred tongue, all-day nausea and the kettle drum in his head the next day had been enough to convince him drinking alcohol was a mug's game.

The water would be good to carry. He took out the chocolate. On the desk were small bags of crisps and a packet of savoury bites. He crunched the salt-laden bites and ripped off the wrapper from a half-size chocolate bar with caramel and nuts, appreciating the rich choc/caramel scent. At least the high sugar content would give him a touch of energy, even if it was short term. He savoured the mixture of flavours as he stripped off his clothes and stumbled to the bathroom on jellified legs. The full-on shower was pure bliss as hot jets pummelled into his skin.

A close examination of his body revealed the extent of the damage incurred over the past few days. The torn out canula left shredded skin, a streak of blood and a dark bruise. Neat stiches in his scrotum were not much darker than the bruise. Holy Moley, no wonder it hurt so much. There were too many paler bruises left behind by Amanda and the side of his face was red and sore from Johansson's punch. No doubt the area will be black by morning. Inside didn't feel a whole lot better. Leant against the tiles for support, he shampooed his hair, shaved off too many days of growth from his chin, took care to soap his body and rinse away until the water ran clear. He lingered another few minutes to lap up the luxury of pulsing water and the freshness of clean skin. When it was a struggle to find a clean set of clothes, he realised he would need to find a laundromat, or at least a new hotel with laundry services. Or maybe buy new clothes. Hmm, new clothes would be better if they were of a style he never wore. Baggy, to hide his build, or weird. Nah, he didn't do weird.

Nausea hit, along with a serious cold sweat. It was pure luck he reached the hallowed porcelain bowl before his stomach ejected the small amount of food he'd eaten. Too late, he understood the reason behind the doctor's comment about no solid food. Satisfied there wasn't a skerrick left to eject, he staggered upright on legs that had turned into soggy marshmallows, wiped the sweat from his face with a cold face washer and rinsed his mouth out several times but not game to drink any. He had to use both hands on the walls to maintain his balance as he reeled back to the bed where he dropped onto the mattress and groaned with one arm over his eyes. Too weak to move, he decided he didn't much care if one of his father's men found him here and ended his life. Right now death would be a reprieve from this weakness and pain, most of it self-inflicted. Eyes shut he switched off his brain.

Seven

'Hey - psst. Boss.'

The voice came in a dream but when an object hit his face, Matteo shot upright. 'Ugh? What?' As he picked up the small ball of screwed-up paper, he turned his head, blinked and stared, unable to believe who stood on the other side of the bars. It wasn't a dream but a real live person, one of his men. 'Pug, what the hell... how did you get in?'

'Shh, keep your voice down.' Paul Messina, alias Pug because of his unrepaired broken nose, planted one finger against his mouth and shook his head. A quick glance to his right, he took one step back, crept towards the door to the entry and stood hidden behind the wall as though to listen. At the silence, he hurried back and beckoned Matteo to the bars.

'You have to get me out of here.' Matteo kept his voice to a whisper as he hid the paper behind the pillow, went the entire two steps to the bars where the two shook hands.

'I'm working on it. What happened? I can't believe how many have been nabbed.'

'How many?' Matteo gripped the bars so tight his knuckles turned white.

'Dozens, almost everyone I know about. You should hear the hum going through every station.'

Matteo swore, turned his back to the bars in disgust. The fingers of one hand tore through his hair. He shivered at the oiliness, wiped his hand down the side of his outfit. On a hiss he turned back, re-gripped the bars. 'Unbelievable. Who grassed? Do you know?'

'Don't have a clue.'

'You have to find out but in the meantime, tell me what you know.'

'*The Haven* got raided. All the girls and staff were bundled into paddy wagons. I managed to escape detection because I'd gone to get take-away. When I got back, hell, the uproar. Blue lights everywhere. At least a dozen police cars and wagons. More coppers than customers and girls put together.'

'You weren't in uniform?'

'Hell no, never am when I go to collect.'

'Did you get the takings?'

'No. I'd left Justine to consolidate the books and package the bills. Ten minutes. I was away no more than ten minutes. But maybe it was a good thing for I would have been caught too if I had been there.'

'What happened to the cash?'

'Cops must have it. They turned the place over after they'd taken the girls away. I hid in a doorway three buildings down. Saw them cart out several huge brown paper bags along with the computer. Figured I needed to disappear quick smart. Called your son-in-law, Tony. His wife answered. Tony was unavailable. I've since learnt he'd also been taken in.'

'Not Lucy? She's free?'

'Yeah, sure, well, she was home when I phoned. Why would she be arrested? She's not in the know is she?'

'No, although sometimes I have my doubts. What about Maria and Peter?' From what Sylvie mentioned, Matteo already figured his other son-in-law was also behind bars. Hmm, where? Could even be in here.

'Don't know. I have no reason to call them.'

'What about the other parlours?'

'Don't know that either. I wasn't game to visit any of the others. Already collected from *Serenity*. Banked the cash. Not due at the others until the day after tomorrow.'

'What else?'

'There's an A.P.B. on Rico. Jumped parole.'

'Yeah, yeah, I know this.' Matteo loosened a white-knuckled hand from the bar to wave in the general direction. 'He went west. Won't be back. Failed his test. He's being dealt with.'

Pug staggered backwards. 'Your own son?'

'If any man fails a test, you know the rules. Rico is no different. I need clothes, a phone, transport. Untraceable of course. And to get the hell out of here. Soon. Before they take me to court and shove me in Long Bay.' The thought of Long Bay prison sent the acid in his stomach upwards. It was difficult to swallow it down.

'Clothes, yeah, maybe a uniform would be best. Easier to walk out if you look like one of the guys. Or loose pants and top to fit over what you've got on. Mine should fit you. Not sure when I can get back. Had to pull a few strings. Supposed to be on duty at my station.'

'Give me your phone.'

'Can't. I had to leave it at the desk to see you. Along with all weapons.' Pug stood back and swept his arms down his sides to show the absence of all the normal gear they wore when on duty. 'This place is tighter than Fort Knox.'

'Why? You're a copper.'

Pug snorted. 'Why? You're in here. A District Court judge in a cell. Crime gang bigwig, they call you. The entire force is humming like a beehive the size of Mount Everest.'

'What about the other guys who are on the force?'

When Pug reeled off a list of names of those who had been arrested, Matteo stumbled backwards, plonked onto the mattress and buried his head in outstretched hands. How did they find out? Apart from him, nobody in the organisation knew so much. Rico? No way. He'd been out of action for five years and wouldn't have a clue about some of these names. The organisation had changed and grown in those five years. His sons-in-law? Nah, impossible. Even they weren't privy to every detail. Matteo wasn't stupid. He gave enough information to any one person so they could carry out their jobs with utmost efficiency. Peter was in charge of the drugs side of things. Tony, all the brothels. It was probable they talked together, exchanged info and stories but the protection racket? Nah. No way. And one of these named coppers is an enforcer in the protection section. Hmm, Lucy had asked quite a few subtle questions. Did she know more than he realised? He shot back to the cell bars.

'Can you find out where all the info came from? There must be details somewhere.'

The shock on Pug's face could never be faked. 'I'm a probie, lowest in the ranks, posted to an outer suburb station. Even my sarge wouldn't be privy to such info.'

'You're not on probation any longer.'

Both men jerked apart at the deep voice of a stranger. Matteo scuttled back to the bed and swore under his breath. It took a few seconds before he was game to lift his eyes then wished he hadn't. The insignia on the huge man's jacket told a story with a grim ending. An inspector's three stars belonged to the protagonist, a man he knew but didn't like because he was such a stickler for correct protocol. A man who would never turn: the type of man Matteo hated. It was impossible to tell if Pug had been set up or if he was in on a sting but Matteo was the antagonist who had just been shot down in flames, tortured and killed off.

'Paul Messina, I am arresting you for consorting, receiving the proceeds of prostitution, being involved in human trafficking and the slavery of underage girls. You were under suspicion but we had no proof. Now we do.' He pointed to a dim corner high up in the ceiling. 'Video evidence of collusion with a criminal and admission of guilt.' He smirked. 'Collection of takings from an illegal brothel, a bent cop on the take for monetary gain. I hear you were desperate to get into the force. Now I know why.' The man nodded his head and stepped to one side.

Another officer, a sergeant this time, held out a pair of handcuffs, his head to one side and a wry grin on his face. Matteo winced at the double click. The poor bugger had been set up, as had he. He mulled over what details each of them had revealed over the past few minutes while he watched Pug being shoved along the corridor. Stupid, stupid, stupid. He damn well knew security cameras were honed onto each gaol cell these days to keep tabs on prisoners who wanted to self-harm or commit suicide. Yet, he hadn't thought. Instead he'd been too gobsmacked by Pug's presence and the chance to get out of this hell hole. Ever since they'd brought him here he'd been too entrenched in his own woes to use logic. Every movement he had made would have been under constant scrutiny.

'Thanks for the admission, it will make your first appearance in court a whole lot easier and quicker.' The inspector stood, feet apart, about a metre in front of the bars. 'As to who grassed? No-one in person but the ream of paperwork we received is a priceless gem. The needle shed off every blade of hay to jump out in all its glory with lights so bright we couldn't miss a single shred of evidence. Someone is right royally pissed off with you. Maybe they couldn't live with a guilty conscience any longer. Maybe they were fed up with doing the dirty work without sufficient renumeration. Maybe you went too far and trod on the wrong person's toes. What I do know for sure is, someone hates your guts. I look forward to your trial.'

A shaft of hope soared. Matteo scoffed. 'Paperwork? Anyone can write whatever they want on a piece of paper. Even you know a few pieces of paper won't hold up in court.'

The inspector turned away, strode along the passage, paused at the doorway and turned back with a return of the smug grin. 'Given you earned a law degree and managed to become a judge, I thought you would be an intelligent man, but it appears I am wrong. Enjoy your day.' The laughter faded as the man went through the doorway: the sort of laughter which wasn't of the humorous kind.

What did the man mean? Since there was nowhere else to go, Matteo lay back on the mattress with both hands clenched under his head on the pillow. At the rustle of paper he turned on one side to face the rear wall. The ball of paper brushed against his cheek. He went to shove it away until he noticed a few letters had been written on it. A spike of adrenalin surged. As surreptitiously as he could, he took utmost care to open out the paper against his chest, ensuring his arm showed little movement. Size was right to indicate it came from an officer's notebook. It was almost impossible to read until he raised his body on bent elbow and pretended to adjust the pillow. He read, gasped, grinned and folded the paper into the smallest possible size. Unsure about where to hide it, he eased it under the elastic cuff of the jumpsuit.

Eight

Rico couldn't recall ever being in such a ridiculous situation. He tried not to catch sight of his image in the mirror but with such a large one in front of him, his reflection was impossible to avoid unless he kept his eyes shut. Silver foils stuck up all over his head resembled the hairdo of some weird punk rocker. A scrunched orange towel draped around his neck over a long waterproof cape. Talk about undignified. The stench of chemicals caused his nose to run and eyes to itch but he had asked for a shaggy hairstyle with blond tips and this was the result. Man, he was glad he wasn't one of those women who did this on a regular basis. On a sigh he shut his eyes and let his mind wander to the past twelve hours.

The two hours of sleep in the hotel had been worth the risk of being found. It not only renewed his energy levels but also cleared his head enough to think with logic. On a phone with full charge it took mere minutes to transfer two files of vital details to a thumb drive which he backed up onto a second. He could have downloaded to his laptop but wasn't game. It was too easy to lose the computer, and the data was too damn important to let some scum find and read. Thumb drives were easier to keep hidden. Not sure how to keep the tiny gadgets safe, he hid one in a pocket inside his backpack and the other on his person.

To make sure it was still there, he patted the front pocket of his jeans and smiled at the small hard bulge.

No-one, not even his father, knew he had the data. A visit to his mother after he'd been released from prison had been fortuitous. At the time Rico thought he would return to his old job as the money man. Now he knew different. A new accountant, a man he hadn't yet met, had been installed and it had been pointed out to Rico there was no chance he would be able to resume his old role. And he could never be a cop again. It was a good job he had more money stashed away than he would ever need. Thank goodness he'd been smart enough to invest in the share market from his very first paycheque, investments no-one else knew about.

Thoughts had seesawed about posting one of the thumb drives to James Ward but since Rico was about to leave the state, it was more important to have the backup on hand in case he lost one. Besides, he'd already given Ward many of the up to date details, although with such time constraints and lack of paper, he hadn't been able to write down all the details. There was no-where he could post the thumb drive to in the east, at least to no-one he trusted. Not now and maybe not ever.

Other less vital information had gone onto his laptop before he dismantled the phone. Not that there had been much since he'd been out of prison for such a short time and hadn't had time to make contact with old pals. With the side of a coin, he had scratched the tiny network of information from the sim card and snapped the card in two.

After he'd checked out of the hotel, he strolled to the river. The large expanse of water was nowhere near as dramatic as the Hawkesbury back home but it was pretty. The main feature he liked was the way no buildings impeded access or the view. The entire riverside was open to the public. There were small boats of all descriptions but compared to Sydney, the number was miniscule. He threw the battery as far out as he could one way, the empty phone another and crushed the pieces of sim card under the heel of his shoe before he'd dropped them amongst the rocks on the edge and watched them sink in a slow spiral, scrape against the side of a slimy green rock and vanish under one of many white jellyfish. He'd had thoughts of putting the lot in a city rubbish bin but if someone spied the latest phone and used it, there was the possibility the poor sucker would have been traced and done away with. Rico couldn't take such a chance.

Clarity of mind meant he visited the car hire centre in person to hand in the keys. An explanation of his hospital stay due to a personal accident went a long way to persuade them to pick the car up from the address he gave. He sweetened the deal with a one hundred dollar extra payment. The already dark smudge on the side of his face had been a bonus to give verity to his pathetic claim. It was worth the money to save him the hours it would take to get to the car and drive back.

Since it had been almost dark, he needed to find a place to stay for the night. Not one of the usual type haunts. His father's men would search those first. Four star hotels were his preference. Never five-star. They were too hoity-toity and required a certain something in speech and characteristics which he neither had, nor could abide. And the exorbitant extra dollars required for the one extra star on stuff he never used or needed, were far better spent on more mundane pleasures like good food and clothes, although, he had to admit, he liked flashy cars, his one vice.

As he headed back to the main city centre he remembered he'd passed a backpackers over the other side of the railway line. The walk across the city had tired his too weak body but he found the place and checked in for the night. They had laundry facilities, which he put to good use, and a decent bed in a private room he was more than willing to pay the extra for. Since it wasn't the sort of place he was known to frequent, he figured it was safer than anywhere else until he could get out of the city. It gave him a chance to give his body the rest it needed.

And now here he sat, rested, but in this ridiculous get-up, bleaching his hair, for goodness sake. Now he was glad he hadn't had time to get overlong hair styled and cut after being released from prison.

After this he needed to purchase enough unique style clothes to get him east and most important, a new phone.

'Let's see how this is going.'

Rico jolted to awareness at the hairdresser's voice. Fingers fiddled on top of his head. He glanced into the mirror to see the young hairdresser unwrap a foil and grin.

'Looks good. Come over to the basin.'

Eager to get this ordeal over, Rico sprang from the chair so fast the seat spun around. He grabbed an arm to stop it before taking the five steps to the basin where he settled into the chair, which was more like a *chaise longue*. They never had these at his favourite barber shop and as for a haircut in prison – well, it wasn't worth the few seconds to think about. Head back, he closed his eyes as foils were removed, warm water rinsed away the gunge and shampoo went on, followed by conditioner that smelt much better than the bleach. It was pure pleasure when long fingers kneaded through every centimetre of his skull for a good five minutes. Absolute bliss. Maybe this was why his sisters went to a salon so often.

Back at the mirror he studied the young woman's actions as she used a hair dryer and fingers to ruffle through his hair. When the strands were half dry she rubbed in some kind of gel and used a narrow round brush to complete the drying process. It was a shock to see the result of a full-bodied hairstyle even though it was what he asked for. Shaggy blond ends hung over his forehead. Such an effortless process changed his appearance far better than he could have imagined but it would take a while to get used to it. He had always preferred a neat cut with his thick black hair swept back from his face. Now there was no more than a centimetre of natural black near the roots.

'Do you like it?' The woman held a mirror at the back so he could see the reflection.

'Perfect, thank you.'

The grin didn't leave t woman's face the entire time he stood at the counter to pay. It widened even further when he bought a tube of the gel and scrunched a twenty-dollar bill in her hand as a tip.

Outside, he threaded his arms through the straps of his backpack and searched both ways along the street for a men's clothing store.

Two pairs of cargo pants later, one khaki, one navy, with four loose linen tops to match, Rico strode along the street unsure about how he felt wearing such baggy clothes. He had always preferred a much sleeker look. And the colours – he didn't do khaki. Yet here he was in light brown baggy pants with bulging outside pockets hanging off his thighs and a darker brown shirt that reached down to cover his backside. No belt. It now resided in the bag with the other new clothes along with the jeans and long-sleeved shirt he'd put on earlier. The clothes he'd bought were stylish and of the latest fashion, so the server said, but it didn't alter the discomfort.

A new phone was next on his list. *Turn left, go to the corner. About a hundred metres along on the right-hand side are a couple of Telco shops*, the same server had told him. Ever alert for sudden attack, Rico merged with a group of business-suited men until they peeled off into a busy eatery a few metres before the corner. The savoury aroma almost made him turn with them but a more urgent need to disappear caused him to turn the corner to discover he was in a mall: a mall he recalled from his first foray into the city after he'd arrived. Was it only two weeks ago? A bit over, he concluded after counting the days on his fingers. Phew, not even three weeks and so much had happened in such a short time. As he moved to the centre of the mall, he began to search for the store he needed. The place seemed to be a hive of activity but nowhere near as busy as the Sydney CBD when it was close to lunchtime.

'Look out!'

Rico paused at the shout from behind. He twisted his upper torso around to see who had yelled and why. With his eyes shooting wide, he swore. A black SUV careened towards him. Sun glinted from the windscreen, blinding him for a second. Before he had time to even think about moving he was rugby-tackled from the side.

Whump. All air left his lungs in an instant as he landed on the hard pavement, a body on top of him. Panic hit when a picture of his father shot through his grey matter. Frazzled brain cells tried to sort themselves out until a loud squealing scrape echoed through the air. With a grunt, Rico shoved at the body on top and managed to get up onto all fours. He lifted his head to see the car sideswipe a large concrete planter box so hard, the tree toppled and soil spread. The car swerved back the other way. Screams, yells and curses rose over the nerve-twanging scrapes as the car rolled onto its side and barged into the tables and chairs of an outside eatery.

'Oh, poor buggers,' he heard in his ear. 'Are you okay?' the same voice said as a large hand appeared in front of his face.

Rico grasped the hand. As he was hauled to his feet, the backpack swung to one side and settled at an awkward angle on his shoulder with a tug on the straps. He hefted his shoulders and adjusted the straps to ease the strain. 'I think so,' he managed to get out between a couple of gasps as his lungs refilled. He eyed the stranger: a tall man dressed in a grey suit – the coat skewed sideways and a large smear of dirt now decorated the lower length of one sleeve.

'Thank you so much. You just saved my life.' Rico brushed a hand down his clothes and winced at the shredded section at one knee. So much for brand new clothes.

'You're bleeding.' The man indicate with a sweep of his hand to the underside of Rico's arm.

He twisted his arm around. Blood oozed through the shirt sleeve at his elbow. He dabbed at it, swore at the sting and pressed hard. More of a large scrape than a deep cut, he figured which meant he wasn't about to pass out with major blood loss and didn't need a visit to a hospital. He was over hospitals. 'Nothing major and you've ruined you coat,' he said with a finger pointed at the smudge.

After a glance at his sleeve, the man shrugged. 'Nothing a visit to a drycleaner won't fix. More important, are you okay?'

The scream of sirens drowned out his response but also sent him an immediate message. Police would want to interview him: something he couldn't risk. He held out one hand to the stranger. 'Name's Joe. I can't thank you enough but right now I need to find a spot alone to let my nerves settle.'

The man grasped his hand and wrapped his other hand around Rico's lower arm in the grip of friendship as they shook. 'Sean. I'm not surprised. My nerves are kind of shot as well. That was way too close for comfort. Take care.'

Two police cars and an ambulance slowed to a crawl, wove past them and made their way through the carnage.

'Looks like there's a couple of folk who weren't so lucky,' Sean said with a nod towards the remnants of the eatery. He stepped to one side, bent down, scooped up the large paper bag with Rico's clothes and held it out. 'You don't want to forget your shopping.'

'Thanks.' Rico took hold of the string handles and turned away. 'I need to sit for a while,' he said over his shoulder before heading towards the upturned car. Number one priority was to check out the driver. There was a strong possibility the accident had been another deliberate attempt to rid the earth of one Enrico Giovannazzo. After a stagger on jelly legs he paused and shook himself while ordering his brain to get his limbs to work as they should. The next step was fine but the grazed leg demanded a limp.

With a step, limp, shuffle syncopation, he wended a way through the ever-increasing crowd of gawkers. As he went, he edged towards the shop fronts so he wouldn't stand out and be noticed. Nausea rose at the sight of two women and an elderly man who were being attended to by paramedics. One woman of middle age had silent tears coursing down her cheeks. She lay on her side in the recovery position with an almost skinless arm being gently wrapped. The other woman had already been loaded onto a stretcher with an oxygen mask over her nose and mouth. Both legs had numerous deep gouges and one foot hung at an awkward angle. Rico sent a silent question skywards to ask that she was unconscious for the pain must have been at a level off the charts.

The gasp from the crowd was loud when a police officer drew a cover over the elderly man's face. A profound silence followed. Many heads bowed. Rico shut his eyes with a single thought. That could have been him if it wasn't for a quick-thinking saviour. The resulting shudder down his entire body stilled him for a moment. Too close, too darn close.

Still afraid to be noticed, he eased closer to the wreckage but had to peer around bodies in the crush of gawkers to catch sight of the driver. The bastard sat leant up against the side of his car, legs bent, feet flat on the ground and with glazed eyes. Rico recognised the stare. The idiot was on a drug high and probably still didn't have a clue what was going on or the carnage he'd just served up to innocent victims. There was one positive about the sight: he didn't recognise the man but it didn't mean Rico hadn't been the target. In the past five years, numerous thugs could have been forced into his father's web of horror. Nausea churned so bad, he turned away and did his best to hide his limp as he went in search of the new phone.

Nine

'Put these on. You've got ten minutes.'

Folded garments landed on Matteo's chest. With one hand, he picked them up, held them high and groaned. Prison greens. Humiliation, mixed with a good dose of regret and anger, shot through his mind. He was used to the finer things in life and such an appalling outfit was not one of them. A snigger came from the doorway at his side. A clang and click followed. Another snigger and, thank goodness, fading footsteps. He waited until the steps disappeared before he was game to turn his head for a peek. As soon as he found out the name of the traitor, he would personally make the man suffer for days before cutting off his balls and forcing them down the bastard's throat. Three bloody nights he'd been here. Three nights of hell.

A sigh of regret blew from his mouth as he sat to spread out the garments on the end of the bed. There were two positives. His own underwear had been included and cotton-knit pants and top were a much better option than this throwaway jumpsuit which was now tatty and grimy after days of wear. There must be a regulation about how long a prisoner could wear such an ignominious garment before they were given real clothes but he'd never cared enough before to find out. Now he sure as hell would find out and press charges the very second he managed to get out of this hell hole.

With his back to the bars, he unsnapped the top of the godawful jumpsuit, withdrew his arms and pulled the green T-shirt over his head. Talk about undignified. Bet the pigs watched every darn movement on the monitor screen. At least the top came down far enough to allow a modicum of dignity while he swept the jumpsuit to the ground, donned his own blessed underwear and stepped into the elastic-waisted thick cotton tracksuit pants. Hell, he never even wore such casual clothes at home on a Saturday afternoon while he watched the footy.

One kick and the jumpsuit landed against the bottom of the bars, as did the folded piece of paper he'd forgotten about. Horrified, he glanced at the camera in the corner. Too late, he realised his actions were way too obvious. To go after the paper would be downright suicidal. With as much nonchalance as he could muster, he took two slow steps towards the bars and bent over.

'Stand back!' a voice yelled.

Matteo glanced up to see a taser pointed at him. As he rose, he shuffled closer to the bars and snuck one foot over the paper. 'I was just going to fold this up.' He pointed to the white jumpsuit.

'Stand back. Two steps.' The officer neared, waved the taser a tad higher. 'Sarge,' he called, as

Matteo shuffled backwards but ensured the paper remained under the pad of his foot.

The same sergeant appeared. 'Perkins? What's the problem?'

'The prisoner, under his foot, paper. I saw it on the monitor.'

As the sergeant neared, his head shook from side-to-side. One eyebrow lifted; the corner of his mouth quirked into a wry smile. 'Sit and lift your feet onto the bed. Perkins, don't be afraid to use your taser if he so much as breathes out of place.' Keys jangled as the sergeant lifted them from his leather belt. Metal chinked on metal. A quiet scrape, the lock snicked open. 'Damn it, Giovannazzo, move back,' the man said as he held the door shut. 'Perkins, aim for the neck.'

Not game for the indignation of being on the receiving end of an electric shock, Matteo moved but managed to slide the paper under the garment before he plonked onto the bed and lifted both feet onto the mattress. Even though his heart thumped like a big bass drum it couldn't move the wodge of fear caught in his throat. His lungs forgot how to work while he watched the sergeant lift the jumpsuit and snaffle up the paper.

The man said nothing, unfolded the paper, read and shook his head again. 'Fat chance,' he hissed as he re-locked the door and left without another word. The constable smirked, replaced the taser in its keeper on his belt and followed his boss.

Matteo swore under his breath as he flopped back on the mattress but shot back up again when some earlier words registered. Ten minutes, but for what? They wouldn't transfer him to Long Bay. Not yet. There hadn't even been a proper interview and Long Bay was for after a trial, not before. Maybe a transfer to some other facility but they couldn't hold him much longer without formal charges and an interview, although they had spouted a list of charges when they arrested him, not that he could remember. Panic at the time had numbed his brain to anything said other than he was under arrest. But he knew the law. Even with the initial charges there was no choice but to give him bail for there was no proof of any of the charges they'd laid against him. He wasn't stupid enough to carry out any of the serious stuff. Any activity could be blamed on the perpetrators. And there was always Rico. Since he had already been eliminated, it would be easy to lay blame on Rico as the mastermind, and the instigator, and the perpetrator of any crime they dared charge Matteo with. A dead man couldn't claim or prove innocence.

Before he had a chance to come up with any more ideas, a scuffle of footsteps caught his attention. Three officers this time, all with staid grim faces. He sat, waited, nerves tensed like a taut piano string ready to ping apart.

'Stand next to the bed,' the sergeant barked.

The other two men stood either side of the sarge. It was almost impossible to hold back a grin when Matteo recognised the newcomer, one of his but he couldn't recall the officer's name. To acknowledge the man would be stupid so he kept his eyes honed on the sergeant.

The door opened. The sergeant held out a pair of cuffs.

Matteo shuddered. 'There's no need for those.'

'There's every need.' The same eyebrow quirked up to an impossible height. 'Hold out your arms with fingers intertwined.'

There were two choices, obey and be meek to prove he is eager to assist, or rebel and make life difficult. When a vision of the taser entered his mind he held out both fisted hands. The snick echoed. Humiliation and hatred simmered and soon boiled. It reached inferno level when the Perkins guy dropped to one knee and wrapped leg irons around Matteo's ankles.

'Come on,' Matteo growled. 'This is ridiculous and unnecessary. I know the law. I'm in a police station, for God's sake. With three armed officers. You can be sure I'll make a formal complaint about my treatment.'

'Walk.' Perkins grabbed Matteo's elbow, jerked him towards the door and shoved. 'Turn right, go to the end of the passage. Interview room one.'

It was almost impossible to take a proper step. Indignation simmered with every shuffle along the corridor, each step accompanied by an echoing clang of metal as it dragged along the floor. Rage like he'd never experienced before, seethed under the surface, desperate to explode. He bit the inside of his cheek to prevent any words bursting out for not a single one would help his cause.

At the door with a rigid plastic label, *Interview Room One,* a hand reached over his shoulder, pushed the door open while another hand settled in the small of his back.

'Get your hands off me,' Matteo snarled. He yanked his body forward to step inside under his own steam. The room was like all interview rooms. This one wore the same coat of depressing grey as the rest of the inner sanctum of the station. A table took up much of the room with the end butted against one wall, two chairs on either side. Modern electronic recording equipment had become the norm. Here, the little red light already flashed to show readiness for the interview to begin. One button was all it needed to start both vision and voice recorders.

A chair was pulled out. He ignored the scrape of metal on industrial linoleum even though the screech sent his nerves on edge as he sat and wriggled on the cold seat. They sure didn't believe in comfort in this place. The sergeant sat opposite with the two constables taking up position against opposite walls, one near the door. At the swish of the door opening behind him, every atom in his body came to a sudden standstill. Who would do the interview? He choked on the held breath when he recognised the uniform on the man who settled next to the sergeant and placed a huge pile of folders against the wall.

'The Feds?' he asked. 'Why? This is becoming more and more ridiculous.'

'Senior Sergeant Sam King, Australian Federal Police. You have the right to a lawyer. Since yours is unavailable we have a legal representative on standby. You indicated earlier that you didn't want one. Now is your chance to change your mind.'

'I am a lawyer. I can represent myself.'

King nodded with a quirk of his brow. 'Very well. Let's get started.' He reached over, pressed the button on the recording outfit.

Everyone present called out their names, numbers and ranks. Ah, Phil, Matteo remembered when his man took his turn but he didn't have time to search his memory bank for details of the man. Matteo added his name at the end, sat back and glared. 'I have nothing to say.'

King laughed. 'You know as well as I do that those people who refuse to comment are the ones with something to hide.'

'You've got nothing on me.'

A large hand with long fingers stretched out, landed with an ominous thump on the pile of files. A wide gold wedding band glinted at Matteo. 'These say different.'

Matteo didn't like the depth of the pile. Where did so much paperwork come from? Nobody in the organisation had anywhere near such an amount of info. A finger tore away at the seam of his pants before he realised he was showing signs of nervousness. Instead, he folded his arms across his chest. 'Paper proves nothing.'

'Bodies do.'

'Excuse me?' Matteo rocked back into the chair. 'I never killed anyone.'

'Yet I am charging you with the murder of AFP officer, Sergeant Michael Simpson.'

Holy hell, how did they find out? Matteo scrambled for the right words. 'Never heard of him.'

'Really? I find that impossible to believe since we found his body on your land.'

'My wife owns the land.'

Both men opposite raised their heads, stared at Matteo and grinned. Matteo realised what he'd done but said nothing aloud. Inside, his brain swore over and over.

'I don't recall me mentioning the property where we found the body yet you seem to know it well. I might point out that we believe your wife when she said she didn't know the particular property is in her name. We had an expert analyse the signature on the paperwork. Your wife's signature was forged.'

'If there's a body on any land my family owns it wasn't me who put it there. But my son, Rico, I wouldn't put it past him to do so.' Matteo unfolded his arms, dropped his hands into his lap and willed taut muscles and strung-out nerves to relax. He'd already made one major stuff up.

'Interesting.' King sent Matteo the slightest of grins: not one that showed humour. 'So you claim your son murdered Sgt Simpson and buried the body on land you own.'

'Yes, he admitted it to me.'

When a stifled snort came from behind, Matteo glanced at the man who stood at ease against the back wall. His eyes were shut but his head shook from side-to-side as though in disbelief. It took a second to unscramble brain cells and realise he'd made another stuff-up.

'I should be shocked at the way you lay blame on your own flesh and blood but given what I've read in the last couple of days about you, I'm not in the least surprised.' King leant forwards. 'Maybe you would like to detail how your son managed to murder a man he'd never met or even heard of, dug a hole on your land and buried the body, when Rico was still incarcerated.' King leant back and folded his own arms.

'He did it the day he got out.'

Both men opposite him laughed out loud while Phil, his man against the wall, groaned. King sobered, leant forwards again. 'No he didn't for Simpson was murdered days before your son was released. You,' a rigid finger pointed at Matteo's head, 'made a monumental mistake. You buried

Simpson's hidden intact mobile phone with him. The one he kept in a pouch inside his trousers. We have recovered every piece of data. Simpson was a smart officer. Unbeknown to you, he recorded every second of the conversation he had with you and your two cohorts. Four distinct voices: Simpson's, yours and two others. We're not sure who the other two are but have our suspicions. A specialist will analyse the voices and compare them with those men we have under arrest. Your voice stood out when you gave orders to break Simpson's fingers, to break his arm, to shoot his kneecap, to… we heard it all. It doesn't matter who fired the last bullet, you were there, you gave the orders. Therefore, you are charged with the cold blooded murder of Sergeant Simpson and you will be held without a chance in hell of getting bail until trial.'

King stood. 'We also have the email sent to Simpson, purportedly from the AFP commissioner which outlined a concocted leak concerning Rico's former wife. An email requesting Simpson to meet with the commissioner to discuss Amanda's new identity.' King leant over so their faces were mere centimetres apart. 'An email the commissioner neither wrote nor sent but which we found on your home office computer files.'

As King straightened, Matteo had the impression the man was as desperate to spit in Matteo's face as he was to punch the arrogant twerp's lights out.

'I'll leave the rest of these charges until later but they aren't pretty.' He laid one finger on the paperwork and stabbed three times. 'We have all the proof we need right here.' Using both hands he picked up the pile, held it against his chest and nodded to the officers, 'Take the bastard away.' He turned back to Matteo. 'You will be sent to another facility as soon as they can clear a cell in solitary confinement. This is for your protection for I imagine if we release you amongst the general prisoners, you won't last more than twenty-four hours, which would be a pity for I want to see you linger in a prison cell for a very long time. It's the least Simpson deserves. He was an excellent officer.' King turned and strode from the room, his back rigid, his boots echoing until the door into the front desk area slammed.

Ten

Even though the strap cut into his shoulder, Rico remained still, leant up against the fence, one leg crossed over the other. The canopy of eucalyptus leaves shadowed him enough to not stand out as he eyed the people going in and out. So far, there had been no-one he recognised. A single crow wailed its macabre song, cicadas trilled in accompaniment. Passing wheels whooshed, the clangs and dings of vehicles being filled with fuel couldn't quite drown out the underlying murmur of voices.

When doubt about his safety eased enough, he straightened, shifted the backpack to the other shoulder, stepped from the leafy shelter and strode across the gravel. Stones crunched until he reached the bitumen concourse, stained with oil drips, spilt liquids and dried food scraps. It had been a while since the area had felt the pressure of a hose to clean it down. Acrid scents from each spill joined with over-heated brakes, baked rubber and strong fuel. The stench caught at the back of his throat until he pushed open the glass door and stepped inside. Chilly air from the air-conditioner was so welcome he sucked in a lung full. More pleasant aromas of coffee and fried food brought welcome saliva to a dry mouth.

Dusty work boots in various dark shades, rubber thongs and petite sandals lined up in front of the glass-fronted food displays. His leather trainers tagged on the end as he peered at the hot food between travel-worn heads. Not much appealed. The next cabinet along was better. Fresh rolls, wraps and sandwiches stuffed with various proteins and salads were more to his liking, especially in this heat. The aroma of fresh brewed coffee won the war on what to drink although he added two bottles of chilled water to his order.

Tables were in short supply in such a busy roadhouse unless one sat outside to bake. None inside were vacant so he settled his food on the edge of yellow Formica on the nearest table and nodded at the sole occupant, a teenager with brown hair tied back in a ponytail. A denim jacket stood out as it was too hot for such a garment. It hid most of her mid-blue T-shirt. 'Do you mind if we share the table? I won't be here long.'

The young woman's head shot up. Fear swept through her eyes before a forced smile masked it. She glanced around, shrugged her shoulders and indicated the opposite chair. 'Sure.'

It was pure relief to drop the backpack to the floor. He rolled his sore shoulder three times to ease the ache, lifted the chair out to not add to the noise and sank into it. Bliss. He savoured every mouthful of ham and salad crammed into a fresh, crusty roll, taking his time to chew and swallow. Even when it was gone, he used one finger to pick up escapee lettuce and carrot strands from the paper wrapper. It could be a while before the next meal. The black coffee was strong and hot. Far better than the last poor excuse for a brew at the East Perth station where he'd caught the country bus. Pity it came no further than this but at least he was out of the city and in a remote roadhouse where it was unlikely he'd be recognised. As he sipped, he eyed the woman who sat head down while she picked at a bowl of fruit salad. The other hand twitched and tapped in a nervous staccato on the edge of the table.

'Are you okay?' he asked.

Brown eyes flicked up and stared. 'What's it to you?'

He shrugged. 'You seem nervous.'

She didn't succeed in masking the quick hiss of a sucked in breath. 'I'm fine.'

He laughed. 'I've learnt from experience that when a woman says she's fine, it's rarely true.' When she glanced over his shoulder and swore under her breath, Rico turned his head to see what had startled her. A wodge of fear lodged itself in his throat. It was impossible to not recognise the leather jacket laced over a plaid shirt. Multiple tattoos covered every centimetre of skin not covered by clothes. Long, greasy hair hung over the shoulders but didn't hide the multiple pieces of scrap metal pierced all over the rugged face. Knee-high leather boots studded with dozens of silver discs left a short strip of dirty denim thighs on display. The man swept his eyes around the room and back: eyes Rico recognised.

'Is he after you?' Rico spun back to find the woman cowered under the table. He stood to hide her. 'Let's get out of here.' He shoved both bottles of water down the inside of his shirt, hefted the backpack onto one shoulder and sidled around the table.

'I can't,' whimpered from the chair. A backpack similar to his sat on the other side.

'Sure you can. You're tiny enough he won't see you if you walk in front of me. There's a side door to your right. Come on.'

With her head still on the chair, she twisted her neck, caught his eye. 'Why would you want to help me? Who the hell are you?'

'Escape first, talk later. Grab your bag before he comes closer.'

The words had an instant effect. One skinny arm shot out, hefted the bag. She screwed around as she stood and wriggled upright to ensure she kept him between her and the bikie. Rico planted one hand in the small of her back and shuffled her the five metres to the door. Once outside, he grasped her hand and tugged.

'You got a vehicle?' he asked as he headed towards the truck he'd already tagged as suitable.

'No, do you?'

'No, I planned on hitching a ride with a truckie.'

'So did I.'

'Damn, come on.' He'd already scouted around for the most suitable road train that faced east, sussed out the drivers to ensure they weren't known to him but hell, it had been five years. He didn't have a clue about who took underhand cash payments from his father to cart *extra* cargo nowadays. This little snaffu meant he'd have to change tactics. He wouldn't be able to sit up front with this young woman in tow. No driver would take two of them. Maybe he should leave her. Or find her another truck.

A door swished. He grabbed the woman around her shoulders and hauled her around the back of a trailer. She stumbled, swore, but found her balance and kept in step with him until he plastered her against the side of the trailer, their legs hidden by a pair of large tyres. 'Stay there while I check.'

With a nod of her head, she turned to face the truck, her bag hugged against her stomach. Rico crept back to the tail end, peered around. The bikie stood, arms folded, less than two metres from the entry to the ladies toilets. Dugite, he remembered the bikie's gang name, held a mobile phone in his hand. In between glances at the screen, he studied the toilet block and the door they'd just come through. How in hell's name did such a young kid get mixed up with him? In the past, Dugite's gang made big purchases of illegal substances from the bastard. If he still did, Rico didn't have a clue.

As he returned to the woman, he knocked on the trailer and checked the locks. Too hard to get into. But the front trailer was an open tray stacked with two rows of large metal pipes and a huge grader. Getting on would be easy but the ride unpleasant. At least until the truck stopped again when he could find her another, better ride. It would be dicey to clamber on without being seen. In theory, the truckie should check the load before he climbed into the cab so Rico would have to wait until the driver was aboard before he could get them on the back.

On his haunches he peered under the tray and studied the scuffed, well-worn leather bikie boots. They shifted from side-to-side, began to pace. As escape time shortened, nerves tightened. Footsteps crunched, neared. Brown steel-caps came into view. A fist banged against the rear door and echoed. Straps on the front tray twanged as they were checked for tautness. It was a check, of sorts but not very thorough. The very second the cabin door squeaked open Rico grabbed both backpacks. 'Come on, we must hurry.' Two lopes to the back end of the tray, he heaved the packs up then followed with a leap. He held out a hand. Cold fingers wrapped around his wrist. He tugged her up. 'Keep to the middle of the tray. The driver has wide side mirrors. Crawl under the grader, sit hunched next to the tyres, passenger side.'

It was a mad scramble with tangled limbs. Rico shoved the two bags over their feet to hide them, wrapped one arm around his companion's shoulders and held his breath until the truck pulled onto the highway after a long wait for another, single-trailer rig to pull out ahead of them. 'Don't move. Keep your eye out for your friend.'

'Friend?' A snort followed the high-pitched screech.

It wasn't until they'd gone about a kilometre before Rico released his hold on the woman. 'Move to the other wheels.'

'Why?'

'So we can't be seen by drivers coming the other way. These tyres are big enough to keep us hidden.' He had to raise his voice to be heard over the rush of wind, rumble of tyres and numerous gear changes until they were up to speed. This time he placed the bags under their bent legs to give them something to rest on and prevent the bags sliding away should the truck lurch. 'Now, I need some details. What's your name?'

The sucked in breath was audible above the noise. 'Why do you wanna know?'

'Come on, I just saved your arse back there. We're going to be stuck together until this rig stops. At least let's be comfortable with each other. I'm Joe.'

'Ella.'

'How old are you?'

'Twenty.'

'Hell, just a kid. What's a kid like you doing with someone like Dugite?'

Eyes wide and mouth agape, Ella stared at him. 'You know him?'

'Not personally, no. Know of him. Hell, he's notorious. Has his ugly mug in the paper oodles of times. What's the relationship?'

'Are you crazy? There is no relationship.'

'Then why was he looking for you?'

'Umm, It could be I might have something he wants.'

Rico swore, twisted to face Ella whose eyes stared at a spot on the metal tray. 'You need to tell me the story. If he's after you, he won't give up until he finds you and when he does, it won't be pretty.'

'How do you know?'

'He's the bloody leader of a notorious bikie gang. These guys don't get to be leader by being nice.'

'He's not nice.'

'This I know, spill the beans so I know what I'm up against when he catches up with us.'

Her eyes widened as she turned her head and stared at him. 'You think he'll find us?'

'He knew where you were. How?'

'Don't know.' Tears flooded across her eyes. She swept them away with a closed fist, sniffed and shuddered.

'Story, please.' Rico reached out, placed one hand over her clenched fist. Tension radiated through stiff fingers.

'Okay. I began to date a guy.'

'Name?'

'Jai. I didn't know he was involved with any gang. Had no tats. Seemed nice. We were about to go out for a meal. I was in the bathroom at his place when I heard bangs, crashes and yells. I didn't know what was happening or what to do. I cracked the door open a weenie bit. Saw that guy,' she wavered her hand in the direction they'd just come, 'stomp into the family room. He had a long thick metal bar in his hand. You know, one of those tyre thingummy jigs. Two other scary guys dressed in black followed. Heard them demand the package. They wanted a package.'

'Of what?'

Ella shrugged. 'Dunno.'

'Keep going.'

'Jai screamed and screamed and screamed. There were thuds, crashes, broken glass. I panicked and began to search for some sort of weapon. I opened the cupboard under the basin. Right at the back was a parcel, wrapped in... umm, you know, that sticky brown tape. Round and round. I don't know why, but I grabbed the parcel, slid the window open above the vanity, noticed Jai's phone on the top. Took it so I could phone a friend or a taxi to come and get me. I was so scared I wriggled through the window and ran for my life. Over the side fence, across the neighbour's lawn and just ran. Later - much later, I tried to ring him until I realised I had his phone.' When she turned her face towards him, a river of tears ran down both cheeks. 'A couple of hours later I found the word Mum on his call list so I rang her. She… she… Jai's dead.'

Rico swore and wrapped his arms around Ella. 'God, I'm so sorry.' He eased back a fraction. 'So how come you were at the servo and how did you get there?'

'I was at my place, too scared to go outside, still trying to figure out what to do when Jai's phone rang. I answered. A real creepy voice said, "I know where you are. I want the parcel you stole." I panicked, packed a few clothes and snuck away from my place. I had no idea what to do but figured I needed to leave the city so I caught the train to Midland, got on a bus to Mundaring. I began to walk east. A nice lady picked me up, took me to the roadhouse. It's as far as she was going.'

'So how did Dugite know how to find you?'

'I don't know.' A new bout of tears flowed.

Rico held her head against his shoulder and let her weep out her fear while he thought. 'Damn, do you still have the phone?'

She eased away, sniffed and used the bottom of her T-shirt to wipe away the moisture. 'Yes.'

'Show it to me.'

'Why?'

Rico beckoned with one finger. 'Let me check it, I think I know how they tracked you.'

His heart played kettle drums while she unzipped her backpack. One drum boomed when a brown-taped package fell out. Even though he wished he didn't, he knew what was under the tape. The drums beat double time when he saw the phone she held out. Same brand and model as the one he'd had. He snatched it from her fingers, removed the sim card and battery.'

She made a grab for it. 'What are you doing?' she screeched. 'That's a brand new phone.'

'These phones have a device in them so you can track down your phone if it gets lost or stolen. I'm almost certain Dugite followed you via this phone.' Since he wasn't sure how the tracker worked, he heaved the battery into the scrub. The sim card was crunched under the heel of his shoe before it went roadside. He prayed it got crushed under hundreds of wheels. On his knees, he crawled to the end of the trailer and dropped the phone in front of the wheels. A satisfying crunch followed. Within seconds he was back next to a fierce-faced Ella.

'Now what am I supposed to do. I needed that phone.'

'You needed it as much as you need a bullet in your head, which is what would have happened if Dugite found you. We're not out of the woods yet. He would have tracked the phone going this way.' He picked up the package. 'Have you opened this?'

'No.'

'Do you know what's in it?'

'I can guess.'

'Drugs. Ice or cocaine. Why in hell's name did you bring it with you?'

'I need the money.'

'You were going to sell it?' Rico ran a hand through his hair on a long huffed out breath of disbelief. He turned back to face Ella. 'Do you often sell drugs?'

'No way. I've never even tried any.'

'Then why…' he couldn't finish. 'Never mind.' He opened his own backpack, scuffled around and took out the new pocket knife. He'd prefer a stiletto but since they were banned they were hard to get a hold of unless you knew someone with illegal contraband. A grip with fingernails and the longest blade eased out. Ella swore but he ignored her. One stab, a slash, the packet opened. Had to be at least a kilo of coke. 'You can't keep this. It'll bring you nothing but serious trouble.'

A hand made a grab for the parcel. 'It's all I've got.'

Rico held the parcel to one side, away from her. He reached over, made the cut bigger and moved back to the rear of the tray where he lowered the package towards the ground and let the wind catch the dribble of powder, ensuring it blew under the tray and not at them. When it had emptied he scrunched the paper into a tight ball and hurled it towards the bush before he crawled back to Ella.

'It's a death sentence: your death first when you get involved with crooks you attempt to sell it to, followed by the death of the users. Once you get involved in such an evil world, pigs like Dugite will never let you out.'

'I need the money. Now I'm almost broke.'

'You sure as hell don't need money from drugs. It will buy you nothing but grief. I'll cover you for anything you need until we get to wherever we end up. I'll give you enough to pay for accommodation and expenses for a couple of weeks. You find a job, a real job, away from scum.'

'You have money?'

'More than I need.'

'Then why are you on this damn truck getting blown to smithereens, burnt to a crisp, more bruises than a squishy pear, out in the middle of a damn desert?'

Rico couldn't hold back a shout of laughter. 'Good question.'

Eleven

'Giovannazzo, time to go.'

Matteo shot upright so fast one foot knocked the tray of leftover food he'd placed on the floor in disgust at the blandness. The clatter echoed, followed by a second *whump* as a pair of shoes landed nearby. His shoes, with no laces. The same socks he'd had on when he'd been arrested were shoved in each shoe.

'Put the shoes on,' said the same insufferable sergeant in his la-di-dah Pommy accent.

A sensation of filth slithered up his spine as Matteo settled on the side of the bed and pulled unwashed socks over bare feet that hadn't seen a shower for two days. He could have washed them in the stainless steel basin but couldn't stomach the indignity of the perverts watching him on their damned cameras. Never before had he put grimy feet into socks. Never before had he donned a pair of unwashed socks. Nausea rose at the image but the shoes would be unbearable without socks. Once the warm wool covered his feet, he pressed both into the shoes and stood.

'Stand against the bed, facing me.' The order was barked, the kind of tone no other soul had ever dared to use when they spoke to Matteo.

Ready to explode, Matteo complied. The door opened; handcuffs were held out. Hatred simmered from him at the nod towards his wrists. When he fisted his hands he thought about using them. Now would be the perfect time to make a break. A punch to the mid-section and a kick to the groin was all it would take. The door was open. He knew the layout of this place. Down the passage, around the corner, race past the edge of the counter, across the floor and through the door then mingle with the pedestrians outside. It wouldn't be easy but with the element of surprise he could make it.

Head down, muscles taut, he waited for the sergeant to move close enough. Come on, come on. When no boots appeared in his line of vision he dared a glance upwards. Two other officers had arrived. Damn it. Head down again, he grinned. One of them was Phil. Details shot back into his grey matter. A recent convert. What was the hold they had over the man? Ah, yes, he'd gotten himself into a massive gambling debt at one of the family's regular poker nights. High stakes. You win, you win big but the losses were massive. God, let the man have a plan.

Metal went around his wrists. The clicks sounded too loud. Both were tugged to check they were tight with no wiggle room to free his hands.

'Walk towards the door.' With a taser aimed at Matteo, the sergeant moved behind him, put a hand in the small of Matteo's back and shoved.

With no laces to hold the shoes on tight, he had to shuffle with an officer either side of him and one behind. Certain the taser was still aimed at him, he dismissed the idea of making a break for the nearest door leading outside. At least there were no leg irons this time. When they reached a door he was familiar with, he knew where he was headed. Central Police Station is located near the rear of the Court House with access for prisoners through the blocked off Central Street. At last he would have the opportunity to gain bail. About bloody time.

The 'L' shape building in rendered brick has wrought iron balconies in the inner angle. He glanced up at the raked corrugated iron roof and squinted at the glare. The brightness was welcome but even more so the warmth of natural sun. What delighted him even more were the constant thrum of nearby traffic and exhaust-filled air. Far better than the stuffy cell with lingering remnants of previous tenants an abomination to his senses.

There were three bays, the one he came out of, the central one recessed between two stone columns which supported a classical entablature over which the words *Central Police Station* is printed in raised letters. A glance one way and he caught sight of the heavy cast iron gates which prevented any entry by vehicles but they also prevented an escape on foot by a prisoner lucky enough to not be guided by three armed officers. The door of the right bay opened, two more officers came out and stood each side of it, both with a hand on their pistol and a smirk on their face. As if he was stupid enough to try to escape from this position. Bet the pigs prayed he would make an attempt so they had an excuse to all draw their weapons at the same time and turn him into a colander.

'Move it.' He bit back a curse when he stumbled at the shove in his back. A single snigger came from behind.

'Take it easy, no need for any rough stuff,' came from his left. His man. There wasn't much Phil could do if he wanted his status to remain secret but the comment of support, little as it was, deserved a Brownie point.

The prisoner holding room was a familiar sight but never from this aspect. How many times had he consulted with a prisoner as their lawyer? A time when he had always been super-confident. He scoffed under his breath. His confidence might be a little dented but within the hour, he would walk out of here on bail. At the thought, he threw his shoulders back, lifted his head and quickened his stride. He would not be seen to cower or show his disdain.

Phil rushed ahead, opened a door, stepped inside and held the door wide. Matteo strode in but stopped in his tracks when the mumble of voices ceased. Dead silence ensued in an instant. Matteo shut his eyes to convince his brain he hadn't seen a courtroom full of members of the media and general nosey bastards. Before daring to open his eyes, he dropped his head but immediately lifted it again and stared straight ahead. He would not give any of them the satisfaction of seeing him beaten.

As he was ushered into the small rectangle designated for prisoners, the rumble of voices began again and rose until the orderly called for everyone to stand. Voices quietened but were accompanied by the rustle of clothes, shoes and seats. The musty scent of old sweat, coffee and stale cigarettes lingered even though no food or smoking is allowed in any court. How often had he seen a crowd of reporters gulp down a takeaway coffee or have frantic multiple puffs before they rushed inside at the last minute.

The judge entered, caught Matteo's eye and shook his head with a tightening of his mouth. Matteo detested this man who had been an arrogant prosecution lawyer. They'd had too many run-ins on opposite sides of many legal cases. Well, the old prick wouldn't win today. He had no choice but to grant bail for they had not a single shred of actual proof that Matteo had committed any crime.

At the call to order, silence reigned. The judge sat and rifled through a wad of papers while the horde shuffled and mumbled as they found their seats again. The size of the pile was a tad scary. Why was the file so thick? Where did they get all these papers? Is it the same pile the fed had? Is it actual evidence or was it a just pretend file to make him believe they had evidence? He wouldn't put it past them to try trickery.

'Will the prisoner please stand?' Such an officious voice.

Matteo stood, almost facing the rear wall so the gawkers couldn't make out any changes in his facial features. His eyes were in the direction of the judge but there wasn't a chance in hell he would catch the bastard's eye again. Instead, he studied the top architrave of the door over the judge's shoulder, noticed the need for paint and the dust along the top.

'Matteo Giovannazzo, at this stage you are charged with twelve counts of murder…'

His jaw dropped and head buzzed with a million mosquitoes. He flopped back onto the seat. Two officers hauled him to his feet again but he had to lean on the bench in front of him to keep upright. The list went on and on and on but few words registered. *Money laundering* came out clear along with the word *brothel*. All he could think of were twelve bodies. How did they know and how come the number was only twelve? *At this stage*. The words finally registered. Holy, holy, holy. They'd dug up twelve bodies but how did they even find them? A picture of the five-acre block of bushland centred in his mind. The bodies had been scattered, no two anywhere near each other. All in dense bush, many so old the bones would now be tangled with the roots of massive trees.

A jab to his ribs. Matteo swung his head towards the perpetrator. 'Get your hands off me.'

'Answer the question.' The officer pointed to the judge.

'Huh?' A slight twist of his head, he noticed the judge had a questioning look on his face. 'Sorry, I didn't hear.'

'How do you plead to the murder of Sergeant Simpson?'

'Not guilty.'

'Really?'

'I never murdered anyone. Not guilty to all charges.'

An uproar came from the masses.

'Silence in the court,' the usher bellowed over the ruckus.

Matteo searched the faces. Many he recognised. Most reporters had heads down as they scribbled notes. A couple whispered into mobile phones. One man, whom he knew from experience, had a large pad on his knees. A piece of charcoal made quick slashes on the paper as eyes swung from Matteo to the pad. The indignity brought a surge of acid to his gullet.

'I've spent the past couple of days reading every item in this file,' said the judge as he stabbed a finger on the way too high pile. 'The contents beggar belief. The proof is indisputable. I've listened to the recording on Sgt Simpson's phone so many times I can almost quote it word for word. Scientific analysis of the voices prove you gave the orders and yet you plead not guilty? Really?'

'I did not kill anyone.'

'You gave the orders. It is still cold-blooded murder and you gave the orders to kidnap, torture and kill Sally Bowers, the lawyer for your son's ex-wife.'

Matteo's mouth opened and closed several times but no sound came out. He shuddered, shook his head and forced his brain to work. 'I did not kill any lawyer and have no idea what you are talking about.'

This time a laugh escaped the judge's mouth before he could pull his face back into a severe frown. 'Did you not hear any of the charges we just spent the last fifteen minutes reading out aloud?'

Fifteen minutes? 'Err, no. I was so shocked by these ridiculous charges my brain went into overdrive.'

'I suggest you obtain the services of a top lawyer who will take you through every charge and explain the finer details but to re-iterate this particular charge, we have the person who carried out your orders to murder Miss Bowers. He gave us a signed statement. The same person who detailed the events of several murders of the bodies we have so far found on your property. You will be held in custody until you appear in court at a date to be determined.'

'You can't hold me in gaol for an indefinite time without proof. I deny guilt in all charges and request bail.'

'Bail is denied.' The words seemed to echo around the room then continued to echo in his head. 'Take him away,' the judge added with a definite scowl. He stood so fast, the court orderly was caught unawares and had to scramble to his feet.

'All stand,' the orderly called as the judge strode through the door to his private chambers without waiting for the traditional nods of respect.

Voices rose in an instant. Glares were speared in Matteo's direction before four officers surrounded him, grasped him by the arms and hurried him from the room so fast, his feet barely had a chance to hit the ground.

'Arsehole,' was spat in his right ear with a definite tightening of fingers into his upper arm. Maybe he should find a lawyer to take photos of the bruises and charge this idiot with police brutality. And he needed to get a hold of the charges, study them and come up with a logical defence.

'Take it easy, fellas,' said his man.

'Take it easy?' another muttered. 'I'd like to tether him spread-eagled in the desert and take my time to pour boiling tar over his skin then leave him to the ants and crows.' A harsh jerk on his arm and Matteo stumbled.

'Come on, guys, we can't be caught doing anything wrong. It's not worth it,' said the one man who wasn't game to cross Matteo.

Back in his cell, he was unshackled and shoved so hard, he fell to his knees and cracked the front of his head on the edge of the hard bed. Matteo gritted his lips together to prevent the escape of a single word until he was alone when he sent the two finger salute in the direction of the camera.

He crawled onto the bed with one thought centred in his brain. Johannsen is a dead man. You talk, you die and Johannsen more than talked: he spilt his guts. He'd better not have mentioned Rico's death.

Twelve

It was almost impossible to stand after hours of being shaken to the core, but it was such a relief to be off the truck. After finding his balance on jellified legs, Rico strapped his backpack across his shoulders, grabbed Ella's pack in one hand and her elbow in the other. 'Let's get out of here.'

'But we need to keep going east.'

'The driver will camp here overnight. There is a limit on the hours a truckie is allowed to drive before he has to take a good eight hours of sleep.'

'Oh, I didn't know. So what can we do? Find another truck?'

'No. We'll stay here in Kalgoorlie for the night. We also need to catch some shut eye.'

'But where? The bikie passed us. He might be on the lookout for me.'

Rico tugged Ella into the shadows at the side of the service station. 'I should have asked this before. Did Dugite see you at your boyfriends' house? Describe the layout, what you saw and what happened.'

'I don't think he saw me. I opened the bathroom door about a centimetre, peeked through the crack. The big family room where Jai was, is opposite the bathroom. I saw three men in the room but they had their eyes on Jai. They just laid into him.' She shuddered with her eyes shut. 'Beat him to a pulp. He didn't have time to move. Two had their backs to me. The other one, Dugite, faced me. I caught a quick peek at his face one time when he glanced up but he wasn't looking at me. He swung his eyes between the other two guys as he yelled orders. So I guess it's possible but I was so scared I closed the door and that's when I panicked and got out.'

'So it's possible he won't recognise you.'

'More like probable but then why is he here? You got rid of the phone.'

'You were headed in this direction with at least a kilo of cocaine. Logic says he would be desperate to get it back but I don't think it his main reason.'

'What do you mean?'

'He knows someone else was in the house for you took Jai's phone. You are a witness to a serious crime he committed and these guys don't leave witnesses behind. He may not even be here. Once he couldn't get any more location signals from the phone, he may have given up and gone home.'

'But he didn't pass us again.'

'He might have. We were in the pipes most of the way. I slept for a while. Did you?'

'Yeah, sure since there wasn't anything else to do, but such a loud bike would have woken us. It sure roared when it passed us the first time.'

Rico laughed. 'Maybe not. We got used to the howling wind, the constant rattles and squeaks and managed to sleep. Other vehicles that passed while we slept didn't wake us so let's hope the bikie returned. Now, we need to find somewhere to spend the night and get a decent meal. A shower would be welcome as well.'

'A hot shower sounds real good but where? Besides, I don't have much money.'

'I'll pay. Come on.' Rico settled the palm of his hand in Ella's back and gave a gentle shove. 'If Dugite is here, he'll be looking for a single person so if we stick close together he'll dismiss us if he spies us. Best place to hide is right under a person's nose. If we look furtive it will bring attention to us, so look confident.'

'Easy for you to say. I'm downright terrified,' Ella muttered as she sidled against his body.

He couldn't suppress a smile at the way she stuck against his side like a limpet but he figured she was more than a little scared after what she had witnessed. It must have been horrific for her. It was possible she was still in shock. As they walked, Rico scanned the streets on the lookout for a particular bikie and a decent place to stay. They turned a corner next to a rowdy pub, one of many in the town and the sort of place a bikie would frequent. Kalgoorlie was famous for its pubs and with the number of miners in the town the pubs were always full, especially in the evenings. Further up the street stood the Plaza hotel. Perfect. Close to the centre of town and a little more luxurious where it was unlikely a bikie, dressed the way Dugite had been dressed, would be welcome. The sort of place where they would say the hotel was full to a man of

Dugite's calibre. Let's hope it isn't full, Rico thought as he steered Ella towards it.

She tugged him to a halt when he turned into the forecourt. 'This looks expensive. I don't mind something less... less glamorous.'

'It's okay, I can afford it. Plus it's not the sort of place a bikie would be welcome.'

'Oh, okay, if you're sure.'

Rico smiled at Ella's insecurity. For someone who'd had the nous to climb through a bathroom window and escape such a ghastly experience, then take on a trek across the country without any plans, he realised she must have acted on a pure adrenalin spike. She was nothing more than a naïve kid who had little experience of the reality of the big wide world. She might be twenty in age but he doubted she was twenty in experience. 'Have you got a job or are you a student?' he asked.

'Had a job. I left a message to say I had an emergency over east and couldn't get to work.'

'What was the job?'

'Server in a restaurant. I know it's not the most highfalutin job but I could work as many hours as I wanted and it paid the bills.'

'All work is valuable. Better than the dole. You learn skills in any job: skills you can take to another job as you climb the ladder. My first job was delivering the local rag on my bicycle.' Rico pushed the glass door open and headed towards the reception desk; Ella still stuck close to his side.

'Do you have a double room with single beds?' he asked when the receptionist eyed him.

'We have several double rooms.' She scrolled on her computer. Two with king beds, one queen…'

'You might think it's okay for a man to share a bed with his teenage daughter, but I sure as hell don't,' Rico growled. When Ella squeaked beside him, he nudged her. She didn't make another sound.

'Oh, sorry, I thought…'

'I know what you thought. It was inappropriate.'

'Sorry, I apologise. We've got a room with a queen and a single.'

'I'll take it. I presume you have a restaurant.'

'Of course.'

'What about room service?'

'Twenty-four hour room service but a limited menu after 10p.m. Do you want breakfast added?'

'Yes, please.'

'Name?'

'Joe Russo.'

'And your daughter's name?'

'Is that necessary?'

'It's the law.'

'Emma.' Ella squeaked again, this time a little quieter. He glanced at her and smiled. Her eyes were wide but a tiny grin appeared. He made sure he took out the correct credit card, one of three he always carried with him, each with a different name. Rico Giovannazzo couldn't leave a money trail. He could sense a buzz in Ella's demeanour as they crossed to the elevator. The very second the door locked them into the small space she spun around.

'Emma? Your daughter?'

'Better to use a different name and Dugite won't look for a father and daughter.'

'But you aren't old enough to be my father. You don't think the receptionist believed you?'

'She doesn't have a choice. We didn't give your age. You can easily pass for a fourteen-year-old. I'm thirty-four so it's possible but it doesn't matter. We'll be here for one night and I figured you would be too scared to spend the night alone.'

'Good point. I wouldn't be able to sleep.'

The elevator stopped with a tiny jerk. The doors opened. Rico peered both ways along the passage to search for room numbers. 'This way.' He left Ella to follow and smiled at how close she stayed, almost scraping his heels with her toes. A quick glance around to ensure no-one saw them, he slid the key card into the slot and opened the door. The room was larger and more up-market than he expected, with a wide window that overlooked the main city centre and the forecourt below. The big bed sat in the centre with the single against the far wall. Ella ran the few steps to the single and dropped her backpack on it.

'You can sleep on the big bed,' said Rico.

'No way. I'm much smaller and you paid. What happens now?'

'To keep out of sight we order room service. You can shower while we wait for the food. While we eat I want to discuss an idea I've been thinking about for a couple of hours. We can watch TV for a while but I need a good night's sleep, in something more comfortable than a shuddering water pipe.'

A giggle escaped from Ella's mouth. 'It was a bit shuddery wasn't it, and noisy, and stuffy.'

'I've slept in worse places but now let's search the menu and order.'

While Ella used the bathroom, Rico searched on his new phone for flights back to Perth for Ella and ways he could get east. He wasn't game to fly for it was the first place his father's men would seek him out. Maybe not when he left Kalgoorlie under an alias but there was every possibility spies would be at Sydney airport waiting for him to arrive, although he had no idea how many or who had been arrested. Plus there would be new guys in the organisation he would never recognise.

The food arrived seconds before Ella came out of the bathroom. A red tracksuit covered her from neck to ankle and damp clean hair hung loose. She looked so damn young. Rico set the food out on the small round table, which he dragged close to the bigger bed. He settled Ella into the sole chair and perched himself on the end of the bed. Ella's burger was so big it seemed too much to fit into her tiny body but she hoed in. The steak on his plate was cooked to perfection and smelt as good as it tasted. He was glad he'd ordered vegetables rather than fries for his body was in desperate need of a decent feed of nourishing food. All they'd shared on the five hour truck journey were the two bottles of water he'd bought way back when they'd met.

Ella must have been equally as hungry for the burger, fries and small salad didn't last long. He was now glad he'd added two bowls of fresh fruit salad to the order.

'You want tea or coffee?' Ella asked as she bounced up from the chair and moved to the tray of fixings for hot drinks.

'Coffee sounds good. Black, no sugar.' Rico stacked the empty plates on the tray and set it on the floor near the door. He'd add the fruit dishes later. 'I want to fly you back to Perth.'

Ella spun around with the open jug held high, her mouth agape and eyes huge. 'No way. Why?'

'I've thought about this, tossed all sorts of ideas around in my head. I can't take you with me.'

'Why not?'

'I've got too much going on in my life right now. Important things to sort, which means I won't be able to keep you safe.'

With the jug still in her hand, Ella shot back to the chair and sat. 'But it's not safe for me in Perth. I can't…'

'And you can't stay on this journey east alone. I can put you in touch with a lawyer who will keep

116

you safe and guide you on the best course of action. You witnessed a murder by three bikies. You can put them in gaol. This lawyer can help you.'

'But… but…'

Rico held up one hand in the stop position. 'Hear me out. I'm almost certain Dugite won't know who you are. He won't expect you to return to Perth so won't search for you there and besides, he can't track you now. You said you hadn't long been dating Jai.'

'Yes.'

'How often had you been in Jai's house before?'

'Maybe three times but I never slept with him.'

'So there would be little indication of who you are. No photos lying around?'

'No, but Jai had my phone number and email address.'

'On the phone; the one you stole.'

'Well, yes.'

'Which tells me none of these bikies will ever recognise you as the other person in the house.'

'But they knew I had the drugs.'

'Not for certain. I'd say they tipped Jai's place to search for the package. There is a single item tying you to Jai - his phone. At a guess, I'd say they sent him messages on his phone and kept tabs on him by the tracking device. They knew where he lived, knew he was at home. But they knew nothing about you or who you are.'

'They might have had a lookout who kept watch on his place. They would have seen me go in with him.'

'Possible. I hadn't thought of that. How long had you been there before they entered?'

'About half an hour. We had a drink and Jai had a shower. We were about to leave but I needed to go to the loo before we left.'

'Half an hour, which means if someone had been there watching, they would have rushed in straight away.'

'The lookout might have had to wait for the others to arrive.'

'You're a smart kid. A logical thinker.'

'I think I'm offended. I'm twenty, not a kid.'

Rico grinned at the way one hand went onto her hip and nose turned up in the air at the insult. 'My apologies but to me you're still young. Too young to be caught up in such a horrible mess and there's one thing you didn't think about.'

'What?'

'If they knew you were in there, they would have hunted you down first. And believe me, there is no way they would have let you escape unharmed. The very fact they didn't look for you tells me they didn't know you were there. Now, let me ring the lawyer I know. He's a good man. Helped someone close to me. Got her out of a serious predicament. Let me get his advice on the best way to handle this.'

'Okay but if I don't like what he says, I'm not going back.' She stood and went into the bathroom to fill the jug.

Rico lay back on the bed and took out his phone, the simplest version of a modern mobile that still did all the things he needed without the added benefit of a tracking device. It was easy to find James Ward's number since it was the only one he had entered in the address book to date. He dialled, waited and heaved a sigh of relief when James gave his name.

'James, JR here. I have a problem and need your advice.'

'What have you done now?'

'Now, now, it's nothing I've done. Do you know of a bikie with the nickname of Dugite.'

'Please don't tell me you're involved with that piece of scum.'

'No, I've never met him but I've got a young girl here with me who is running scared. Yesterday, she witnessed a murder carried out by him and two of his cohorts and is now in need of some serious advice and help.'

'Where are you?'

'Kalgoorlie.'

'Excuse me? How the… never mind. Give me the details.'

While Rico related every detail, Ella made hot drinks and placed a mug of steaming coffee on the bedside table next to him. It smelt so good he took a cautious sip while Ella retreated to the chair where she perched with her feet on the seat and her hands wrapped around her own mug. Wisps of steam rose in front of her nose. Her eyes bored a hole in his head.

'I want to put her on a plane back to Perth tomorrow. She doesn't have the experience to handle this on her own or to flee to the east alone. She doesn't have any money to start with.' Rico grinned at her scrunched up features which sent him the dead-eye look. 'She has a regular job or had until this morning but I'm sure she can get it back if she hasn't been away for more than a day or two. She can phone her boss from here. Would you be able to meet her at the airport and take her under your wing? Guide her on how to handle this. There's every chance Dugite had tracked down where she lived so maybe it's best if she doesn't return to her digs.'

'I'm too busy.'

'Yes I know you are but maybe put her onto another lawyer. I'll pay any fees she incurs. I can transfer a retainer. Hell, James, she's just a twenty-year-old sweet young woman who inadvertently witnessed a ghastly murder. Ella doesn't deserve to be in such a pickle. Plus, I'm sure the cops would love to have first-hand proof to put Dugite away for a few years. I've already sussed out a flight for tomorrow.'

'Okay, send me the flight details. I'll meet the plane and take her to someone I trust. I know a few detectives who will be delighted to talk to her. I take it you are on your way back to Sydney.'

'Yes, because I need my passport, organise the sale of my home and settle a few things.'

'Keep me informed on your whereabouts in case we need more details.'

'I'll keep in touch and thank you. Send me an account number for the retainer. Before you hang up, do you know what happened about Johansson?'

'They caught him as he was about to get on a plane. He's been arrested for aggravated assault of a police officer. Tried to cut a deal by spilling his guts about your old man.'

'You could add attempted murder of a patient.'

'A bit hard when you aren't here to lay charges but I could try.'

'He's a paid assassin. And the guard. Did they find him? Is he okay?'

'He has a skull fracture but should make a full recovery. They found him unconscious, stuffed in a toilet stall.'

'I'm glad he's okay. Thanks for the info.' As he hung up, Rico caught sight of Ella's glare.

'I'm not getting on any plane.'

Thirteen

It had taken a lot to convince her but Rico managed to see Ella boarded on the early morning flight to Perth. He hated leaving himself exposed at the airport but to ensure Ella didn't sneak away, he remained at the departure door until the small jet lifted from the ground.

Relieved with the outcome he turned and searched the area for signs of covert eyes trained in his direction. 'Getting paranoid, my man,' he said to himself before making a beeline for the exit through the almost empty terminal. When he realised most people had already left, he increased his speed and eased into the sole cab before it took off to seek a more lucrative place to pick up a fare. Destination given he relaxed back against the seat, his thoughts on the young woman.

Even though James had promised to keep her safe and ensure her witness statement was given to the right people, poor kid was still terrified and had every right to be. When he thought about it, she was in much the same position as him – daring to give eye-witness details against the low-life of this world when they committed some heinous crime. He sniggered at the low-life thought, for in reality, he could shove himself in the same basket. It wasn't often he trusted anyone but himself, yet he trusted James would do everything in his power to keep Ella's identity secret. The man was too darn perfect while Rico had so many black marks against his name, he doubted he could ever aspire to be half the man. You can choose your friends but when it came to parents you had to live with what you were served. He was caught in the middle with the worst possible father and the best of mothers.

Thoughts of dear, sweet Mama centred in his mind as the taxi stopped and started through chaotic early morning traffic and pedestrians, all on their way to various jobs. For a small city stuck out on the edge of the desert, there seemed to be an abundance of vehicles and people hurrying in a confused melee. Kalgoorlie had been the centre of the gold mining industry for a century and featured an enormous open pit.

All Rico had to do was fill the day before it was time to board the Indian Pacific; after he'd managed to secure a vacant cabin to Adelaide where he would transfer to the Overland train to Melbourne. For the final leg to Sydney he intended to hire a car and drive. It would have been a darn sight easier and quicker to train direct to Sydney but he wasn't game to take the chance. Sydney Central train station was as risky as Sydney airport for a man wanted by police as well as unscrupulous members of the underworld. They would all be on the lookout for him, especially his father's men, even though he didn't have a clue how many were on the loose. No doubt Johnny Thomas knew Rico was still alive. Johannsen would have messaged Johnny. Or maybe not. To fail at a task meant death. Johannsen might have kept his mouth shut in the hope he could get to his family, pack and leave. But he might have been stupid enough to ask questions to ensure what Rico had told him was true. Had they arrested Thomas? He should have asked James but didn't think about it at the time. Man, all this uncertainty was doing his head in.

'Thanks, mate,' he said to the driver as he handed over a twenty dollar note. 'Keep the change,' he added before easing from the rear seat. Upright, he stretched and winced. Too many body parts still hadn't recovered and the truck journey had added a few more creaks to tender muscles and joints. Who knew a five hundred kilometre journey on the back of a truck would be so rough and noisy. It wasn't something he wanted to repeat – ever.

He turned towards the hotel entry and stalled. The black motorcycle glinted in the already hot sun, which seemed to highlight the polished chrome with intent. Couldn't be, his brain cells said but his gut argued and he trusted his gut instinct. The calm he'd managed to achieve overnight, melted away as fast as an ice block would on the already baked steel of the bike. It took several seconds to gather together the scattered pieces of his mind, jumble them up then sort them into logical thought before clarity evolved. It was possible the bike's owner was making general enquiries at every accommodation venue in town. He could be visiting a mate or even booking in. Other logical reasons flittered though his brain. Breakfast in the restaurant, coffee and cake? Each one was more ridiculous than the previous and he bet not one was true. For him to hide would make it obvious he held secrets. To face this little snaffu head-on would be far better but not a solution with which he was enamoured.

Decision made, Rico shoved his shoulders back, winced at the pain, and strode towards the door as though he didn't have a heavy steel beam pressed down on his shoulders. Nobody, or at least he hoped nobody, in this town knew a damn thing about him. The glass doors parted at his approach. Not game to pause, he quickened his pace the moment he was inside and headed towards the elevators.

A hand landed on his shoulder. Eyes shut, he paused, huffed air from his mouth and took his time to turn. 'Excuse me,' he said in such a way it wasn't a question, as he raised his chin and glared.

'You were at the servo back at The Lakes.'

The tangled brain cells returned. Was he supposed to admit it or act dumb? Lies caught up with you. 'So?' Keep it simple.

'You were with a young tart.'

'Excuse me?' Rico pressed a finger into the other man's chest despite the shiver of disgust and pure terror that managed to weave through his innards. 'That young tart, as you call her, happens to be my daughter and I can assure you she is a fine innocent young lady with decent morals. Not what you are

125

referring.' Nerves stretched to their limit, he turned towards the elevators again but the hand grabbed his shoulder and twisted him back around.

'Get your hand off me,' he snarled.

'Where is she?'

'None of your damned business.'

To prove he was a big man who must be obeyed, the bikie thrust his chest out in an attempt to threaten. 'Where is she?'

Instead of answering, Rico took out his phone and pressed in the emergency number.

'What the hell are you doing?' Dugite asked.

'Calling the cops.

'What the hell, why?'

'Because your tone and questions are a threat to both me and my daughter. I have no idea what the hell you want with her since neither of us have ever met you before but I happen to know who you are. Your ugly mug gets plastered over the papers on a regular basis. I can assure you, no daughter of mine would ever associate with the likes of you. Especially an innocent fourteen-year-old. Now get lost or I press the call button.' With his index finger hovered over the green button he held the phone in the air out of the bastard's reach. 'Three seconds,' he said. 'Two.'

Dugite turned away, took three steps, turned back. 'I'll be waiting for you and her, outside.'

Rico laughed. 'Big threats, little boy.' The fierce ugly glare was a definite threat but he managed to keep his face impassive until he turned back to the elevators with breath held. It was a fight to keep his gait normal while he waited for the oaf to retaliate. The gut instinct he relied upon shot out a dire warning. When the silver doors whooshed open, he'd never been so glad to step into a confined space and after five years housed in a cell, he detested confined spaces. Before the doors closed he dared a glance across the foyer. The bikie stood outside at the bottom of the steps; arms folded across his leather-clad chest; eyes planted on the door. With such brightness outside Dugite would find it difficult to see in but his glare held such pure menace a shiver wove itself down Rico's spine.

In the rising car, Rico redialled and held the phone to his ear.

'James here. I'm a little tired of your calls, Ri… er, J.R. Every single one seems to bring me trouble.'

Rico couldn't help laughing. 'I just had an uncomfortable meeting with the bikie young Ella witnessed killing her boyfriend. Since he has threatened me and is now waiting outside my hotel for either me or Ella to appear, I'd appreciate if you could maybe call one of your in-the-know legal fraternity friends to have him arrested sometime in the immediate future. He demanded to know where Ella was. Lord knows how he put two and two together but he recognised me from the servo where I met Ella. Maybe he is grasping at straws in the hope Ella might be his target. Glad I managed to get her on the early morning flight before he recovered from a hangover. He stunk like a stale brewery.'

'You sure know how to get yourself into pickles. Such an interesting life.'

'Funny man. I'm doubled over with laughter. Is there anything you can do?'

'I'll do my best and let you know. I'm on my way to the airport now. Is Ella still okay with this?'

'To be honest, she's scared spitless. She might be twenty in age but her naivety deems her much younger. Please keep her safe?'

'Do you think your bikie friend knows who she is?'

'Dugite isn't any friend of mine. Until a minute ago, I'd never met or spoken to him. To answer your question, I doubt it. Told him she was my daughter and he doesn't have a clue who I am. I registered under my alias and didn't use Ella's real name. So if he continues to search he'll ask for an Emma Russo and won't find her.'

'Smart thinking.'

'Yeah, well, I've had years of practise, too many years. I'll keep an ear and eye out for your friends in blue. Please make it before seven tonight when I'm booked to leave. And thank you again – for everything.'

'I can't say you're welcome but good luck. I'll keep you informed.'

It didn't take as long as he thought before sirens sounded. Less than thirty minutes. Not game to return downstairs for a much wanted machine brewed coffee, Rico had ensconced himself in his room. When the sirens ceased, he shut down his laptop and went to the window. From two storeys up the entire space in front of the hotel was visible. Bystanders from the pathway had already created a huddle, eyes on six officers and three marked cars that had surrounded both man and bike.

Two officers held tasers high while the other four grappled with a furious Dugite who didn't appear to be in the mood to give up without a fight. Arms flew every-which-way and legs seemed to be in a tangle. A loud roar erupted from Dugite when the precious motor cycle crashed to the ground. Rico couldn't hold back a grin, which widened when the electrodes from a taser caused the man to stagger, fall and shudder.

Even after he was hauled to his feet, Dugite sure put up a fight as he was dragged to the paddy wagon. Although he was ensconced in the confines of his closed room, Rico could make out the raft of swear words and claims of innocence, although he didn't hear whether or not the man had been arrested for murder. The vicious kick aimed towards one officer was evaded but by the way the van shook after the door had been locked, he figured the man was in the throes of a major hissy fit.

Rico rang James. 'Let Ella know Dugite has just been arrested. He's not a happy man and I think a certain paddy wagon might need to go in to be panel -beaten. I appreciate your help. Thank you.'

'For this you are welcome. My friend, the commissioner, is overjoyed. They've been trying to pin something major on this jerk for a long time. Ella's plane has landed. I'm waiting at the door for her now. I'll pass on the message and the commissioner has promised to keep Ella's identity a secret. He, at least, is a happy man in regard to this. You might get another tick of approval towards your redemption. Enjoy the train ride.'

'How the hell did you know?'

'It's why I was smart enough to become a lawyer – pure deduction skills.' Wicked laughter came through the phone before it was shut down on the other end.

Fourteen

The charges on the list were so accurate, Matteo shook his head in disbelief as he turned the stapled sheets of paper back so he could study them again in order to figure out who could have known so many details. Every damn section of the family business was printed in black and white. It would take months to figure out logical defence tactics to prove his innocence and lay blame on other individuals, but he was certain it could be achieved. All he needed was the list of names of who had been arrested. Although the traitor could also be in gaol as a red herring or maybe protective custody.

Both sons-in-law were a good place to start. Matteo considered both in detail. Neither would dare contradict him, not if they wanted to live. He knew every aspect of their lives right down to the numbers and names of their secret bank accounts. Easy to create arrows directed towards them. The brothels were a cinch since he'd never stepped foot in any of them. There wasn't a paper trail to lead any brothel to him. But Tony was in charge of the brothels, visited often, dealt with any problems, recruited the girls and it was possible he slept with every single one of them. Each one could verify Tony's involvement. Easy peasy, one problem solved.

After a second read of the first page he closed his eyes on a long huff. Twelve murder charges with two bodies named, which meant those in authority hadn't yet matched DNA to missing persons and were unlikely to. He wriggled back on the bed to get more comfortable, shoulders leant against the wall with knees bent and sock clad feet flat on the mattress. He could sure do with a chair, and a table. A computer to research would be mighty handy right now, along with a bottle of red and some decent food: not the crap they seemed to delight in serving - on cardboard plates, for heaven's sake.

It had been a surprise when the information had been given to him this morning after his initial request. No arguments, no excuses. Although there was a smart comment about his entitlement to such information since he was to act as his own lawyer. Now he was glad he hadn't yet done as the smart-arse judge suggested to retain a top lawyer, but he would. He just had to figure out who to ask. Who would be game enough to act as his defence lawyer? Had to be a QC or a KC as they were now since the old biddy passed away. Many lawyers didn't much care who they acted for as long as they were paid enough and he bet his bill would be a mile high. Now who was more interested in big dollars than in true justice? Several names came to mind, two in particular. A few of the bikie gangs had excellent defence lawyers but it might be best to avoid them. He didn't need the association right now.

Hmm, there might be a shortage of heroin and smack at the moment with him out of action. Let's add eccy to the list. And the shipment of weed had been due in last week. Had it been picked up and stashed away? There were still good supplies of coke, ice and GHB stashed in the self-storage unit. Not that he would be able to make the order to distribute at the moment and even if he could he didn't have a clue how many distributors were still on the loose. Unless he could get visitors he had no way to contact a damn soul.

'Okay, Giovannazzo, time to go.'

At the sudden command, Matteo jerked back, bumped his head on the wall and swore. The papers flew from his lap and landed on the floor in a messy heap.

'Go where?' A quick scramble from the bed, he shoved feet into shoes and bent to retrieve the papers, which he folded into three and wriggled them into the waist band of his pants. The taut elastic pressed the edges into his skin but held them tight enough they wouldn't fall out or slide down his leg.

'Where you belong, thank goodness.' The sergeant from the first day came to a standstill in front of the barred doorway. Keys rattled. The door emitted a metallic grinding squeak as it swung open. 'Arms out in front.' The dreaded handcuffs replaced the bundle of keys and were held out between him and the officer.

Now was his chance.

'Don't even think about it,' the sergeant said with a certain wry humour. 'Show yourselves, fellas,' he called louder.

At the scuffle of feet, Matteo didn't bother to lift his head. Had to be a least two others but when a thought came, he fisted his hands and held out both arms at the same time he dared a look. With a large, bulky paper bag in his hand, Phil stood at the back and gave an almost imperceptible shake of his head: a movement neither other officer would see. A glimmer of hope shimmied through Matteo's body.

There was an ominous click as the cuffs closed, followed by the sergeant's hands as they wrapped around the cuffs and jiggled to ensure they were tight. Matteo bit the inside of his cheek to prevent the escape of even a whisper of sound.

'Okay, let's go. Perkins, bring up the rear with taser ready in case our prisoner gets any smart ideas.'

The grip on his upper arm hurt, with all fingers squeezed tight enough to leave a bruise. Matteo was swung around so he was in front of the sergeant. One hand pressed into the small of his back.

'Walk.'

To walk as normal as he wanted was difficult with lace-less shoes. The smooth leather heel slid and scraped at each step, forcing him to shuffle rather than step in order to keep the shoes on. The ignominy was almost unbearable but no way would he comment or complain, for he was certain it would result in some smart remark meant to bring him even more indignity. Wouldn't they love it. Even more they would love him to make an attempt to escape so they could pepper him with bullets and turn him into a fountain spurting blood.

The four man parade passed the now closed door to the front counter at a pace Matteo set. Arseholes could match his speed. When he went to turn right, the same way they had gone before, he was yanked left. One officer went ahead, opened a steel door at the end of the short passage. A cold draft of air swept in, along with a rancid stench of mustiness and something he couldn't place. Maybe a dead animal, it was so bad.

'Down two steps, turn right.'

Matteo paused on the top step, glanced around. They were in a dim, covered alleyway. The dusty bitumen had rills of dead leaves mixed with rubbish, blown in through the bars of a metal gate. The walls were bare dark brick. Brightness came from the gated entry about ten metres ahead. A small prison truck, engine humming, faced the gate ready to go. The rear door hung open. He didn't have to ask the question. He was to be transferred to another facility, to be locked in isolation. A shiver of unease wove its way across his shoulders.

'Move.' A taser point pressed into the small of his back the same time the single word order hissed into his ear with a spray of spittle that sent a shudder through him. He fought the urge to turn and spit back for such action would be greeted with an electric shock he had no desire to experience.

With lips clamped together, he swallowed down the spit, moved, stepped forward, down both steps and paused while he searched for some means of escape. The area was small, big enough for the van and maybe one other vehicle. Bigger vans would fit. There were no windows. Only the barred gate. Outside the gate was another laneway that ran at right-angles, with a grim concrete wall opposite.

'Keep going.'

A push to his back caused him to stumble forward but he straightened and held his head high. He would not show cowardice. He climbed the steps into the van. It was rank, as though it hadn't been cleaned of urine and other unmentionables. On purpose, he bet to himself.

'Move right in, shoulder against the end wall.'

Matteo studied the end. A small window sat in a recess so the officers in the cabin could keep an eye on the prisoners but so far he hadn't seen any prison officers. All he'd seen were police. Maybe they were yet to arrive. Could be a ploy to have him sit in the stuffy van for hours. He settled on the bench, shuffled his backside along and leant back against the side wall. The sergeant knelt next to him, clamped a leg iron around his left ankle with the other end snapped to a solid steel bar that held the seat to the floor. Even though severe punishment would be meted out he thought of giving the arsehole a hefty kick. It took a monumental effort to keep his feet centred on the steel floor.

After the sergeant exited, Matteo waited for the rest of the prisoners but the door slammed shut with an echo that vibrated along the steel walls. At the ominous click of a lock, Matteo let loose with a raft of four letter words.

The van bounced, a shadow crossed over the small window, doors slammed. A few seconds later, the engine revved. The van crept forward at the grind of the gate sliding across the entry. He knew when they were out in the open for the light brightened all of a sudden. At the same time, cold air blew from somewhere. He searched around, spied some vents high around the edge of the roof and noticed two small, square windows with toughened dark glass in the side wall opposite. A snort escaped at the size of the windows, so damn small the only part of the body able to reach out would be an arm.

Since he had no idea to which prison they were headed, he leant against the wall and relaxed, determined to enjoy the last few minutes of outside life until he could get this whole mess sorted. Eyes shut, he forced his grey matter to concentrate and figure out who the snitch was. Family members, he dismissed in an instant. There was no way Rico could have known any of the events from the past five years. Sylvie had already shown she didn't have a clue about any of the *family* enterprises. Peter and Tony were in the same predicament as him. Both knew about the property, had even been there when bodies had been buried but neither would say a word about their involvement. They weren't stupid. If they were to squeal they would do so from another country after they had fled and since they were both ensconced in hell holes, there wasn't a chance. The girls? He was certain neither had a clue about the family business although young Lucy had asked a few too many questions about subjects she shouldn't know. Had Tony gabbed to his wife? Nah, couldn't have. He knew the consequences if he talked. Hell, he'd even personally eliminated a couple of snitches who said too much. As for Maria, she was afraid of her own shadow, let alone get involved in anything unsavoury. She would be too scared to ask questions and Peter was super protective of her and their two youngsters. Plus he knew how to keep her in line.

The ride was smooth, with a regular flashes of shadow through the two tiny windows each time they passed a larger vehicle. They were going fast enough he didn't have time to make out shops and buildings but he could visualise where they were as they paused at or passed through intersections. After a few more left and right hand turns he lost track of which direction they were headed, to which gaol he would be stuck in. Correctional centres, they now called them. Ha, what a joke. He had no doubt it would be maximum security centre. Maybe Goulburn, or Hunter, or Lithgow but they could all be too far away to get him back to Sydney for court appearances. Parklea was much closer. They hadn't gone over the harbour bridge so maybe they were going via Parramatta, he figured but with his luck over the past few days he could even be headed to another state, since the Feds were now involved.

Too scared to even think about another prison cell, he turned his thoughts back to on whom he could lay blame. The newcomers, like the officer back there in central, didn't know half of what had been spouted to Matteo so far. None would have known about Simpson. Matteo snapped his fingers. Simpson. Maybe he was the key. Who knew about him? Zappacosta for sure since he was present and had done the deed, but he had been caught in the west. Hmm, maybe he had spilled his guts to make a deal. Nah, he was in way too deep and had too much to lose.

His lawyer, Guido? Couldn't be for he didn't know about Simpson and besides, he had also been arrested. Damn, Guido's son, Luke. Had to be. He kept the books, knew where the money went. A large payment to Zappacosta went out when he'd made a termination. Luke would know such details. And he sure as hell knew more than anyone else. It must be him for it couldn't be anyone else. But had he also been arrested? Maybe not. If he is the traitor, he would keep his involvement quiet and the Fed had said no person had blabbed. They had a pile of papers. Had Luke printed off all the files and sent them in anonymously?

Matteo sank back against the wall and huffed every atom of air from his lungs. The thought of all the details Luke Bianchi could lay his fingers on, to photocopy and pass on to the police, was way too much to contemplate. Surely not. But no-one else, not even his two sons-in-law, would have access to nor any idea about so many details. In particular, the overseas bank accounts Sylvie had mentioned. One man knew – Luke Bianchi.

Pop. The truck lurched. Matteo shot upright, glanced at the narrow window into the cabin. A shadow reached across to the driver's side. The truck veered the other way, threw Matteo off balance. As he struggled upright a bigger shadow moved across the pane of glass. It blocked his view until bright light replaced the darkness. What the hell happened?

His body slammed against the wall at another jerk. He fell sideways onto the seat. The leg-iron cut into his ankle until he wriggled back along the seat to ease the tension. Another lurch. He toppled forwards and yelped as he bounced on the floor with shackled hands caught under him and his leg skewed at an awkward angle. The truck jolted as it came to a sudden stop. A few seconds later he was certain one of the front doors opened and someone got out for the springs swung up and down. Not sure whether or not to get back on the seat he instead managed to scramble into a sitting position on the floor, which eased the pain of twisted ligaments in his shackled leg.

A door closed. The truck rocked. A roar of the engine, another jolt, they were moving again. Sure it was now safe to do so, he took his time to get back on the seat where he waited for some indication as to what had just happened. Was it an engine malfunction? A tyre? Couldn't be a tyre for the truck now ran too smooth for it to have a flat, although if they were dual wheels it wouldn't make much difference. And who got out? Or did they? Might have let out a pesky bug. But the pop?

When too many what if's and maybe's scrambled his brain, Matteo figured it didn't matter. He was still stuck in the back of a prison van, handcuffed and tethered to a solid steel bar. He wasn't going anywhere other than to another prison cell.

After what couldn't have been more than three minutes the truck slowed, turned, crept along and stuttered to a standstill with a rev and sudden brake. Sunlight turned to shadow. The sudden silence when the engine ceased its rumble, sent a quiver of fear down his spine. They couldn't have reached Parklea yet so where the hell were they?

Matteo honed his ears to any sound. The driver's door opened. Footsteps crunched from front to back. A rattle at the rear door. It opened. A man appeared: one he knew.

'What the hell happened?' Matteo asked.

'Had to get rid of Perkins.'

'You shot him?'

'How else could I get you out?' The man climbed in with the large bulky paper bag and held out a bunch of keys. 'There's a car across the park. Silver Mazda. Clothes in the boot. These are your clothes from the gaol and the car key, but you'll have to be quick. I have to get away from here.' He inserted a key in the leg iron, released the lock.

Matteo kicked the chain away and shook his leg, overjoyed at the rattle of freedom. 'Stolen car?'

'Yes.'

'Number plate?'

'False.'

'Good man.' Matteo rubbed the red chafe marks on both wrists as each cuff dropped away. 'I'll need your gun.'

'Huh? Why?' His saviour rocked back on his heels.

'If you turn up still armed, no-one will believe you were attacked from the outside. You would have fired shots and been dis-armed.'

'I fired a shot.'

Matteo held out his hand. 'Gun, and to make it look real, give me your taser as well.' It was a relief when both weapons sat in his hands. He pocketed the gun, grabbed the bag and shoved it under his arm as he rushed to the door and jumped to the ground. Phil followed. 'Where's the car and where are we?'

A finger pointed over Matteo's shoulder. 'This is Parramatta Park. The car's behind the toilet block. It's the best I could manage.'

'I appreciate everything you've done,' said Matteo as he spun around and fired the taser into Phil's neck. Poor guy's eyes boggled in shock before he dropped to the ground and convulsed as the electric waves swept through him. The crotch of his trousers darkened from navy to black. 'I'm sorry, but this has to look real or you will be blamed and arrested.'

While Phil was still in the throes of shock, Matteo took the pistol from his pocket, lifted and pulled the trigger.

Bang.

'Why?' The squeak came from the contorted mouth of the man folded on the ground. Crimson blossomed through the blue fabric of the pale blue shirt.

'To make it appear authentic.'

To shut out the sight of the dying man, Matteo turned away from the van parked under a small grove of trees. Phil had pulled onto the verge of a narrow road. The tang of eucalyptus and freshly mown lawn was a welcome relief from the putrid stuffiness of incarceration. He tried to run towards the car but with such loose shoes, a wonky lope was all he could manage. Within twenty metres he discovered fifty-six years of a good life had reduced his fitness level more than he liked. Scattered thoughts tangled themselves as he crossed the bitumen carpark covered in potholes, uneven patches and mounds of dead leaves held together by dried mud.

First, he had to ditch the prison tracksuit: it was too obvious. Did he have time to get the clothes from the boot and change in the ablution block? Nah, it would take too long but the coppers would search for a man in prison greens. If he left the outfit here they would know to look for a man in a suit since it would be obvious he had the bag of his own clothes but it might take a while for them to figure it out. It would be quicker to stay dressed as he was until he was a long way from here, but he needed to change soon.

Beyond the toilet block was what looked to be a bowling green. He paused for a second when he noticed a few cars parked next to it. A quick search of the green told him no-one was outside so maybe they were at a meeting in the clubrooms. He prayed they all sat around a table engrossed in a speaker's sage words but at the knowledge of other people nearby, he quickened his pace with head down. Had they heard the gunshot? Too bad if they did for there wasn't a damn thing he could do about it but with luck, the bang would have registered as a car backfire, after all, gunshots weren't a regular occurrence in Australian cities and most people wouldn't recognise the noise for what it was, especially city folk.

When he reached the driver's door he clicked the remote attached to the single key. The car was recent model with all new-fangled electronic devices, unlike his classic Jaguar. At the click he grabbed the door handle, tugged and dived inside. The gun landed on the passenger seat with the bag over the top to hide it before he buckled the seat belt.

Sirens sounded. Already? How would they know? Damn, there must have been a witness at the bowling club. A sudden wave of sweat flooded his brow. An adrenalin surge caused him to fumble with the key which dropped onto his lap. Nerves twitched. His pulse pounded as frantic fingers found the key. Somehow he got the car started and wasted no time to reverse, grind the gears into first and tear out of the car park with a squeal as rubber burnt. He shot across the first intersection and increased his speed. A train on a parallel line raced past in the opposite direction and drowned out the wail of sirens for a few seconds. The second intersection was clear but he eased his foot from the accelerator a tad when he realised he was going way too fast. To get pulled over for speeding would be suicidal.

Hunched over to hide his top, he passed an open area that heaved with pedestrians milling on a paved mall between modern buildings. He swore at raised eyes from various people when plain logic told him not one person would be suspicious of a man in a car as it drove past them. Head turned away, he drove on until he ran out of road at a T junction and had to turn left. The traffic was horrendous, sending a wave of fear across his shoulders but at least the drivers would be too darn busy concentrating on getting to their own destination than to worry about how any other driver was dressed.

Two police cars, sirens blaring, shot past him. Expletives spewed from his mouth as he drove over a bridge to cross the river before he dared to glance in the rear vision mirror to ensure a car hadn't turned around. Although, why would they even know to follow an ordinary, common hatchback when they hadn't yet arrived at the scene to suss things out? A weird sensation swept over him: one he couldn't put a name to. Maybe he should feel some sort of remorse but it was an alien concept. He blew out his cheeks in an attempt to ease the tension in strung out muscles and nerves as he studied the road ahead to figure out where to go.

Unfamiliar with the layout of Parramatta, he wove through streets in a general northerly direction. There were plenty of places in Gosford, Wyong or maybe even in the Wollemi National Park where he could hide long enough to sort out what the hell he could do now.

He almost turned onto a tollway but passed by when he figured it wasn't such a great idea since he had no money and there were very intrusive cameras to take pictures of recalcitrant drivers who failed to pay or didn't have little gadgets attached to their windscreens which automatically deducted money from the account of the car owner. He scanned the front window, saw no such gadget but he did spy a screen in the centre of the dashboard, which meant he could log onto a navigation aid, if he could figure out how to use it. A phone was easy but he had yet to search the bag for his phone and wasn't game to stop, even for a few seconds, to retrieve it.

A less direct route through minor roads was needed to get away from the area, but he kept the car headed norther. At the sign for Pitt Town and Scheyville National Park, he veered right, passed a sign - *The Vintage Pantry. Oakville Harvest Farm Shop*. A good place to find food but without money it could be difficult to obtain any. It might be worth a good scout around to see how many people were present. He wasn't above stealing what he needed. It wouldn't be the first time.

Half a kilometre in he decided he needed to find somewhere to stop for a while so he could gather his thoughts and make plans. His laugh was wry when he realised his desperation to escape over-rode even a single plan on what he was supposed to do once he did manage to get free. This deep panic wasn't on the agenda. Nor was the realisation that every law enforcement officer in the state would be on the lookout for him. Home would be under constant scrutiny. The one place where he could get clothes, money, documents and a decent feed.

He decreased the speed to a crawl through the forest until he found a clear area with picnic tables and an ablution block. A quick search with his eyes told him he was alone apart from an empty vehicle parked a good hundred metres across the other side. He pulled to a stop at the near end of the brick building, found the lever to open the boot and gave it a hitch. Another quick glance around to ensure there were no onlookers, he unfolded from the seat, stood and stretched. An earthy aroma greeted him. It wasn't unpleasant but reminded him of the block in Forestville. He shuddered at the memory and turned to the rear where he lifted the boot. A low groan rumbled from deep down. A bloody police uniform, with a pair of police-issue black boots. Didn't the man have any sense?

Disgusted, he returned to the car and tore open the paper bag. His suit and shirt tumbled out along with his watch, wallet and a handful of coins. He grinned. A wallet meant money and credit cards. One problem sorted. Phone. It should be with his things. He scrabbled through the small pile, shook out the shirt, tie, coat, belt and trousers then patted the bag and swore at the emptiness. The bastards had kept his phone. To see how much cash he had, he rifled through the wallet and smiled – three hundred and forty-five dollars would get him some decent food and maybe a bed until he could make better plans. As he fingered the two credit cards the smile widened into a grin. More money than he would need sat safe in both accounts.

Nerves tightened and twitched when a young couple emerged from the bush less than twenty metres to his left. Both waved. He lifted his arm to wave back but noticed the sleeve of his top and swore. A quick tug and the sleeve came to his elbow before he plastered a smile to his face and gave a brief wave of acknowledgement. When the couple parted and each entered the relevant door of the ablution block, he tore off the putrid green top and shoved it under the seat. Within seconds he had both arms in the sleeves of his business shirt and was doing up the last of the buttons when the man emerged and headed for the car across the clearing. Matteo whistled out a long breath of relief through clenched teeth.

In the two minutes before the woman stepped out from the door nearest to him, he had the suit coat draped across the passenger seat over all the other items and had managed to get the radio to work. To make out he was busy he fiddled with the buttons and dials as though in search for a station. His heart forgot how to work when the woman paused and gave the appearance she was about to come towards him. A toot from the other car, she stepped away, turned and jogged across the grass. His heart raced to catch up the missed beats as he wrapped his arms around the steering wheel and flopped his head on top. Too damn close.

It seemed to take forever but at last, the engine of the other car rumbled to life. Head down, he stilled until the wheels crunched over loose gravel as it passed within metres of him. Relief surged when the rumble faded and silence reigned. At last, he was alone. He remained where he was to gather the frayed edges of his nerves together and let the adrenalin surge run its course.

Calmer, he lifted his head. The first thing to catch his eye was the brick building. Now he could change his pants. Clothes in hand, he entered the male section and cringed at the stench. God, he hated public toilets but he had the chance to make full use of the facilities. When would be the next opportunity? At least, here, he could close a damn door and have a modicum of privacy.

Suit trousers on, he washed his hands and buried his face in a scoop of water. Even though it was icy, he gave his face and neck a good rub until the skin prickled with cold and the sense of gaol filth had eased. Since he had no towel he used the gaol issue pants to pat his skin dry. There was no mirror to see so he brushed damp fingers through his thick unwashed hair and patted it down. A comb would be appreciated but he hadn't used one for days. They hadn't even trusted him with a damn comb. On the way out, he scrunched up the large paper bag and stuffed it into the too-small rubbish bin.

The return to the car with shuffles, scrapes and swear words sent the definite message to try the boots. They at least would do up – if they fitted. With his backside perched on the edge of the open hatch floor, he tugged on the first boot, placed his foot on the ground, wriggled his toes in and stood. A tad tight but not too bad. Length was okay with enough room his toes didn't scrape at the end. A smile broke out and remained in place while he put on the other boot. He was free and had decent strong footwear. He sat a while longer to toss ideas through his head on what to do next. Food was needed: decent food. Not the insipid crap they served in the hell hole. And decent coffee, hot and strong, from a machine. Not the acrid powdered husk shavings from the filthy floor of some foreign coffee producer.

With little option on what to do, he figured it was time to suss out the farm shop. Eyes skittered left and right on the lookout for vehicles or people as he retraced his path but there was little to see except a fringe of dense bush along both sides of the road. The bushes hid the boles of tall eucalypts with the upper canopy allowing little light through. Weird shadows danced along the road in front of him as he coasted the distance at low speed.

On his right, the bush vanished, replaced by vegetable crops and a much brighter light, unfiltered by foliage. He turned into a driveway, drifted towards a shed with a sign *Oakville Harvest Farm Shop*. Nerves twanged as he eased from the car. So far he'd not seen any humans, not that it mattered for it was too soon for his description to be advertised. Even though he straightened and strode with confidence towards the door, his innards were all dithery and awkward. One step inside the large doorway, he paused to cast his eyes over the contents. No customers, thank goodness. Wide, box-like shelves displayed fresh vegetables and fruit. Behind a counter sat what he most needed, a coffee machine. Order the coffee first, he figured, While it brewed, he could grab something to eat, pay for them all at once and skedaddle.

It was impossible to evade the wide brown stare and sparkle of light from the young woman who stood behind the counter with an expectant lift to the corner of her brow. 'Very hot long black in the biggest take-away you have,' he said as he approached. He would have preferred an espresso but a quick gulp wasn't enough. What he needed was a lingering taste sensation to eradicate the memory of the muck he'd had to put up with over the past few days.

'I'll see what takes my fancy to eat,' he added. There wasn't a lot to choose from since he had neither the implements nor facilities to prepare a meal from fresh products. He pounced on a transparent plastic bag of six cheese and bacon rolls. An already prepared Greek salad bowl said, *pick me, pick me*, so he picked up two and added two packets of biltong dried beef slices since he couldn't spot any other meat products. Plain salad would never be enough. He was a meat man, always had been and was proud of it. A large container of juice and six bananas completed his purchase. The ready coffee sent up tantalising wafts of saliva inducing aroma when he returned to the counter. Eager to get away, he took a credit card from his wallet and held it over the machine.

'Just a minute, I need to add it up,' said the server as she tapped buttons on the till. 'That will be fifty five dollars and eighty five cents. Credit or savings?' she added with a rise of one eyebrow.

'Savings. I can just tap?'

'Sure.'

He tapped the little silver icon against the machine and waited for the beep. When none came, he glared at the machine and tapped again.

'Umm, it seems your card has been declined.' The woman pointed towards the tiny readout window.

'Huh? Can't be,' he said at the same time a bright spotlight lit up his brain cells. It was possible his account had been frozen. To cover his humiliation, he glanced at his card. 'Oops, sorry, I picked up my old card instead of the new one. But I've got cash,' he added as he delved into his wallet and withdrew a fifty and a twenty dollar note. Even though he was desperate to get away, he waited for the change because he would now need every cent of cash he had if what he suspected was true. Although he had his other credit card in another name there was no way would he attempt to use it here. He couldn't make up a second excuse without raising suspicion.

'Do you need a bag?' the woman asked as he fumbled with the purchases.

'No, I'll manage.' He shoved the biltong in his trousers pockets, hooked the juice on a little finger, stacked the two round plastic domes on top of each other and held them in place with his chin while he managed to bundle the bananas in the crook of one elbow and secured the twisted end of the plastic bun bag between two fingers of the same hand which left one hand free for the precious coffee. All he could manage was an awkward gait as he hurried outside and half-ran, half-hobbled to the car where he plonked everything on the bonnet to get the remote, which, of course, had to be at the very depth of his trousers pocket.

Nerves had stretched to panic status by the time he managed to get all items in the car without dropping the lot. Engine on, he crunched the gear into reverse, planted his foot on the accelerator and took off, with a spray of gravel left in his wake. Two deep breaths later, he eased off the accelerator until the car slowed to a reasonable speed. It was unlikely there would be speed cops this far out but he wasn't about to take a chance. He turned left to return to the park where he could take the time to search the inbuilt Navman for a route back to Sydney without using major roads. Somehow, he had to get home to find money, clothes and suss out at least one person who hadn't been arrested, to help him hide long enough for him to sort out what in hell's name he was supposed to do now.

Back in the parking area, he fiddled with buttons on the dashboard until the navigation screen blinked on. Couldn't be much different than the phone, he figured while he studied the buttons, pressed, cursed, pressed again. While he savoured sips of hot coffee, he managed to type in the destination via no toll roads or major highways. The route through the park held promise for along such a route he wouldn't encounter too many cars or people since at least forty kilometres was within a national park.

His head shot up at the distant sound of sirens. He twisted his head around, wound down the window to figure out from which direction the wail came. It sounded as though they came from where he'd just been but how could they be after him so fast? Gut instinct sent him a definite message to scoot. After he managed to nestle the coffee in the console, he turned the key, reversed and followed the directions on the screen.

NE on Avondale Rd, TR onto Dural. 0.9km

His speed was so fast he almost missed the turn but spun right at the last minute, skidded, panicked and straightened with a squeal of tyres. Coffee sloshed from the lid into the console.

Heart pumping at a furious rate, he slowed a tad, glanced at the screen. The twelve kilometres along Cattai Ridge Rd gave him a chance to force strung-out nerves to ease.

TR onto Old Northern Rd. 3.1km. flashed on the screen at the same time the engine stuttered, ran smooth and stuttered again. A quick glance at the fuel gauge and he swore.

'Bloody idiot didn't fill the flaming car,' he yelled with a fist pound on top of the steering wheel. As he steered the stuttering car onto the verge, his brain cells were quick enough to tell him he needed to hide the car in the bush. He peered through the shrub, spotted a clearer patch, wove between trees, threaded a way around the densest bushes until the car shuddered to a halt on the last gasp of fuel.

Past experience told him what to do next. He bolted from the car, tore a hefty branch from the nearest shrub and retraced the tyre marks to the road. Walking backwards, he swept away all tracks and even scattered litter and leaves over where he'd been. At the few bushes with torn foliage, he jiggled the branches to hide the tears until he was back at the car. Even though every cell in his body spun in panic, he managed to circle the car as he faced the road, to ensure he couldn't see where the road was. Happy he was hidden well enough to not be noticed by a passing vehicle, he folded into the front seat where he cursed the world and everyone in it. Since it would soon be night, there was no choice but to sleep in the car until the sun rose far enough he could see where to go.

He feasted on half the food he'd bought, peed behind a tree, tugged the prison greens over his clothes for a modicum of warmth and curled up on the back seat.

Sixteen

Nature's dawn calls of tweets and chirps woke Matteo from a cramped cold sleep but at least he'd gained more shut eye than he'd had in days. The padded back seat was a damn sight more comfortable than cold steel and the thick seat cover had retained his body heat. Two layers of clothes had helped keep in the warmth while the cushion of the police uniform he'd retrieved at ridiculous o'clock in the night, kept his head warm and comfortable.

As he eased from the seat, he groaned at the twinges of pain from muscles which had stiffened overnight. He stretched tall as he stood on dew drenched ground, bent sideways to his right and then left with arms stretched skywards, fingers gripped together. Head and shoulder rolls caused a few creaks but seemed to lessen the stiffness. A spot behind a tree for bladder relief was not his favourite toilet but at least it didn't stink like the public facilities at the park. And, more important, he had privacy. When his body shivered from the cold, he moved to the front seat of the car, turned on the radio and took a swig of juice. A glance at his watch showed him exactly how early it was. At home, he would roll over, tug the Doona around his ears and grab at least another thirty minutes of shut eye.

Instead, he twiddled with the tuner buttons on the radio in search of the national broadcaster, the ABC, for a news bulletin. While he listened to doom and gloom in the world, he picked out the tomatoes, feta cheese and olives from the remaining Greek salad.

Police are still searching the area near Pitt Town for any sign of Matteo Giovannazzo who is the mastermind of a highly sophisticated criminal gang. He escaped from a prison van after shooting two police officers yesterday afternoon. He is believed to be driving a silver Mazda sedan and was last seen when he purchased food at the Oakville Farmer Harvest Shop on the edge of Scheyville Forest late yesterday. He wore dark suit pants and a white business shirt but could also have access to mid-green knit-cotton track pants and top. He is believed to be armed. If seen, do not approach but please contact…

Matteo stabbed the off button. Frantic brain cells went on a rampage as he tried to figure out what to do. With no fuel he couldn't drive. There was one option open to him. He had to leg it. At least the bush was dense enough to keep him hidden until he reached more built-up areas when he could travel at night and find somewhere to shack up during the day. At least until he could find a phone. The shirt and pants had to go, as did the prison clothes. Might as well leave them in the car. Nah, that wouldn't work for if they found the car, they would know he had a different outfit. Better to let them search for a man in shirt and trousers while he would change into the uniform. They wouldn't be on the lookout for a copper.

Desperate to not waste another minute, he shot from the car, yanked the rear door open, stripped down to his underwear and shivered as the chilled air kissed his skin. He thrust legs into the navy trousers and pulled them up. They almost fitted. A bit baggy was better than too tight. He threaded his belt through the loops and tugged in the extra few centimetres of fabric. Shirt next. The sleeves were a tad too long but a single turn back on the cuffs and he wriggled his arms to find it was just right like in the tale of Goldilocks. Nothing else, however, was even remotely right, he thought as he tucked in the shirt tails and tightened the belt. The food was essential as was the fruit juice but with no bag to carry it in he had a major problem. He swore at the memory of the large bag he'd left in the bin.

At the sight of the prison greens a light bulb flashed in his brain. He tied the sleeves of the top together, fashioned a sling, put the created circle over his head and eased one arm through the tight loop. With the tail curled up against his body and tucked into the neckline of the police shirt, he was able to form a large pocket. He moved to the passenger side, opened the door and scooped up what was left of the food. To see how well he could pack it together, he laid every item out on the car hood. Most important was the gun, which he eased into the waistband of the trousers. Biltong pieces packed into the domed plastic salad tub, along with three bananas. He settled it into the makeshift pocket and pressed it into place as a test. Not bad. There were four bread rolls left. Since they were essential but light, he opened out the top of the plastic bag, fed the ends through the side of his belt and tied them together. The two litre juice bottle was more of a problem even though he'd already drunk half. Liquids were a must but it would be awkward to carry, especially when he needed to also carry all the clothes, at least far enough away before he could bury them.

It took two minutes to fold the clothes into the smallest possible pack before he figured out a solution. He fed the handle of the plastic bottle through the other side of his belt and let the bottle hang from the back of his hip. One of his own shoes went in each pocket of the trousers, the other two bananas curled inside each other on top of the salad bowl and he was able to pack the clothes in the top of his makeshift carry bag even though it reached almost to his chin. Happy, he searched the sky for the sun, calculated the directions, turned south and began the trek through the forest.

Within minutes, he discovered early morning dew was much thicker and stuck around a lot longer in a forest than it did in a suburban backyard. The thick layer of dank, rotted leaf litter he had to wade through didn't help. At least the leather boots kept his toes warm but moisture soon soaked the hem of the trousers. It took half an hour before the sun rose high enough to make its presence felt but he didn't like the way leaden clouds insisted on hiding the warmth from the sun in spasms as they swept across the sky. Instead, humidity increased with such rapidity sweat began to trickle down his torso. All the sun became useful for was a marker to keep him headed southwards.

Earlier fresh scents of eucalyptus and cool air turned to dank heat and the unpleasantness of his own stale sweat from a body which hadn't been washed for too long. Unbrushed teeth added to his misery to the extent he paused to drink but swished the juice around his mouth and gargled before spitting it on the ground between spread feet. The next mouthful he swallowed and followed it with a banana to kill the fetid sensation of bad breath.

He trudged until noon, all the time with his mind calculating distances. The navigation system in the car had indicated it was about fifty-five kilometres to Sydney. He'd driven around twenty-two kilometres which left about thirty-three. At the steady pace he'd maintained he calculated he might have covered five k's so far for it wasn't easy going. It took twice as many steps to go around thick impenetrable scrub and big grey rocks than it would if he were on a well-maintained track. At this rate he would be lucky to reach Sydney in three days.

To top it all off, he didn't like the way the black clouds kept banking on top of each other or the way the humidity seemed to intensify so much he knew, to the depths of his soul, Mother Nature was about to make life even more miserable. Sydney, at the end of summer and onset of autumn, could imitate the tropics and dump monsoon-like downpours on the city. He might not be in the city but was close enough.

He paused, leant up against a tree, to indulge in a tasty bacon and cheese topped bun. While he chewed and savoured he figured this was a good place to bury business shoes which were useless without laces and maybe the white shirt. The trousers could come in handy if what he wore became too wet. He used a stout dead stick to scratch a hole under a bush. Since he was in the middle of nowhere it didn't need to be very deep, just far enough down to cover the clothes with dirt. To finish the job, he scraped mouldy leaf litter over the top, along with a hefty rock to prevent foraging animals from digging up the clothes.

Before he set off again, he adjusted the loop around his neck, checked everything he needed was still attached and took his bearings from the little he could see of the sun at its most northern aspect. He had to keep it behind him now so he followed his shadow, but still had to dodge this way and that around native flora, none of which he appreciated as bush walkers would. He hated the lot. Hated the thorns, the twigs stuck out far enough to catch raw flesh and the wet leaves. He hated the constant green, the dank smell of rotted ground litter and increasing wetness of his clothes. Even more he hated the rising humidity and sudden rumble of thunder. God was up there rolling bowling balls along a very long, loud lane as he laughed at Matteo's predicament.

Even though he knew it would happen, the first flash of lightning caused him to jump and stumble. After the bright flash, the sky seemed to darken even more as the thunder rolled within seconds. He let loose with a raft of swear words at the first drops of rain: heavy plops, not a fine sprinkle. They didn't cease but increased with such rapidity he was soon drenched. The cold didn't edge its way into his skin but shot through as though from a cannon. Still he trudged on since there was no point to stop for there was nowhere to hide. Just trees, bushes and boulders. No caves, cliffs or even an overhang to hide under. Further east would be more hills but hills needed to be climbed. He kept south.

Mother Nature was intent on increasing the ferocity of the storm. A wild wind turned the rain horizontal, tore leaves and small branches from their fragile hold on parent trees and flayed his frozen skin with whipping lower branches. He paused mid-stride when he spotted a small mob of frantic sheep. Black faced, their long wool hung in saturated dreadlocks as they bounded in a huddle, tripping over each other in their desperation to keep together but at the same time flee the melee. When they disappeared, Matteo turned towards the direction from which they had come. Farm animals meant some sort of property, which meant a shed or house where he could find cover, dry out and rest.

Massive trees had lost their grip of the earth, too weak to fight the horrific elements that had left the soil sodden. He had to fight a way through drenched bushes on ground which had become a quagmire with no ability to soak in any more water. The climb over fallen trees sapped his energy too much so he veered around them. The one good aspect was the way the undergrowth thinned all of a sudden, as though it had been cleared to a certain extent. Civilisation was close. He trudged on, desperate to get rid of the sour whiff of wet clothes, to find warmth and hot food.

A tree had fallen over a fence, flattened the posts and wires. Maybe where the sheep had escaped. Matteo paused to stare through the sheet of water. In the gloom, he made out the most amazing sight – a house. Not giving a damn about being seen, he changed direction and headed straight for it. He was over hiding, over life.

Of course, the very moment he came within centimetres of cover, the rain had to cease with the same suddenness it had begun. He stepped onto a wooden veranda, edged around the wall and peered into every window as he passed. The place had an aura of emptiness but inside looked so damn homely, dry and warm. At the back door, he studied the lock, grinned and took out his wallet. With the now useless credit card, he eased it into the crack, jiggled, slid it up and down. The lock snicked. He pushed the door open.

'Hello,' he called, to be met with blessed silence.

With a wide grin, he toed off sodden boots and unhooked the wet bundle from his neck. Still on the wooden slats of the veranda, he undressed and bundled all the clothes into a pile. Right inside the door sat a washing machine with a drier on top. He wasn't above using them if he could figure out how. It wasn't something he'd ever had to do before. That's what wives were for.

He untied the track top sleeves, left the rest of the gear on the veranda and stepped inside. Clothes in the machine, he dribbled in two scoops of laundry powder, studied the dials, pressed what he hoped were the right ones, grinned at the rumble of machinery and went in search of a bathroom. It was across the passage but there was no shower stall, only a bath. Not even a shower head stood over the bath. He turned the hot tap on full, adjusted the heat level with cold, stepped into the porcelain tub and eased back with eyes closed to wait for the tub to fill. Ever so slow, the warm water eased up the sides. At the same rate, the warmth eased the chill in his body.

Because they were the same tone, it was difficult to make out what was mud and what was hair as he picked at the gunge smeared over his lower legs.

The warm bath water softened most of the mud but stubborn bits still gripped each hair, determined to not be dislodged. A slather of soap and vigorous rub with the flannel turned the water almost black but satisfied most of the mud had gone, he gave up, lay back and relaxed, although with knees folded in the tub too short for a man unless he was a midget, and a tap poked into his neck, relaxation wasn't on the agenda. Who didn't have a shower stall these days, he thought as he huffed out a long breath, twitched his neck to one side and closed tired eyes. He couldn't remember the last time he'd sat in a bath tub – if ever.

The rustle of leaves outside had eased to whispers with the occasional louder brush against the glass pane. He scratched at the itch of two-day-old whiskers and ran his fingers through hair which also needed a trim. Soon, he thought. Soon, he could find his way home and get back to normalcy, although it was impossible to figure out what normal meant.

A loud screech followed by a bang had him bolt upright. He stepped over the bath edge and searched for a towel. A grin and sigh escaped when he spied the bright pink of the single towel on the rail. The toes of his big feet hung over the edge of the poor excuse for a bathmat as he wrenched the towel from the rail, hitched it around his hips and tucked the top edge into a sort of knot. At the sight of his reflection in the mirror over the vanity he swore under his breath. Raw scratches down one side of his face had turned a ferocious red from the heat but at least they were now clean. He couldn't recall when he'd been scratched but he'd been so damn cold the stings hadn't registered. Thick dark hair hung in limp strands still dripping from the three doses of shampoo he'd needed to rid it of thick mud, twigs and oodles of unrecognizable bits from the bush. To ensure it was clean, he had rinsed it under the flowing tap water since the bath now resembled a muddy dam.

Another thump. He eased the door open and crept along the passage to the kitchen. When he reached for the handle of the door which led to the back veranda, the door swung open and a man stepped inside. He was huge and very wet. A battered bush hat hung so low it hid the man's eyes. Water poured from an oilskin coat to create a puddle on the floor at the man's booted feet. Everything about the interloper was dark and brooding. It sent out an instant message – danger. Every atom in Matteo's body jolted to alert status.

'What the hell did you do with my sheep?' the man bellowed as he raised his head. Eyes boggled while his mouth imitated a guppy as it opened and closed several times. No sound came out until he coughed. 'Who the hell are you?' he stuttered as he glanced around. 'Where's Suzy?'

'Probably glad she isn't here if she was supposed to be on the receiving end of your aggression.' At least Matteo now had a name. Suzy. And better still, this man wasn't after him. Relief was instant. He held out one hand in the traditional handshake even though he should get the hell out of there but since he stood in the kitchen with a scanty pink towel draped around the private parts, he had no choice but to make out he had a right to be there. 'Jack's the name,' he lied, using the first name that came to mind. Can't be too careful especially since he'd been caught in the flesh. He sniggered at the thought – too much damn flesh. He tightened the grip on the knot. 'As to sheep, I don't have a clue.'

The man screwed his eyes with lips pursed as though a piece of sour lemon swept over them. 'Where's Suzy?'

'I don't know.'

'What are you doing in Suzy's house?'

Matteo lowered his eyes, brushed one hand down his still dripping chest. 'Getting cleaned up.'

'Why?'

Matteo wanted to roll his eyes but instead stared at the man and waved a hand in the direction of the open door. 'Think, storm of the century. Thunder loud enough to rip eardrums to shreds, lightning so close the air sizzled with electricity and enough rain to fill the biggest of dams in less than a day.' He indicated the man's coat. 'I wasn't fortunate enough to have an oilskin on hand.'

'But why here and where are my sheep?'

'Here was the closest haven and sheep? Black faced?'

'Yeah.'

'Might be the twenty or so I came across about two clicks that way.' His hand wavered in the direction behind him.'

'Two k's! Why the hell are they so far away?'

With a firm grip on the knot, Matteo placed one finger against the side of his cheek as though in thought. 'Could be the storm scared them enough to run for their lives through the fence flattened by fallen trees. You can't have missed the mess out there.'

'Which is why I came to check on my sheep.' The man swore, turned away and vanished, leaving the door open.

The slam of a car door, an engine roared to life, wheels rumbled as they spun in the same saturated mud Matteo had waded through less than an hour ago. He wasn't sure but got the impression the car fish-tailed before it hit an object but he didn't much care. A search of the area outside the door ensured the man had gone. After closing the door, he turned the key to prevent any more sudden invasions and went to check the washing machine, thankful the cycle had finished. He withdrew his now clean clothes and shoved them into the dryer. It was a miracle the electricity still flowed but maybe this new estate of small rural lots had underground power. He shut the dryer door but paused.

It might be a stupid idea but he retrieved the boots, hosed them off in the basin, shook the worst of the water off and shoved them in with the clothes. They wouldn't dry well, but half-dry was better than squelchy splats at each step.

To kill time, he searched for something to eat. The fridge yielded little in the way of stodge to fill an empty stomach but a stick of celery, half a carrot, a tomato and handful of mixed greens meant a few of the right minerals and vitamins entered his bloodstream. There wasn't a skerrick of much needed protein, not even milk, which meant black coffee but at least it was via a coffee machine and sent up a rich aroma as he sipped and sighed at the rich, full flavour. In the neatest pantry he'd ever seen, the sole packet of biscuits were of the water cracker type. He scoffed the entire package, found a small box of nutrition bars and put them aside. Two apples, a banana and orange in the fruit bowl had seen better days but when you were hungry, it didn't much matter. Food was food. He downed all of the squishy banana but set the other pieces of fruit next to the box of bars although he wasn't sure how he would carry them all.

When he found a small notepad on the end of a bench, he wrote a note to the missing Suzy.

Sorry to invade your home. Got caught in the storm. Your house was a Godsend. I apologise for

using your bath to clean off the
mud and both washing machine
and dryer to clean my clothes. I
also ate a little of your food. I
suggest you get a decent lock on
your back door. If I could get in,
so can anyone else, including the
aggressive sheep owner, who
didn't have the manners to knock.

He remembered to sign Jack at the bottom before he took care to place the note in the centre of the table, held in place with a vase containing three droopy rosebuds. Suzy hadn't been away longer than a few days. The wallet he'd taken from his trousers pocket was damp on the outside. None of the contents had been affected by the elements.

The warmth of dry clothes straight from the machine sent a shiver of appreciation through his body. The shoes weren't too bad but he reset the timer while he cleaned the mess left by Mr Grump and swished out the ring of black in the bath. After another glimpse of his mug in the mirror, he searched the cabinet, found a packet of razors, withdrew one and, using the soap to soften the bristles, scraped his face clean. Pink was good, he decided, if it meant he could feel human again. When he spied the toothpaste, he used his finger to scrub away several days of grot from his teeth. There wasn't a lot he could do about the wet towel but hung it straight on the rail and draped the rinsed out flannel where he'd found it over the side of the bath. Maybe the mysterious Suzy wouldn't be home for a while if she could get through the storm debris at all. But Mr Grump had driven through so maybe the roads weren't in the same disastrous condition as the route he'd taken.

Happy the bathroom was as pristine as he'd found it, he checked all the machines were switched off, donned warm, almost dry shoes and was ready to go. He took a last glance around the kitchen and spotted a phone on the wall. Did he dare?

Caution, be damned. He needed help. In his mind, he ran through a list of people he could call. Family was out for he was certain calls to any family member would be traced. He would trace them if he was a copper.

An idea edge its way into the forefront of his mind. Luke Bianchi.

He dialled, waited, and waited.

'Hello, who is this?' The familiar voice sounded cautious.

'Luke?'

'Who's asking?'

The tone didn't sit well, but Matteo figured Luke would be sitting on a nest of nasty European wasps. 'Matteo, of course.'

'Holy hell, Mr G. Where are you? The whole world has gone crazy. Dad's in gaol. They won't let

173

me visit. I thought you were too. Have they let you make a phone call?'

'Calm down, my man. I need your help. I escaped but you must come and get me.'

'Where are you, Mr G? How did you escape?'

'No time for questions. I have to find a safe spot to hide but first you have to pick me up. I'm… hang on… I'm not sure… give me a minute.' Matteo scrabbled through items on the kitchen bench, found a couple of opened letters, glanced at the address on the envelope and smiled. 'Okay, here's the address but I'll walk down the road a bit and keep out of sight. When I see your car, I'll wave you down. Please hurry. The weather's not great. How come the coppers haven't arrested you?'

'Cops came, questioned me about Dad's association with you but I can act dumb. I've got a legit job. They don't have a clue about my work for you. I've kept the two well separated. Keep none of your stuff at home or work. Not sure where you can hide, though.'

'I've got an idea. See you within the hour.' Matteo hung up and growled. Lying bastard would pay.

Seventeen

Still two days short of Sydney, Rico took small sips of the beer even though he wasn't a lover of the beverage, plus he'd sworn off alcohol. The humidity of an impending summer storm had led him to order the lager, because it was ice cold. Now he regretted it for the bitter aftertaste on his tongue negated any sense of refreshment. He sat alone on a stool at the tiny bar of the licenced Café 828, refreshment car on the Overland Train. In a railway carriage there wasn't room for anything larger, hence most patrons purchased their favourite tipple and returned to more comfortable seats.

An undertone of a thin continuous screech of steel wheels on steel rails accompanied the rumble of voices, interrupted with occasional shouts of laughter. A round of applause from a group of older travellers dressed in smart attire indicated some sort of celebration. Wine glasses and two open bags of crisps sat between them. Rico couldn't think of anything worse than to celebrate on a train.

Although… a sudden memory came to him. There was the train trip he went on with his mother and two younger sisters way back. It was hard to remember how old he had been when they travelled by train to the Sunshine Coast in Queensland where they'd spent a week in a cabin perched behind a dune, which had been within and easy stroll to the beach. Maybe six or seven. Neither of his sisters had been babies for they walked hand-in-hand along a well-worn track with Mama close behind. She carried an overladen basket, filled with food, drinks and beachside essentials. He recalled the orange and white striped towel around his neck while the girls both had pink towels. Maybe he'd been seven with Maria five and Lucy around three. The week had been brilliant and carefree. Could be because his father hadn't been with them to issue constant orders and make demands. At seven, he hadn't realised the demands were those of a bully. They were just a normal part of life: a life of fear, he now knew. He still hadn't figured it out at twelve. It wasn't until he had spent a year in high school and they'd been given talks on how to handle bullies when the message hit home but constant threats and fear kept him under the harsh thumb of an autocrat all through his teenage years. In reality, it had taken him almost thirty years to stop and say, no more, although he hadn't yet voiced this new determination. He'd made the decision when he met Amanda but five years in prison had got in the way. Now, he'd been foolish enough to end his father's regime by becoming the ultimate traitor.

'You want another one?'

Rico jolted at the voice and twisted his head towards the bartender. 'No thanks. I don't really want this one.'

'Then, why did you order it?'

'Figured it would be the coldest. Why is it so hot in here?' He swiped at the sweat on his brow and wiped his hand on the bar towel.

'Having trouble with the air con.'

'Brilliant. Just this carriage or the entire train?'

'Not sure but customers have complained when they come in so might be this car. I can give you a glass of ice and water if it helps.'

'Thanks, I would appreciate it.' He took another sip of the beer, winced at the taste and pushed the half-full glass away. On the laminate wall behind the bar, pictures of Victorian tourist spots caught his eye. The frames were a bit tatty and a closer study of the wall's surface indicated regular polish did its best to hide the need for refurbishment. Maybe why the air-con didn't work. The entire carriage needed a thorough update: a new carriage would be better. Surely Victoria Rail could do better than this on the popular Overlander.

The two nights and single day on the Indian Pacific had been much better, perfect in fact. He'd slept most of the way, not because he wanted to but it seemed his battered body demanded it. He hadn't felt this refreshed in weeks. Sore muscles had eased to occasional twinges, dark bruises were now much paler, most turned to a sick yellow but it was better than black and indigo.

He had woken at sunrise on the Nullarbor to a spectacular scene of low scrub, dark against the salmon sky. The way the colours had changed as the sun rose, from pinks, through purples and gold was something to behold and had kept him entranced until hunger pangs drove him from the cabin to a five-star breakfast in the dining car. At the stop in the old town of Cook, he'd kept away from the other passengers who were eager participants in the historical talk he had no interested in. Instead, he'd taken the opportunity to power-walk to one end of the kilometre long train and back again in an attempt to regain a modicum of fitness and work out too many kinks. About twenty metres from the side of the train, a pair of magnificent wedge-tailed eagles, their dark bronze feathers glistening in the sunshine, didn't scatter at his nearness but remained feasting on a recently culled kangaroo, probably hit by a train. Both had stilled and eyed him for about thirty seconds before the fresh meat had got the better of them and they tore off large shreds and devoured them.

After a second night of solid sleep, there had been no time for breakfast for those alighting before they pulled into the Adelaide Parklands terminal right on time at 8.15 a.m. The transfer to this train went like clockwork but breakfast wasn't anywhere near as luxurious which was a disappointment. But still, he'd eaten good solid meals, which his battered body appreciated.

'Here you go.' The bartender's voice broke his reverie.

Droplets of condensation on the new glass were a welcome sight. 'Thanks, mate.' Rico lifted the glass and carried it to the other end of the carriage where he settled into a more comfortable seat but it took mere seconds before the heated faux fabric caused sweat to puddle down his back. He stood again, turned and sought out a different chair, one not in the sun, but found none. With a shrug he decided to return to his seat in the passenger car where it hadn't seemed to be quite so putrid. He reached the door, pressed the red button and waited for it to open.

With a grind and rumble, it slid to the side. He took one step. Foot in the air, he jerked sideways and his feet slid from under him. He managed to grab a hold of a handle and yank himself upright while water and ice cubes sloshed over his other arm. The train shuddered. Wheels squealed. He rocked from side-to-side, tightened his hold on the steel handle. New bruises were added to his left side before the train came to a halt and a heavy silence ensued until it was broken by loud voices of query. 'What the hell happened?' the most prominent.

'Please stay where you are,' came across the intercom. 'There's been an accident on the bridge ahead and the train can't get through. We might be here for a while.'

This time the comments from the passengers were more of the four-letter kind. Rico had to smile at some of the more uncouth murmurs, most of which he agreed with. He shook his head from side-to-side, amazed at what fate had served up to him. Since getting out of prison mere weeks ago, this was just one more disaster to add to many others: enough for the thought to edge its way into his mind that prison was a damn sight easier on both body and mind. In a flash, he dismissed the thought as ridiculous for prison had to be one of the worst ways to spend your life. He continued on his way back to his seat in the carriage, where he sat and waited.

Three hours. It had taken three sweltering hours for the authorities to sort out what the hell to do. After it had been determined the way under the bridge wouldn't be cleared for at least twenty-four hours, buses had arrived. They'd all collected their luggage and been loaded onto various coaches to continue their journey by the much longer and slower route by road. While they waited it had been as putrid on the train as it had been off. It didn't matter where they stood or sat, sweat oozed from every body part imaginable the entire time. Now, everyone had a disgruntled aura about them. Rico sat jammed against another man of equal size, halfway down the aisle. These seats weren't built for two broad-shouldered men but the conductors had insisted that unless you travelled with a partner, men sat next to men and women next to women. He understood the social implications but it sucked. To top it all off, there was a strident voice over-riding all other quiet mumbles. A young woman down the back had been talking, full throttle, on her mobile phone for the last half hour. Huffs, harrumphs and raised shoulders, along with serious glares at the perpetrator, hadn't had any effect.

Fed up, Rico rose, turned to the rear and strode to the woman. He grabbed the damn phone and held it high.

'Hey, what do you think you are doing?' the strident voice squealed even louder and higher. There was an instant hush from the passengers.

'Every person on this bus has experienced a hard, aggravating day. The sort of day we wish had never happened and want it to end real soon. We are all pissed to the nth degree and would love a little quiet to stew in peace but instead we have had to listen to you carry on like a pork chop about your boyfriend ditching you. If you treated him with the same disrespect and *I don't care* attitude you have dumped on the rest of your fellow passengers for the past half hour, I'm not surprised he ditched you. Good on him. We would all appreciate it if you turned off your damn phone and shut the hell up.'

To make sure, he pressed the off button, dropped the phone in her lap and returned to his seat amid loud applause and cheers.

'Good onya, mate,' said his fellow seat mate as Rico plonked back into his seat. 'Brave man but thank you. She was driving me insane.'

'She was driving everyone insane. Don't kids learn any manners these days?'

'Some don't. Think they own the world. Now we can all get some shuteye.'

Rico took the comment as a hint and settled back against the back of the seat, despite the squishy closeness but at least this bus had a functional air conditioner. Sleep eluded him but he noticed most of the other passengers managed to doze in the blessed peace as the day turned to night. At least madam up the back wasn't game to talk again.

It was almost mid-night when the bus turned into the passenger terminus. Eager to get off, everyone stood at the same time and squeezed their cramped bodies into a wonky queue. Front and central doors wheezed open at the same time. Hushed murmurs escalated into loud rumbles of relief and complaints about the amount of rain which had fallen over the last hour. It hadn't decreased the humidity level, Rico discovered when he stepped off the bus, for even though they were under cover, a wall of heat hit, which brought out instant sweat to add another level of discomfort from the previous, now dried, layers of sweat. Body odour was abundant in the melee of arms and legs scrambling to find luggage and be first to front the man in the small kiosk who was in charge of finding taxis at this late hour or directing passengers to the nearest accommodation.

The line of tired, bedraggled passengers folded back on itself several times. Rico was lucky enough to grab his sole bag and be in the front section with three people ahead of him. There were no smiles from the first two after they received direction but he figured it was because most people were too exhausted to form a smile. At his turn, he stepped up to the kiosk to be met with steel-blue eyes running up and down his body.

'Budget,' the owner of the eyes said.

Rico bristled as he straightened. 'Excuse me. What do you mean by budget?'

'I've been in this job for seven years. I can tell by demeanour, luggage and clothes what sort of accommodation a passenger wants.'

'Is that so?' Rico turned and swept a hand to indicate the line behind him. 'By demeanour, every person here looks like they've just risen from sleeping in an alley. They've all had a hell of a day.' He turned back and glared at the man. 'I can afford to buy your so-called budget hotel so show a bit of compassion. Lift up your phone there and book me a bed in the nearest five-star hotel. The name's Joe Russo.' He didn't do five-star but when a point had to be made he'd suffer the la-di-dah consequences.

'Sorry, Park Hyatt is a couple of minutes' walk.'

'Book me a single room for tonight but I'll need a late check-out.' Rico had to bite the inside of his cheek to prevent a smile at the sight of the flushed neck and face on the obsequious little twerp who shoved a plum in his mouth when he spoke to the hotel.

Details given to him, he turned, took three steps and pulled to a halt at the sight of two police officers who stood at the entrance. By the way one waved his arms around, it was obvious he was giving directions to an elderly woman. Rico figured these guys wouldn't be on the lookout for him at this time of night. Too tired to care, he was game enough to see this as a great opportunity to find out if his new hairstyle masked his appearance enough. Although there was no real reason they would be looking for him in Melbourne in any case. He strolled past but began to jog when he hit the outside for water still tumbled from the sky, although the intensity had eased from heavy downpour to light shower status. Who cared if he got soaked? He was about to shower in any case and there wasn't a chance in hell he would wear the same sweat-laden clothes any time soon.

Eighteen

Even after such an exhaustive day, Rico woke at dawn, refreshed. The few hours of sleep in the over-sized bed had been solid. Could be because of the softness of the luxurious mattress, he figured as he rolled over to lift his watch to check the time. Not quite six-thirty. Thirty minutes to wait for the room service breakfast he'd ordered. He wriggled upwards, punched the second pillow into submission and wedged it under his shoulders. The time would be useful to catch up on personal messages, emails and what had happened in the rest of the world.

It took mere seconds to boot up the laptop, left to charge overnight along with the new phone. Since he'd had no chance to reconnect with people on social media after his release, he didn't expect any emails. He scanned through tweets, deleted the lot – all utter nonsense. There was nothing on Facebook but ridiculous adverts, all sent to the trash can. Such a boring life. To while away a few more minutes, he logged onto his internet banking, checked his Joe Russo account - agreed with all the debits, smiled at the final balance. The next account had done nothing but collect interest and investment dividends for five years. This time he grinned at the final figure on the bottom of the electronic statement. More money than he would ever need:

more than enough to set up in another country with the purchase of a decent home.

He opened the Rico account, scanned down to check the purchases he'd made while in the west. His eyes stalled on the last debit amount. Ten thousand dollars? He checked the date. Yesterday.

'What the hell?' he yelled. No-one had access to this account. No-one had knowledge of the new password he'd changed it to the day after he'd been released from prison. Frantic fingers scrolled to the top of the statement until he found the number of the bank's call centre. He grabbed his phone, tore out the cable, punched in the number. While he waited for a connection he re-checked the debit amount, certain he'd read it wrong. The number ten with three definite zeroes stared back at him.

A tinny voice came on the line, asked him to press a number. He pressed, waited and was issued with another number to press. He stabbed to hear *brnng, brnng.*

'How can I help you?' This time a human.

'I've just noticed a large sum has been debited from my account.'

'Oh, please give me your account details.'

Rico rattled off the account number.

'Just give me a minute to find your account.' Loud breathing followed. 'Which amount are you concerned about?'

'The last amount, ten thousand dollars. I haven't used this account since the debit before, over a week ago. Who has access to my account? Who authorised this? Have I been scammed? Why wasn't I notified of a large amount being debited?'

'Umm, who are you?'

'What do you mean, who am I? My name is on the account - Enrico Joseph Giovannazzo.'

'There must be some mistake.'

'There sure as hell is. Some stranger has had access to my private, password-protected account. Not a single soul knows my password so please explain how *your* bank has permitted ten grand to be debited without *my* permission?'

'The law allows up to ten thousand dollars to be withdrawn from the account of a dead person to help fund the funeral.'

'Excuse me?' Rico winced at his own screech. 'How can I be dead if I'm speaking to you?'

'How do I know you are Enrico Giovannazzo?'

'Holy… look, if I give you the actual password, will that convince you? I can assure you I am alive. I did have a short stint in hospital last week. I can even give you the number of a well-respected lawyer who I have dealt with over the past few days. Will that be enough?'

'Give me your password.'

Rico fought to settle shot nerves while he spouted off numbers, letters and two characters. 'You do realise, I had to use the same password to log into my account to start with. How else would I have been able to?'

'You have a point.'

'Rather a valid point, I might add.' A thought came to him. 'Are you able to tell me who the money was given to or who requested it and I am certain the law states you need to sight a death certificate before you give access to a person's account?' There was one person who would have the gumption to steal his money. The one man who had given the kill order. But he had to be still locked up. Had he been granted access to a phone?

'Hang on a second, there's a note attached to your account. Let me read it. An authorisation came from a lawyer to confirm your death. The money was to be given to your family accountant as family members were too distraught to attend the bank in person.'

Rico laughed; he couldn't help it. 'Lawyer's name?'

'John H. Watson.'

Rico's laughter increased until he snorted and had to hold his nose in order to stop. 'You've been taken for a ride,' he managed to get out between a few more ungentlemanly snorts.

'What do you mean?'

'Ever heard of Sherlock Holmes?'

'Of course, why?'

'John H. Watson was Sherlock's sidekick. There is no lawyer with that name. Who was authorised to pick up the money?'

'A Mr Luke Bianchi.'

Luke Bianchi? The lawyer's son. What's he got to do with the old man? 'You do realise your bank hasn't acted with due diligence and I expect full restitution. I know access to an account of a person who has passed away cannot ever be granted unless a signed death certificate has been sighted and verified. Let me warn you, if you allow another cent to be taken out of my account without my permission, I will contact consumer protection with a serious complaint. My email address is in my account details. Better note, I've changed my phone number due to an accident with my phone so at the moment you can contact me via my email address. I will be in contact soon, in person, to confirm every detail but at the moment I'm interstate and please be assured – I am very much alive.'

'I am sorry this has happened. I've made note of the details and will have it looked into by our security department A.S.A.P.'

'Thank you. I'll be in contact as soon as I get back to Sydney.' As he hung up he grinned at the audacity of his father but frowned at what this meant. Somehow, his father had gained access to his account. Well, he assumed it was the old man. Mama wouldn't be game or dishonest enough to pull such a stunt. All he had to figure out was why. If the bastard was in gaol, why did he even need ten grand? Rico shrugged. Maybe a lawyer. 'Why my account when the old man had millions stashed away?' he said to the statement on his laptop.

Since there wasn't anything else he could do about the situation, Rico closed down both phone and laptop, rose from the bed and searched for clean clothes. Shower time. A quick glance at his watch - ten minutes until breakfast arrived. Just enough time.

Clean shaven, clean body, clean hair, Rico sat on the padded dining chair at the small rectangular table, took a sip of the fresh orange juice and lifted the aluminium dome from the plate. Bacon-scented steam rose, wafted in a spiral and sent a flood of juices in his mouth. Two crisp rashers draped down one side of the white plate, next to two fried eggs with yellow yolks glistening in perfection. Two hash browns were crispy gold. Toast, wrapped in a paper serviette to keep it warm, sat on a separate small plate with a tiny ceramic bowl filled with butter. Hmm, maybe this five-star treatment was sometimes worth the extra money, he thought as he scraped butter onto the toast, spread it and eased both pieces under the eggs.

Since he hadn't watched television for days, he reached over, scooped up the remote and pressed the on button. Maybe he could catch the local news. While he savoured the food, he watched the destruction from the overnight storm. Seems Mother Nature had been intent on releasing her full fury on the entire southeast of the continent. Puddles were pools, roads had turned to rivers. Saturated engines had stalled in the most ridiculous of situations, to leave the owners stranded. Why people drove in such weather, Rico couldn't understand. There might be some urgent situations where one had to drive but to stay put until the storm ceased would be far more sensible. His eyes rose to stare at the ceiling. Isn't that what he was about to do? Hire a car and drive to Sydney. He was about to click off the T.V. when a thought came. Might be better to see what Mother Nature was going to deal out for the next twenty-four hours.

He swirled the last piece of toast around the plate to scoop up the egg remnants, shoved it into his mouth, chewed and swallowed. The last of the fresh orange juice followed. Now he wished he'd ordered coffee but hadn't because it would have been tepid by the time he got to drink it. Instead, he would go down to the dining room to get a hot fresh brew. Nothing worse than lukewarm coffee. He stacked the dishes on the tray, stood and lifted the tray to place outside the door. As he lifted, he glanced at the screen and almost dropped the tray.

The entire screen was filled with a photo of the bastard. Mouth agape, Rico sank to the chair and stabbed the volume control. '… still searching the Scheyville National Park area for any sign of Matteo Giovannazzo. Police have cordoned off the entire area with roadblocks at every entry. Nearby residents have been warned to not confront Mr Giovannazzo if they spot him but to call the number on the screen as he is believed to be armed and dangerous. Please avoid the area.'

Rico swore, flicked through various channels in search of more information but it seemed the news was over. Desperate, he flicked back to the original news channel to hear the weather report and study the map. Another severe storm band was expected to sweep up from the Victorian south coast, through the Australian Capital Territory and New South Wales. The same exact route Rico had planned to drive. He had little choice but to change plans. Flying was out. There was nothing worse than flying in a storm - if the planes would even be allowed to take off – or land. Another bus trip was not on the agenda any time soon. Couldn't stand the trauma. This left the train.

A search for train times on the internet and he yelped. If he hurried he could get on this morning's train. Clothes were fisted into the backpack, toiletries on top. Laptop slid into its own pocket, cords bundled in a tangle, with phone and wallet shoved into the pockets of his jeans. A quick search around with his eyes to check nothing had been left behind, he ran, avoided the wait for the elevator, took the stairs, two at a time, down three floors.

At the service counter he flung the room keycard on the ledge. 'Joe Russo. Room 317. Gotta hurry. Catch the train. Paid last night. Nothing from the minibar,' he garbled, turned and ran for the main door with backpack hefted over one shoulder. It was fortunate he knew to return to the same place he'd arrived the night before. The three-minute slow midnight run now turned into a two-minute early morning dash.

He flew into the station with eyes scanning the area for a ticket machine or person in a booth. He spied both but figured the woman would be quicker since he wasn't *au fait* with the machines – didn't know what buttons to push and didn't have time to figure it out.

'Train to Sydney,' huffed out as he yanked wallet from pocket, opened it out and took out a credit card but shoved it back in when he realised it was his Rico account. His brain functioned enough to figure it wouldn't work since he ordered the bank to not let anyone take out any more money. Next card was the right one. He held it over the card machine, eyes on the poor woman as she tapped and pressed. At her nod, he lowered the card until it beeped.

'You'll need to hurry,' she said as she slid a ticket through a slot at the base of the Perspex window.

Rico grabbed the ticket, held it against the card and wallet with two fingers, turned and ran. Good job there was a sign – *Trains This Way*. He belted around a corner, skidded the last little bit, regained his balance and pelted along the concourse.

'All aboard,' came from a loudspeaker. 'Train to Sydney leaves in one minute.'

'Wait,' Rico yelled to the guard; ticket, card and wallet waved high. He reached the end of the train, increased his speed, leapt through a closing door and stumbled. He managed to hook an elbow around a steel pole to right himself. His chest heaved, blood thundered and sweat oozed.

'Almost didn't make it, mate.' An age-wrinkled man with thick white hair, lips spread in a wide grin, stared from the seat opposite.

'Almost,' Rico gasped out as he steadied. 'But thank goodness I did,' he added when his lungs found enough air to formulate words. Before finding a seat, he dropped the backpack to the floor, put card in wallet, ticket in shirt pocket, wallet in jeans pocket and twisted all his clothes into the right place. His forearm dealt with the sweat on his face. He leant up against the pole for a couple of minutes to regain some sort of composure, picked up the backpack and went in search of a seat.

The carriage was half full. Most passengers had found seats alone. The two seats at the front end were devoid of passengers. Rico eased into the right-hand seat, wriggled to the wall and set his backpack next to him. If he was lucky he could spend the next eleven hours alone, not like the night before where he was squished against a man of equal size.

Now he had a chance to take note of the world, he realised clouds of lead hung low in the sky giving no chance for the sun to peek through. The side of the track held large black puddles, similar to those he'd seen on the news. The train increased speed with a steel-on-steel whine and a regular rhythm of clicks. Train whistle blew, crossings whizzed past and then the heavens opened in a deluge so strong, water pounded the window as though frantic to get in. This was supposed to be an express train but Rico wondered if it would have to slow if Mother Nature didn't ease up her determination to create havoc.

He settled back against the fabric seat; his head twisted to stare at the outside torment. There was little else he could do as vague shapes raced past, too fuzzy to discern what they were through the cascade of water.

The pictures in his mind were clearer but raced to catch up with each other. The full screen shot of his father fought to take centre stage. How did he escape? Who helped him? Where was he? What about Mama? Did she know? Must do for nobody could miss the photo. No doubt police officers would be stationed outside her home, in wait for the bastard to show his face. And he would, for he relied on Mama for the creature comforts. He wouldn't last two minutes if he had to fend for himself. He'd never cooked a single meal, done a load of washing, swept a floor, made a bed. Rico doubted whether his father even knew where the clean sheets were kept.

Mama. Somehow, he would have to contact her, make sure she was okay. Did she have money?

Maybe not if the family bank account had been frozen. Or it was possible the bastard hadn't wanted to access his own account for fear of his whereabouts being traced through the electronic network. The authorities would be on the lookout for every single transaction. No, the old bastard had used Rico's account instead, to indicate the missing Rico was back in Sydney. Nah, that can't be right for he had been proclaimed dead and there was every possibility nobody knew he was still alive. Johannsen had been caught at the airport, which meant it was possible he hadn't reported in. The bank had been told one Rico Giovannazzo had met his demise but he had disabused them of such a fact. Damn, the authorities would soon know he was alive. Ah, but he'd told the bank he was interstate and the last time he'd used his Rico account had been in the west. Phew.

There were now under eleven hours to fill. It would give him time to search through the rest of the files he'd downloaded, to see what the bastard had been up to over the past five years. It took a few minutes to set up his laptop, search for the thumb drive and wait for it to boot up. Since the battery wouldn't last the entire trip, he scanned through those he'd already read, opened a new file and took his time to read and absorb every word. Eyes boggled, brain cells jerked to awareness and an awful lot of facts came into focus.

Nineteen

The station was abuzz with shoppers and workers desperate to get home. Voices rang out over the scuffle of shoes and background murmur of a busy area. Rivers of humans flowed to and from carriage doors, snaked across the concourse in organised chaos, many with heads down to check phones. Also with his head down to hide his face, Rico fed into a line headed to the nearest outlet. He didn't much care where he came out. What he did care about was to not be recognised by the heavier than usual police presence. Officers stood in pairs, fingers looped through the front of their vests, as their eyes scanned the crowd. He prayed they centred their search on a fifty-six-year-old escapee and not a man with thirty-four years under his belt. His innards hurt from tension while his heart replicated a loud bass drum booming to keep everyone in step.

The train had made good time despite having to slow in some areas when the storm had been at its worst. He figured they'd gone faster between the latter stations to make up for lost time for they'd arrived no more than ten minutes after the designated time of arrival. Relief surged when he shot from the confines of Sydney Central station to see the streets a shimmer with the slick of left over rain. The air had a dank scent but was warmer than he'd expected although, with the amount of

197

moisture in the air, the humidity level had to be high. Lights glinted from puddles as he walked, in search of an eatery. Somewhere he wouldn't be recognised. Not a seedy joint frequented by the underworld nor a highfalutin place loved by the legal fraternity: places he knew from his past. A siren sounded from far away, increased to a shriek and faded again. It didn't concern him for it was a common sound in the city.

As he passed an open door, a rumble of voices surged, accompanied by a saliva inducing aroma. He scanned the inside and paused. Vertical meat skewers rotated over a bench. Flames sizzled and spat. Three men, lightly tanned skin like he had, were busy behind the counter. One with a hair net over his head, shaved meat and piled slivers on a plate. Another spread meat on flat bread and added sauce. The third spread sliced salad and rolled the bread into pockets before he wrapped each in paper. Customers sat in twos and threes around small square tables. The atmosphere held a liveliness and smelt divine. Rico stepped inside, dropped his backpack on an empty table in one corner and read the board menu as he headed for the counter. A young woman with a too large white apron tied around her waist stood from her seat on a stool.

'One beef kebab, please.'

'Sauce?'

'You choose and coffee, long black. Smells so good in here.'

The woman smiled. 'Real traditional food is good.' The strong accent indicated a recent immigrant or maybe a refugee given the state of warfare in her part of the world. Rico fished out cash for the flat fifteen-dollar amount then stood to one side to wait.

'I bring to your table,' the woman said.

'Are you sure?'

'I bring.'

'Okay, thank you.' He sent the woman a wide smile and nod, turned and crossed the small eating area. He sat where he could keep an eye on the people inside as well as those who entered even though his gut sent out no alarm signals. After an intricate study of the files he'd stolen, it had taken several hours on the train to sort out what to do once he reached his home city. First, he wanted to check on Mama. He'd concocted a plan on how to meet up with her for he felt sure there would be discreet surveillance on her every move in case she made a secret rendezvous with her husband. The phone would also be monitored for a call from his father. At least until they recaptured the bastard. He also needed to contact James Ward and more important, book himself into some sort of accommodation even though he had his own riverside home. It too, he was certain, would be under surveillance.

Hostels had come out on top of the list of where to stay. Most customers would be tourists who wouldn't have a clue who he was. No more than one night in any one place and he would use his third bank account in the name of his other alias for he had an identity card with both name and photo to verify he was who he said he was, even though it was fake. There were also sutures which were overdue to be removed. If they were in a more convenient part of his body, he'd do it himself. It would require contortionist abilities and a magnifying glass to find each tiny stitch and a steady hand to snip each away. With his current luck he could do more damage than what had already been done. Instead, he'd find a private practice in some outer suburb, maybe north of the river.

The rich smell of the food arrived three seconds before coffee was placed on the table in front of him.

'Sir, your order. Please enjoy.' A paper plate was set before him, on which sat a stuffed kebab cut in two. Sauce and juices drooled from each cut end.

'Thank you, I'm sure I will.' He lifted one piece, crinkled back the paper, bit off a chunk and rolled his eyes. 'This is delicious,' he called after the woman.

She turned, grinned and continued on to serve a new customer.

Rico took his time to chew so he could savour every bite. He couldn't figure out which flavour made this the tastiest, spiciest and juiciest kebab he'd ever eaten but if he stayed in town long enough he would make sure he returned to try a different meat. Maybe chicken next time.

While he ate, he took out his phone, pressed James's name.

'You do know what time it is over here, J.R. For you to ring in the middle of my dinner, I assume you've got yourself into another pickle.'

Rico laughed. 'No, sorry about the hour. I didn't think about the time distance. Too much on my mind. I saw part of a news bulletin. How did the bastard escape?'

'Ah, I thought you would have known.'

'Life has been a bit hectic which caused plans to go skewwhiff. Got caught in the storm of the century and arrived not long ago.'

'In Sydney?'

'Do I dare tell the truth?'

'Truth is all I deal in.'

'Okay, yes but I still have to keep out of the limelight. I don't have a clue if either the police or Dad's men have me on their radar.'

'I doubt it's either. I'm quite sure the only interest the police will have in you is to get more information. As for your father's hoodlums, how many can be left? Over a hundred arrests have been made Australia wide.'

'Over a hundred. I didn't give you so many names.'

'Some have squealed, given up others as bargaining chips. Not that it will do them any good.'

'My father. How did he escape?'

'Shot two police officers: one dead, the other not quite.'

'How did he get a gun?'

'Stole it from one of the officers.'

'How, when?'

'He was being transported to Parklea a couple of days ago.'

'Car or van?'

'Prison van.'

'Then how did he escape. Were the officers in the van with him?'

'No, they were driving.'

'Doesn't make sense. Why were police officers driving the van? Shouldn't they have been prison officers?'

'Good point. I don't know.'

'Had to have been outside help. What were the officer's names?'

'I don't know that either but it might be worthwhile for you to collate names with those on your list when you do find out. Do you have any more info?'

'Yes. I couldn't get it all written down before I first saw you. I've got a thumb drive but haven't had time to study all the files.' Well he had but wasn't game to admit it.

'How did you get it?'

'Downloaded files from my father's hidden computer when I visited Mama after I had been released. The old man was at work. He doesn't know and I sure as hell don't want him to ever find out.'

'Your mother would tell him.'

'Nope, she doesn't know either. She was too busy creating an Italian feast for lunch as a welcome home for her prodigal son.'

'This hidden computer – would the police have it now?'

'I doubt it. Hidden means well-hidden but I knew where he keeps it. The idiot hadn't changed the password. It will still be there.'

'Can you tell me where it is?'

'No, not yet. Not until I'm sure I'm not about to be re-arrested.'

'I'll see if I can get the authorities to make such an assurance. They should. Let me work on it. Anything else? My dinner is getting cold.'

'Ella. What happened?'

'She's safe. She gave an in-depth interview. Immediately pointed out Dugite from a photo line-up. No hesitation. Police are delighted. When it goes to court, she will testify via electronic means from a remote location. Her name will never be used or released. She has been given a new home, miles from the old one in case our bikie friend honed onto her original location. She's back at work, new job, different suburb. She's one gutsy young woman. Wants to contact you to say thanks. I said I'd ask.'

'Give it time. Let the dust settle. I've got too much on my plate right now. Tell her to leave it until later and let her know I'm proud of her.'

'Will do. Can I go back to my lukewarm stir fry now?'

'Yeah, sure. I'm about to finish the best damn Lebanese food I've ever eaten. Enjoy your cold limp veggies. I'll be in contact.'

'If it's in the middle of my meal, I won't answer.'

Rico laughed and hung up. He glanced at his watch, noted the time, subtracted three hours. 6.30 in the evening. What did the man have to complain about?

Before he made another call, Rico finished his own meal, wiped the juices from his mouth with the scrunched-up paper and set the rubbish aside. He sniffed the coffee before the first sip. Strong, a tad bitter but damn good and still hot.

It took less than five minutes to log onto a central backpackers and book himself a double room. They didn't do singles for individuals, not that he cared much. A double bed was preferable in any case. He wasn't in the space to share in a dormitory.

Room booked, he eased back in the chair, stared at the phone. Mama. Should he, or shouldn't he? He pressed in her mobile phone number, paused with the index finger over the send button. Even though he'd thought this through, run the plan through his mind dozens of times, a niggle of doubt seemed to hover. He pressed, placed the phone next to his ear.

Four rings. Maybe she was asleep.

'Hello.'

'Tia Silvanna.' He spoke in Italian in the hope those who listened wouldn't understand. His second language was needed to make his plan convincing.

'Who is this?'

'Tia, this is Joe Russo, grandson of Guiseppe and Maria Russo.' He paused at his mother's gasp, sure she understood for her parents had no other grandson. Still in Italian, he continued to prevent her from saying his name. 'I have come from Palermo to visit with my Australian relatives. I have news for you, are we able to meet up?'

'*Si, si.*'

'I have tomorrow free but am in Manly. I understand there are regular ferries from Sydney to Manly. Are you able to come to me?'

'*Si*… yes.'

'What time?'

'*Le dieci e trenta.*'

'I will meet the ferry. Thank you. It is too long since we last met.' As he hung up, he was certain he heard a sob, which twisted his heart. Now he was sure it had been the right thing to do.

Twenty

E ven though it was between ferry times, Rico had to stand in a queue to purchase a ticket. Head down, newspaper tucked under one arm, he scoured the wharf in front of his feet. How many people studied the ground, spied the fatty splotches of spilled food, the crushed empty sugar packet, a pale green flattened straw and general grime? How many, like him, didn't want to be recognised?

'Next,' a voice said at the same time someone nudged him in the back.

Rico stepped forward, lifted his head far enough to not be rude to the ticket seller. 'Manly.'

The man in the booth didn't glance up, handed over the ticket, scooped the correct payment in his other hand as if he were a robot. With ten minutes to spare, Rico wandered back to the cafe where he'd spent the last hour eating an okay breakfast. He settled his back against a pillar between two large windows so as to not block the view of the many customers still inside. From here he would spot Mama when she hurried to the ticket booth, head high, handbag caught in the fold of her elbow. It was the way she always walked when in the city or at the local shops. A no-nonsense woman, confident enough to stride with perceived purpose although her eyes often skittered as if in fear, a trait she couldn't hide well. The leather handbag would be more for show than a necessity to hold copious *just in case* belongings. She couldn't see the sense in lugging around lots of unnecessary junk. A pressed handkerchief would be tucked either up a sleeve or in a pocket, dependent on what she wore. Inside the bag would be a wallet with a low-limit credit card and enough cash for the day's needs. Never enough for a robber to delight in, should she be mugged.

A stream of feet fed in and out of the many cafes and eateries around the edges of Circular Quay. The outs would have finished breakfast while the ins would be on the hunt for morning coffee or tea, since it was too early for lunch. With a sudden increase in noise, a tidal wave of humans from the above ground station surged from the escalators with an equally large wave from the various ferries that had just berthed. Many were obvious tourists with cameras or phones held high: the arched bridge the centre of attention one way and the white sails of the opera house the other. Few centred on the famous ferries, yet they had carted passengers across the bay a lot longer in their distinctive yellow and green paint. An abundance of dreaded electric scooters made a nuisance of themselves, almost toppling unsuspecting pedestrians as if the scooters had right of way in a definite pedestrian zone.

Rico spotted her immediately. His heart hitched and smile spread. Today she wore a tailored dress in swirls of green, caught in at the waist with a black belt to match low-heeled shoes. It wasn't new. He'd seen it many times before. Mama wasn't one who demanded a constant new wardrobe of clothes. She had always been frugal in such matters. Carefully coiffed waves, still black despite her age, shone with reflected light. Sunglasses hid her eyes; a black leather bag was held in the crook of one arm. As she made her way to the ticket booth, Rico searched the area behind her.

The surveillance officer wore stylish reflective sunglasses, blue jeans, long-sleeved collared Polo shirt and white runners. It wasn't a man Rico recognised but it was obvious why he was there, tagged on the end of the small queue lined up to purchase tickets for the 10.30 ferry to Manly. Rico would have to be careful.

At the last minute, he strode to the crowd milled at the gates while they waited for the ferry to disburse a huge mob of passengers. Gates clanged, shuffled along steel runners; the noise echoed enough to cause seagulls and bronzewing pigeons to scatter with loud coos and squawks. Rico crept up behind Mama, bent down and dropped a piece of paper, scooped it up and tapped Mama on the shoulder.

'Excuse me, Ma'am, but you dropped this.'
'Ri..'
'Don't talk,' he whispered in her ear. 'Take this paper and read it on the ferry. You are under surveillance by the police.' He pressed the paper into her hand, stepped back to let a couple of other

passengers get between them. Mama had stiffened her stance but he noticed she wrapped her fingers around the paper. He searched for the officer, spied him standing to one side with his eyes sweeping over the crowd. Maybe he hadn't seen the few seconds of contact.

After he'd found a seat inside near the rear, Rico settled back with eyes on Mama, who sat three rows away, her eyes on the opened-out paper. *Wait ten minutes, buy yourself a coffee. Come to the outside seats on bottom level, near the front, facing the south shore.* He knew the words well for it had taken several attempts to get it succinct yet easy to understand.

As he stood, the boat rocked, creaks echoed, metal clanged to herald gates had closed and the gangways were dragged away. The constant hum of the engines accompanied him to the seats he wanted where he would have his back to the metal cabin wall – where they couldn't be observed from the inside. A lurch caused him to stumble. He righted himself as the pier began to fade away. How many times had he experienced this, yet it still sent a thrill through his innards. With most passengers settled he exited the door.

A stiff breeze carried the scent of river brine mixed with diesel exhaust fumes. It was cool but not too cold. After the bleakness yesterday, it was difficult to believe the sky was almost cloudless with the odd wisp of white to remind people of yesterday's deluge. Now the sun was bright, warm on his head and neck without the dense humidity. He passed two hardy passengers who stood at the rail, probably tourists eager to not miss a single detail, and found three vacant slatted seats where he settled in the central one to wait.

The wait was long enough to open out the paper, fold it in half as though it held his interest. Familiar lavender perfume warned him. A flash of green wriggled into the seat next to him. Coffee wafted into his nostrils. A black leather handbag was shoved between them.

'Rico,' whispered in his ear. His heart leapt. God knew how much he missed this woman.

'Mama, pretend you are watching the scenery while you sip your coffee. Don't look at me. I'll pretend to read the paper. Keep your voice down. If anyone comes close, we keep quiet. Maybe you could stand and move to the rail.'

'Why the secrecy?'

'I don't want to be recognised. I skipped parole. Dad forced me to. Not sure if they are on the lookout for me but they are looking for Dad. You know he escaped.'

'Yes, the police came and searched the property. You said I'm under surveillance. How do you know? Why?'

'Tall man. Has on blue jeans, dark blue long-sleeved Polo shirt. To make sure you aren't here to meet up with Dad.'

'How would they know?'

'I have no doubt your phone calls will be monitored. They could even have planted listening devices in the house when they searched it. Would have heard our conversation. Probably suspect you have a secret rendezvous with Dad.' Rico unfolded the paper, turned the page, folded it into a manageable size to prevent the wind from tugging it out of his fingers. He winced at the hiss from his mother.

'Is it all true?'

He didn't have to ask what she meant. 'Whatever they told you is true and more: much more.'

'He killed people?'

'More than you could ever guess.'

'Why?'

'He's evil, Mama. Has no conscience.'

'I want to know everything he's involved in.'

'It's not pretty.'

'This I have already figured out. Secret bank accounts with millions, yet he gives me enough each week to buy food and essentials. Property I never knew about, in my name. Stolen jewellery. You knew?'

'Most, not all.'

'Why didn't you tell me?'

'Because I love you, Mama. To keep you safe.'

'You were involved?'

'Not the bad stuff, no. I never could. It's not me.'

'How involved?'

'Before prison, I maintained the books. Never any bad stuff, I promise.'

'Tony and Peter involved?'

'Yes, Tony is in charge of brothels, Peter deals in drugs. They are in deep. Not the girls.'

Her eyes closed on a soft groan. 'How big is this… err… family business is what the police called it?'

'Mama, think Mafia from the old country.' When she whimpered, he wanted to put his arm around her but blue jeans caught the corner of his eye.

'Stand at the rail.' Head down, he turned the page over, shook the paper, ran the back of his hand over it, shifted in his seat so he was half turned away from Mama, swung one leg over the other knee. At the same time Mama stood, leant over the rail and took a sip of coffee. Blue jeans ambled close. Eyes bored into the top of Rico's head. Legs brushed past his overhanging foot. The brief shadow felt ominous. Blue jeans leant on the rail the other side of Mama. She glanced at the officer, turned away and scuttled away so fast, she was in the door before Rico had a chance to react.

When he noticed her handbag still next to him, he grabbed it. 'Ma'am, your bag,' he called as he stood and followed. She sat at the back, against the wall. The coffee shook in a hand that imitated a force seven earthquake. When Rico neared, he noticed tears had created a stream down her face. His heart stuttered. Not sure what to do, he knelt in front of her but with the sight of blue jeans as they moved to one side he still had to pretend he didn't know her.

'Ma'am, are you okay? You left your handbag outside.'

'Oh, th… thank you.' She pulled a handkerchief from the sleeve of her dress, shook out the pristine folds and bunched it against her eyes. A vicious swipe across both eyes swept away all moisture. When she glanced up her face was fierce.

The coffee dropped to the floor with a splat as Mama rose so sudden Rico fell on his backside. She stormed the few steps to blue jeans.

'Why are you following me?' she yelled so loud there was instant silence in the cabin.

The poor officer reddened as fast as silence evolved. His mouth opened and closed several times. 'I'm a police officer,' he said much quieter than Mama. One hand went into the pocket of his jeans and withdrew his badge.

'This I know.' Mama wasn't so discreet. 'It doesn't explain why you are following me. I go for a nice ferry ride to meet a nephew so I can get away from the turmoil in my life and you have to watch my every move. You going to join me in the loo as well?' She stormed away, spun in a circle to search for said amenities and clomped to the painted metal door under the sign *Ladies*.

Still on his backside, Rico couldn't help but grin at his mother's audacity. His grin widened at the uncouth swear word from the officer before the man climbed the steps three at a time to reach the upper level. Rico figured the man would soon be on his phone. He also figured Mama would be left alone since they were on a damn boat where no-one could get on or off until they reached Manly. As he rose, he picked up the soaked coffee cup and sat next to Mama's abandoned bag.

Now he was inside, his larger than normal sunglasses gave a clear but shadowed view. They didn't have the ability to prevent the penetration of bright reflective glints from waves. He wasn't game to take them off for they masked his features well, especially with a longer than normal fringe of blond almost reaching the lenses. It was difficult to recognise himself in the mirror so he doubted the officer would, since he was probably on the lookout for the bastard.

It was a good ten minutes before Mama emerged. She stood in the open doorway, scanned the entire area with reddened eyes, and finally rested them on him. A smile broke out as she approached.

'Has he gone?'

Rico grinned as he pointed upwards. 'You surprised me but I'm proud of you.'

'Yes, well, I've learnt a lot over the past week and decided to take charge of my life. I don't like the new hairdo but understand. Now where were we? I want all the details.'

While he kept his eyes on the stairs Rico told her as much as he dared but not all.

'Why did you go west?' she asked.

'Dad ordered me to go. Thought Amanda had some files.'

'Amanda? You found her?'

'Yes. She had legally changed her name. Dad found out the details.'

'Do I dare ask how?'

'Not wise.'

She clicked her tongue with a shake of her head. 'And Amanda, what happened?'

'It's a long story. She's fine but Dad sent… umm… people… wanted her done away with.'

Mama hissed, closed her eyes. 'Why?' she asked after a long pause.

'Anyone who crosses him needs to fear for their life.'

'Really?'

'Sorry, Mama, but you need to know he is one mean, nasty bastard.'

'So I have discovered. He won't want to come anywhere near me again.'

Rico stared at her. Where did this determined, strong woman come from? 'How much did you know?'

'Not a lot about this *family business.* That he is a cruel bully? Forever.'

'Why didn't you leave him?'

'Safer to stay. Safer for you three and me.'

'He ever beat you?'

Mama shrugged, turned away. He didn't need the answer. 'I'm sorry. Wish I knew.' He grasped her hand, gave it a squeeze.

'Never again. Amanda – what happened?'

No way would he tell her about the fight. 'She was smart, hid away with the help of a lawyer. I knew some of the men Dad sent over to eliminate her. I set one up, got him arrested.'

'What happened between you and her is what I want to know. She's a beautiful woman. You both loved each other.'

Rico sighed, leant back with one hand across his brow. 'I know and she will always own a corner of my heart but too much damage has been done. Too much pain. Dad even threatened her when I was in prison, to the extent she was given a new identity by the authorities. She's lost all trust; all faith and I don't blame her. Life has been hell for her. Much as I would love to be with her, I need to step away for good.'

A warm hand reached over, grasped his. 'I'm sorry.'

'So am I.'

'What happens now?'

'Not sure. I want to sell my house, start over. I'm serious about leaving the country, maybe go to Italy since I speak the language.'

'I wish I could do the same. I can't afford to. Don't have much money of my own.'

Rico turned, caught his mother's eye. 'Why don't you go back to family? I can give you money but you could sell the house.'

'I can't. It's not mine.'

Rico smiled. 'Yes, it is. The Title Deed is in your name.'

Mama sat forward, turned to him. 'Are you sure? I discovered there is a property in Forestville in my name but I was told they found bodies on it.'

Rico hissed in a breath of regret. 'All properties are in your name, as a form of security. If they found a body, Forestville will be a crime scene until they clear it. You are free to sell your home. Start anew. I know you don't believe in divorce, but you should. Dad doesn't deserve your loyalty. He hasn't been loyal to you.'

'Oh, I've already filled out the forms.'

'You have? Bravo. You could come to Italy with me, spend time with the family you haven't seen for years. I'll pay.'

'I'll think about it. They might not let me leave the country. I'm certain they suspect I knew about everything.'

'I've met a lawyer in the west. Gave him the details I knew. I assured him you were never aware of any of the bad stuff.'

'A lawyer? Why?'

'Before I answer, did you tell Dad I was in hospital?'

'Uh, yes. He ordered me to get you back. I had to give the message to Johnny. Why?'

'I don't know how to say this but he sent one of his men to get rid of me. I was attacked in the hospital.'

Mama surged from the seat. Her hands swept to her head, grasped the sides of her face. A scary long moan rumbled from deep down. She walked away, spun around and came back. 'I will never forgive myself. There's something you...'

The ferry bumped the jetty. Blue jeans bounded down the steps, swung his eyes between both of them.

'I'll be in contact,' said Rico as he walked to the gate. Passengers crowded around him, all eager to be first off. Nerves twanged the entire time it took for gangways to be positioned. He stepped onto the creaking metal, twisted to search for Mama. Caught sight of her. Blue jeans was jammed at the rear. 'Ciao, Tia Sylvanna,' he yelled and waved at the startled officer before increasing his pace with a wide grin.

He hailed the first taxi queued in a higgledy-piggledy line in the hope all the passengers wanted a ride to somewhere. 'Sydney CBD,' he instructed, not concerned about the horrendous cost, even though it was no more than about fifteen kilometres and would take half the time the ferry did. Locals preferred the ferry for it was cheaper with no torturous traffic snarls while the millions of visitors knew it was an amazing must-do experience.

Twenty-One

*B*rrng, brrng.

The ring of his phone was such a surprise Rico ignored it until a picture of James Ward centred in his still dozy brain. James was the one person who had this new number. As he turned over, he reached out, snatched the phone from the poor excuse of a bedside cupboard. When the phone didn't reach his head, he swore under his breath and unhooked the cable. Now able to put the phone to his ear, he pressed the green button.

'Isn't it a bit early for you to be awake?' he said since it would still be the middle of the night in the west.

'Rico.'

At the female voice he shot up from the mattress and leant against the bedhead until he remembered there was no bedhead, only a wall smeared with a gross greasy mark. He didn't want to think about what the mark was made of. If some person's hair was so filthy it was scary to think of what bugs they left behind. He'd checked for bedbugs even though they weren't as common in Australia as in some countries. The lack of the nasty little critters was the one redeeming feature of this particular abode.

'Mama. How did you get this number?' He swung his legs over the thin mattress so he wasn't tempted to lean back but when he noticed the condition of the floor, a shiver raced across his shoulders. In an instant he shuffled his backside backwards, planted both feet on the bed and leant over his knees. Dust bunnies, mixed with grains of dirt, added to the grim story about the cleanliness of this youth hostel. Checking in at the last minute to avoid detection had knobs on it, he now decided.

'It showed up on my phone when you rang the night before last. I wrote it down.'

A thought jostled not yet awake brain cells and shook them to alertness. The authorities might now have this number. Especially if Mama had phoned from home. Yet he had purchased the phone under his Joe pseudonym, which gave credence to his story about being a relative. He blew out his cheeks on a long sigh in gratitude but winced when he realised it wouldn't take much research for the police to discover the purchase was recent and made in the west. Might need to buy a cheap burner phone.

'Where are you?' he asked with a slight relaxation of stomach muscles that had tightened as though they were piano strings on a finely tuned instrument.

'In a café. I borrowed a friend's phone. Gina's in the queue waiting to order. I thought about what you said. You know, about my calls being monitored. I'm not stupid, Rico.'

He laughed, more from relief than humour. 'Stupid is never a word I would attribute to you. You are a lot smarter than you let on. Sorry I left you stranded at the ferry but I couldn't take the risk of being recognised. Were you hassled by your guardian?'

'I enjoyed the way he winced when I waved to him across the other side of the café where I indulged in apple strudel and coffee before I caught the next ferry home. I might add, I enjoyed my day out. Enjoyed the freedom without having to explain where I was and why. On the ferry, he asked who you were.'

'And?' he asked with a frown at the implication of her words.

'Told him to replay my *private* phone call with my nephew. He went red.'

Rico couldn't hold back a shout of laughter. 'I like my new Mama – a lot. Is there a purpose for this call?'

'Might be I want to hear the voice of my favourite son.'

Rico smiled at the old family joke. 'I'm your only son. What is the real reason?'

'Still my favourite. I want to sell this house. It holds few good memories. Do you know where the Title Deed is?'

'In the safe.'

'I don't know how to open it. I think the police might have. They had a locksmith here. Searched every nook, cranny and tiny crack, twice now. It was embarrassing.' When her voice cracked, Rico closed his eyes on a sucked in hiss. 'They might even have taken the Deed, along with umpteen boxes of stuff.'

'I'm sorry. Wish I could have been there for you. What about the girls? Did they come?' Surely his sisters would have given support, or maybe not. They sure showed no support to him.

'They have their own problems. Police did the same to them. The little ones were terrified. This is all such a mess. I don't know what to do. I'm even too scared to go out into the garden. There's a car parked out the front, across the road. Even at night. Men watch every move I make. There could even be someone lurking around here as well.'

'I doubt they are interested in you as a person. More like waiting for Dad to turn up. He will try. My guess is he'll try to sneak in in the middle of the night. If he does, phone me straight away.'

'He'd better not or I might be the one in gaol.'

'Now, now, Mama, he's not worth it. I can give you the code to the safe; if it's still the same. If the Title Deed isn't there, contact the police and ask them for it. You can get a certified copy but it will take time. I can organise a real estate agent. It's on my list of things to do today. I've made up my mind to sell up as soon as I can. The one thing to keep me here at the moment is you.'

'Not your sisters?'

'They didn't care enough to visit me even once over the past five years. You did, every week. You have no idea what it meant to me.'

A sniffle tore at his heart. 'Please, you are my son. Of course I visited. None of what happened was your fault. There is one person to blame. I know what he did, about the steroids. Told him it was stupid. Would he listen? Of course not. Oh.'

Another sob, louder. His heart shredded.

'This is too much. I'm so confused, so… I don't know.'

'Mama, please don't cry? Wish I could be there for you. Maybe we can meet up again. Let me think of another plan. Have you got paper and pen with you?'

Sniff. 'Yes. Why?'

'Write down the code for the safe. Try it. Write down every detail. Don't hurry when you do it. Pause for a couple of seconds between each step. Okay?'

She blew her nose, sniffed and cleared her throat. 'Okay. Go ahead.'

He made her repeat each detail after he'd given it, to ensure she got it right. The safe was old, not one of these new-fangled electronic ones. 'Phone me if it's not there, but not on your phone and not from the house. The girl's phones might be monitored as well.'

'They can do this? Invade my privacy without telling me?' There was more stridency to her voice – a hint of anger, which pleased him. A determined Mama was much better than one who was sad and weepy.

'Yes. In serious matters the police apply to the courts for permission to tap phones.'

'You think this is serious?'

Rico searched the ceiling for inspiration on what to say. A shudder wove across his shoulders at the network of dark spider webs dangling from the single bare lightbulb. Gross. Why didn't he check out this room before he handed over his credit card to make payment? The good thing about this place was that no-one would think to look for him in such a run-down hovel. It was a wonder they were still able to operate as a youth hostel. Local council couldn't have regular health checks.

'Rico.'

'Sorry, Mama. Yes, this is serious. You have no idea how serious,' he added in an undertone.

'Tell me.' The two words were a demand.

'You already know a lot.'

'A lot doesn't mean all. I want every detail but before you do there's something I need to tell… umm, Gina's coming back, I'll call again when I can. I love you, son. Ciao.'

'Love you too, Mama. Ciao.' He flopped back onto the mattress with brain cells jostling around in confusion. How could he sort this mess and protect Mama? There was little chance the police would let her leave the country, at least not until after a trial. Such a major trial would take forever to prepare and months to unfold unless the bastard pleaded guilty to all charges. A rude snort escaped at the mere idea.

Fat chance. 'They've got to find the bastard first,' he said to the dusty ceiling. 'And I need to get out of this disgusting joint,' he added as he rolled over and began to collect his bits and pieces on the wonky bedside table without putting his feet on the floor.

Before he left, he needed to shower and shave, because he didn't have a clue when next he would have a chance to get clean. Good job he'd made use of a washing machine and drier before he'd left the previous backpackers.

He took socks and sneakers to the bathroom to avoid having to put clean feet on the filthy floor. The communal shower facilities weren't a lot cleaner than his room, but at least he'd been first in so didn't have to wade through other people's soggy puddles, hair strands or toothpaste dollops. When he left the bathroom, it was cleaner than he'd found it. His good deed for the day. Bag packed, he stripped the bed, folded the linen as instructed and dumped the items in a laundry basket next to the counter where he checked out. The thought of eating breakfast, or even making a coffee in this particular facility sent a wave of nausea though his innards.

While he enjoyed a substantial cooked breakfast in a busy café, he searched the internet for a suitable private medical facility to get his sutures removed: a task he could no longer put off. A phone call for an appointment gave him a time and the area on the north shore where he would also search for an estate agent. Might as well do both at the same time.

The man at the next table folded the newspaper he'd been reading, shoved it to one side. Rico leant over. 'Is this your paper?'

'Nah, belongs here.' A shaken head and dismissive flick of the knobbly wrinkled hand.

'Do you mind if I take it? You finished with it?'

'Go ahead. Not very exciting. All doom and gloom. Even the cricket. Stupid team can't win a single game.'

Rico wasn't interested in cricket; he was more of a soccer fan. The game was played, won or lost in under two hours, not days. He took the paper from the table, unfolded it. 'Thanks, mate.' The front page highlighted the recent storm with the discovery of a young kid's body stuck in a storm drain. He now understood the doom and gloom throwaway. The article wasn't what he was interested in. As he turned each page, he scanned the headings.

Matteo Giovannazzo had been relegated to page five. Still no sight of him. Be on the lookout. Don't approach. Armed and dangerous. Found the stolen car he'd driven into dense bush. Still in the confines of the national park.

The same bare facts told him a big fat zero. He read again, slower, to absorb each word, the police section of his mind working out what hadn't been stated. If there was no sight of him, the bastard would be hidden away somewhere. He didn't have the ability to survive out in the wild for long. Too used to his creature comforts and being waited on at the click of a finger. To be hidden in a safe place he would have needed outside assistance. To gain assistance he needed some method of contact. Stolen phone? Possible. Who, of all his cronies, would still be at large to render assistance? It had to be someone on the payroll. Since Rico didn't know who had been arrested, it was impossible to figure out where the old bastard could be. Not in the city for sure. Unless he tried to get home, which was unlikely since he must know the police would have the house under constant surveillance. Mama hadn't seen him yet. A smile broke out at the thought of the reception he would get if he was game enough to show up at home. The smile turned to a frown at the memory of her unspoken shrug as an answer to his question about her being on the receiving end of physical violence. How bad had it been? He hadn't lived at home for over twelve years. He shook his head to chase away the grim images his mind wanted to paint.

'I wonder who they are looking for?'

Rico jerked his head towards Mr Cricket Man. 'Who?' he asked.

'Two coppers at the door, scanning the room.'

A big bass drum boomed in Rico's chest. 'Might be the escapee. You're about his age,' Rico quipped as he lowered his head to make out he was engrossed in an article. He ran a finger down the paper, stabbed it on the most important item.

'Not funny, young man. Can you believe he was a judge? Can't trust anyone these days. Even those two coppers could be on the take.'

Rico had to fight from letting a snicker escape. If only this guy knew how many bent coppers, lawyers and high-brow professionals were on the take. All for pure greed and status. Even when they had plenty it was never enough. He could never figure out what the thrill was. Power to be sure. Control – definitely. Egotism played a big part as did pure narcissism. A scoff slipped out when he thought of his own bank balance. Sure he had more than he would ever need but he'd played the stock market since his first pay not long after he turned fourteen. Even though he stuck in the main to blue chip companies he'd been lucky with a couple of start-up telcos and computer companies. Those early investments now brought in healthy dividends but he didn't class himself as an egotist, or power seeker and certainly not a narcissist.

The only way he would see if the two officers were still there, was to turn around. He wasn't game. He did glance at his new friend. 'They find their man?'

'Nah, they've gone. Standing outside. One on his two-way.'

The big bass drum boomed again. Had he been spotted? Were they waiting for him to emerge? Rico folded the paper and stood. 'Are there any amenities in this place?' A back entrance would be preferable.

'Sure, rear left-hand corner. You never been in here before? Best eatery for miles, which is why it's always packed.'

'No, I'm from interstate. On my way north.' He shouldered his backpack. 'Have to agree about the food. And the coffee. If the coffee's crap, you can guarantee the food's not a lot better. Have a great day.' Not game to wait for a response, Rico kept his back to the door as he wove a way through the cramped table and chairs to the bathroom. He couldn't figure out why it was supposed to be acceptable to call the toilet a bathroom when there were no bathing facilities in the poky rooms, which usually stank in public loos.

After making full use of the facilities in the spotless room, Rico opened the door and glanced both ways along the short corridor. There was no back door which meant he would have to brave the front entrance.

No boys in blue stood outside. It didn't mean they weren't still nearby. Rico crossed the floor of the café and paused in the open doorway while he searched both ways along the street. Nerves ratcheted to pinging point. Shoppers bustled along the footpath, none in a blue uniform. A bus pulled into a bay ten metres along. Not the best move for they had CCTV cameras but a short journey would get him away from here. He yelled, waved one hand in the air and bolted. It was fortunate three people got on before him, which gave him time to step on before the doors shut. He had to scrabble around to find a few coins in his pocket. The driver didn't appear to be pleased at having to issue a ticket since most passengers these days had electronic gizmos. Rico ignored the *harrumph* of displeasure, picked up the ticket and moved down the aisle to stand next to the rear door with his back to the CCTV he had sussed out. Five stops later, he pinged the button and alighted to search for a taxi to take him in the opposite direction. He needed to go north, not south.

Twenty Two

It was ridiculous to feel vulnerable but the sensation overwhelmed him with his genitals exposed and him flat on his back, not game to move a single centimetre in case the tiny scalpel blade slipped. To keep his mind off what was happening down below he studied the white ceiling. Not a skerrick of dust and no months-old hanging spider webs. The high rail around the bed to hold a curtain seemed a ridiculous item for he was in a doctor's small room. He couldn't see any reason for such privacy when it was only a doctor and patient.

'The surgeon did a good job. What happened?' *Snick.*

'Accident.' Rico winced at the tug. He wasn't about to say more about the humiliating experience.

'Nasty. It must have hurt.'

'Excruciating.' *Snick.*

'You know you can get a prothesis to balance the appearance.' Tug.

'It was explained to me. Need the area to heal first. Go easy there,' he hissed at another tug.

'Sorry, bit of a delicate position.' A wry half-grin played around the doctor's mouth.

Rico rolled his eyes in response while forcing taut muscles to relax at the next *snick.* It didn't help. The tug stung.

'All done, you can relax now. I'll just swab it with antiseptic. It has healed well. No infection.

You might find a couple of tiny spots of blood from where the sutures were taken out. Keep it as clean and dry as possible for a couple of days.'

The cold from the antiseptic caused a shiver to wend upwards. Glad the ordeal was over, Rico eased to a sitting position, swung both legs over the edge of the bench, bed, couch. He didn't know what to call the narrow, hard structure with little stuffing under the thick vinyl cover. It wasn't comfortable and so narrow his arms dangled over the side until he gripped his hands together across his stomach.

'I appreciate your help,' he said as he stood and dragged up his underwear and jeans. His phone rang before he could buckle the belt ends together. Had to be either James or Mama. Neither would be good news. 'I need to take this,' he said as he eased the phone from the back pocket of his jeans with one hand and slid the leather strap through the buckle with the other and held it in place since he needed two hands to buckle it.

'Hello.'

'Err, Joe.' Rico jerked at the wail and went on full alert at his mother's use of Joe. Danger, his brain yelled.

'What is it?'

'There are two police officers here.' A loud sniff indicated her distress.

'Why, what do they want?'

'To arrest me unless I tell them where Rico is but how can I tell them when I don't know? Last I heard, he was in Perth.'

Rico reeled backwards, hit a chair and grabbed it, letting go of his pants. 'Sounds like blackmail to me. They can't arrest you if you've committed no crime. Ask them what the charges are.' Phone held against his ear with his shoulder, he managed to get the belt buckled and shirt tugged into place as he listened but couldn't make out the officer's answer. 'What did they say?'

'I'm aiding and abetting a fugitive.'

'Bullshit. Give me a second.' He ignored his mother's hiss at his uncouth word as he turned to the waiting doctor. 'Sorry, this is important. My mother is in a bit of strife. Gotta go. Thank you. I'll pay as I leave. Appreciate your help.' He hoisted his backpack over one shoulder while holding the phone to his ear with the other hand. In the reception area, he cast his eyes around the almost full room of patients. Most gave the indication of being fed up. One held a tissue to a bloody nose. A young kid had a make-shift sling while his father looked on with a disgruntled frown. A seat in the back corner was as far away from other patients he could get. In case the officers could hear the conversation he figured he needed to keep up the nephew persona, so spoke in Italian.

'Tia Sylvanna. Abetting means you are assisting a fugitive but if you don't know where the fugitive is, how can you be assisting?'

'They don't believe me. Oh, God, please help me?' It wasn't often Rico had heard his mother sob. A spear shredded his heart at the sound.

'No!' she screamed.

'What is it?'

'He's got open handcuffs in front of him.' This didn't sound right to Rico. The actions were downright fishy. You didn't arrest a person for suspicion they might be doing something wrong. You needed proof.

'Ask them what proof they have. They need proof.' As he listened to the stuttered question, he racked his brains to figure out what was going on. A crazy idea came.

'They say you are Rico and I know where Rico is.'

'They have no proof. What are the officer's names? Speak in Italian.'

'*Si*, I don't know.'

'Are they in uniform?'

'*Si*.'

'They should have a name badge on their shirt and they should have revealed their names and shown you their badges when they arrived. Did they?'

'No.'

This was not good. 'Read the names to me.' With one hand he yanked his laptop from the outside pocket of the backpack, opened it out on his knee and booted it up. As she gave the names, he wrestled the thumb drive from the fob pocket of his jeans and plugged it in. The few seconds it took to respond felt like an hour.

'What do I do?' Mama asked.

'Give me a few seconds, I need to check my computer for some details.' He pressed on the icon, opened the file, ran his eyes down the list, pressed to open the right document, scanned the names, certain he had seen one of the officer's names before. 'Bingo,' he said with a cringe. The bloody officer was on his father's payroll. What the hell could he do? If he let on he knew, Mama would be in danger.

'Joe.'

'Listen hard. Can the officer hear me?'

'No.'

'Take a couple of slow steps backwards. No more than two, to ensure he can't hear but make sure you don't look as though you are about to make a run for it. You won't like what I'm about to say but to keep you safe, you *must* do what I'm about to tell you. Let them arrest you.'

'What, why?'

'One of those officers is on Dad's payroll. I doubt they have orders to arrest you. I'm almost certain this is a ruse to find me. Could be on Dad's orders. Please, whatever you do, don't tell them you know where I am. These strong-arm tactics are to intimidate you so they can get to me. If you agree to be arrested they will have to back down because, if they take you in, they will be roasted for making a wrongful arrest. If the police had any proof you are involved in Dad's skulduggery, you would already be in gaol. Do you understand?'

'*Si.*'

'I will need to get another phone. It's more than possible they have begun to track the signals to this one so I have to hang up and move. I will be in touch with a lawyer in the west as soon as possible. If they do arrest you, go with them. Don't fight. Be the meek and mild woman I know you can be. The lawyer will get you out. He will also have that particular officer arrested in the near future but you must act dumb. *Capiche*? Love you.'

'*Capisco. Ciao.*'

'Arrest me,' were the last words he heard before a scuffle.

'I know who you are and where you are,' growled a deep voice in Rico's ear.

'And I know who you are,' Rico said in Italian before he hung up.

Certain his phone number was in the process of being triangulated, he shoved everything into his backpack, went to the counter with his third, so far unused debit card held out. 'I'm in a hurry. How much do I owe you?' Now he was glad he'd gone with his gut and registered in the same name as the debit card. At least, this card wouldn't be traced, since it was possible the less than savoury authorities were in the process of tracking down Joe Russo transactions. Persona number three had taken over his life.

An invoice was placed in front of him. Thank goodness it had been prepared in the few minutes he spoke to Mama. It took too many precious seconds to make the payment. Nerves notched to high alert, he went to the door, searched the area outside and stepped onto the pavement. The street wasn't anywhere near busy enough. There were no crowds to hide in. Too few vehicles drove along the bitumen. There was no way he could remain in the area to visit a real estate agent as planned. With nerves strung tight, he power-walked to the corner, jogged across the road, with a pause long enough to let the single sedan pass. A rubbish bin in front of an old house with *Accountant* on the gate at the next corner was handy. He dropped the phone in the slot.

There wasn't a taxi or bus to be seen. The idyllic leafy suburb in an up-market area was replete with large older style homes renovated to luxury status. Most houses still sat on decent sized blocks. No infill around here with backyards sectioned off into teeny blocks filled with two-storey monstrosities. Tailored gardens with trim, green lawns, well-shaped shrubs and filled garden beds must keep the local gardeners busy and their pockets full.

To run would attract unwanted attention so he strode past gorgeous properties to the next corner, turned right into an even quieter street. At least with houses, there wouldn't be any CCTV cameras, although most homes would have their own security cameras honed onto their front yards. He shoved sunglasses over his eyes, kept his head down and maintained a steady pace on the outside edge of the paved sidewalk until the end of the block where he turned right again. On the other side of the road a fenced sport arena sat at one end of the shady park. A small kiddies' playground and smart painted ablution block with not a single scrawled graffiti mark, graced the end nearest him with a strip of parking bays along the edge. It would be a pleasant area to live.

He veered into the male section of the ablution block to make use of the facilities. Had to be the cleanest, sweetest smelling public toilets to ever exist. So clean, you would be too darn scared to drop a piece of tissue on the floor or misaim. The fact there were no security cameras on the outside said a lot about the area. At the door, he checked there were no boys in blue before he headed to the playground where a young couple sat at a picnic table, their eyes on two youngsters who climbed a small jungle gym.

'Excuse me, I'm new to the area. Are there any shops nearby? I've lost my phone and need to buy a new one so I can make an urgent call.' He held out his hand in greeting towards the man. 'Chris is the name,' he lied. It was the first name to enter his head: the name of the officer who threatened his mother.

'Sean, and this is my wife, Tara.' The grip was solid: not too hard and not limp. 'Nearest phone shop is about half a kilometre that way.' Sean pointed west. 'Turn left at the end of the oval. Do you need to make a call? I can lend you my phone.'

The offer was perfect. 'If you don't mind, it would be much appreciated.' He sat at the end of the bench, searched the pocket of his backpack for James's business card. It might not be such a good idea to ring the man's mobile phone since it was possible the authorities had traced the numbers Joe Russo had called. He checked the time, deducted three hours. Eight thirty. Would James be at work?

He pressed the man's office numbers, waited.

'Hello.' He blew out his breath at the sound of the familiar voice.

'James, I need your help.'

'Ri... er J.R. This is a different number.'

'Borrowed phone. Mama's in trouble. Two police offers threatened to arrest her for abetting a fugitive. One of the men is on a certain payroll. My bet is he's searching for Rico on orders from his boss.'

'You got ears near you?'

'Yes.'

'How do you know the officer is one of you father's men?'

'I've had more time to study in detail the files I downloaded. Recruited in the past couple of years. I've never met him. Standover man, from what I can gather. Big bucks paid. Tens of thousands.'

'Your mother. Was she arrested?'

'Don't know. I suggested she go with them if they insisted. Blackmail tactics. Tell where Rico is or arrest. She was smart. Spoke in Italian to her nephew, Joe Russo. Are you able to ensure she's released and left alone? I also need written assurance I'm not on the arrest list in exchange for the whereabouts of a certain computer which has every last detail. This o… er man needs to be stopped. Certain Matteo has been in contact with him. Could even be the one… God, this is hard.'

'Who has given him a place to hide?'

'Yeah.'

'Name.'

'Christopher Hudson.'

'Status?'

'Don't know. Uniform.'

'I'll make a call but can't wait for an answer. Due in court at ten. Be there all day. If I hear, I'll text you a message.'

'I've lost my phone, hence the borrowed one. Need to purchase a new one. I'll message the number as soon as I can.

'Lost or dumped again?'

241

Lord, but this man was smarter than most. 'The latter. Possible triangulation. Hence no call to your mobile.'

'I understand. I'll be on the lookout. Thanks for the warning. You know you can download a VPN on your phone to prevent it being tracked?'

'No, been out of the loop to keep up with modern technology. How does it work?'

'It encrypts your internet traffic and hides your IPS address. Might be worth it. You okay?'

'So far. Sorry to land this on you but there's no-one else I trust. Maybe find me a source in the upper echelon over this way. Someone I can trust. I'm barely a step ahead.'

'I'll see what I can do. Give me a number as soon as you can. Maybe email it to me via the office. You still got my card?'

'Not game to lose it. Thanks again. Enjoy your day.'

'Oh, I will. Another bent government official about to spend twenty years locked away.'

'Bye.' Rico hung up, hefted his shoulders on a long sigh, turned to hand the phone back, to see the couple had moved over to their kids. Not sure whether it was a good sign or the opposite, he wandered over to them. 'Thanks for the phone. It was important.'

'Your mother okay? Sorry, I overheard the first bit before we moved away,' said the young man with a sheepish look.

'She will be. She's being hassled because she happens to know a person who has disappeared but doesn't know much about them. I guess we have all had contact with people yet know little about them. I appreciate your help. Now I need to go find me a new phone.'

He waved over his shoulder as he strode to the next corner where he turned left at the same time sirens sounded in the distance. They grew louder with each second. Too loud. At least two cars. The final blast of the siren came from behind. Too close. A quick search around the area while he recalled the directions he'd walked. He swore under his breath when he realised he'd doubled back and there was only one block between him and his ditched phone.

Twenty Three

On a diagonal, he jogged across the oval. An out and out run would be too obvious. Near the rear fence, he cut behind the small brick building he thought might be some sort of club rooms. Tall trees shrouded the wide strip of dark soil covered in ancient wood chips. A few clumps of dead wild oats, flattened by the recent storm, poked from clearer patches. Seems the local gardeners weren't employed by the council. He passed through the trees, came to a wire fence, six feet high in the old language, strung between steel supports all the way along the edge of the block. The diamond-shaped holes were big enough for handholds. He reached up, grabbed, scrambled up and over. Dropped to the ground to land in a crouch with backpack skewed to one side.

The sound of a nearby siren twanged his nerves tight. He shot up, twisted to resettle the pack, peered around. This side of the road had no footpath but was covered in leaf litter, sticks and a sparse layer of more grey wood chips. Smart houses lined up on the other side. To continue south, as suggested, would make him too visible for there was no cover. He kept to the fence-line along the verge, trotted back past the oval, the playground, the toilet block. Turn right to maybe come out at the rear of the shops. Was it a large centre or a local grocery store?

A siren wail was too loud, too close. Instead of turning right he shot across the intersection, belted up the gentle incline, past houses a little less grandiose. Sweat oozed, breath huffed. He reached the top, paused and gasped, bent over at the waist. Tyres squealed. From the corner of his eye he spied the flash of a blue light as it sped through the intersection he'd just been on. Had they found his phone? Had the couple given him away? Or the medical facility? Eyes wide, he searched the area for somewhere to hide. Houses, houses and more houses, both sides of the road. Trees marched in a straight line along the verge his side, electricity poles along the other. Brain cells seemed to scramble themselves into eddies until another siren sounded, chasing after the first or maybe the same car. It was hard to tell.

Logic leapt out. He was headed east which meant water was nearby. Almost anywhere in the northern suburbs meant water wasn't far away, be it ocean or the river with its wide expanses and many tributaries. He knew where he was, sort of, but was unfamiliar with details of the area. Even though he'd spent his entire life in Sydney, it wasn't often he visited the north shore area. Even the property they owned in Forestville, he'd been to a few times as a child and once with Amanda. A snort escaped. Now, it would be the last place to be anywhere near.

Over the hill, he ran, full pelt, down, down, down. Kept to the fence line, hoped the foliage shaded him enough. Ahead, he spied a glimpse of water beyond a wide strip of ancient eucalypts. Better still, the base of the trunks were hidden by dense bushland. His pulse pounded; breath gasped. It ceased altogether at the scream of a siren. Louder, louder it shrieked. Everything inside tightened, including his gut, which yelled for him to hide.

A quick glance to his left. He spun in the same direction, hurtled along a concrete driveway, wriggled in the space between fence and garage. Stuck because of the bulk on his back, he squirmed one arm from the straps, twisted in the tight space and managed to ease the backpack to one side. With it held out behind him, he sidestepped further along the narrow gap.

The roar of an engine stilled him. As he twisted his head towards the road, he swore. The flash of blue and red lights arrived a split second before the marked police car shot past, its siren so loud his eardrums hurt. A prayer of hope was all he had to convince his mind he hadn't been spotted. He wriggled further, centimetre by centimetre, left arm with backpack dangling, right arm led the way.

A slight squeal of brakes came from nearby. Car doors opened, followed by a pause before they snicked shut.

'I'll search this one, you go next door,' said a male voice.

Rico kept his eyes honed onto the road as he sidled. At last, the end, a final step was all he needed. He paused, afraid of what or who he would meet in the backyard. Many images flew through his mind. Friend or foe? Animal or human? Although a dog would have an easy escape through this gap so maybe not some vicious Alsatian or Doberman intent on tearing him to shreds. It was obvious the police were searching for someone. With him sneaking into a stranger's backyard, it was even more obvious he was the target.

Since he couldn't retreat, there was little choice but to take a chance. He eased from the gap, backed around the corner, paused, sent his eyes scanning the backyard. Harsh reflected light lanced onto his retinas from the pool water. He blinked, turned his head from the glare. It took a few seconds for his eyes to adjust and clear. Bowling green lawn covered the entire area apart from the pool and metre-wide pavement around the edge. Not a single bush to hide behind or under. Wrong house for a fugitive. Except, maybe – he eyed the slope towards the rear, behind a steel pool safety fence. The stumps holding up the rear of the house, hadn't been boarded in.

The sort of silence he needed, reigned. No human sounds, no radio or television. No chatting. No frantic barks. Somewhere in the distance two kookaburras laughed at his predicament, a few musical tweets of smaller birds echoed and sirens had ceased. The lack of sirens wasn't an advantage for police officers had to be searching individual properties. It wouldn't be long before they came here.

Eyes and ears alert, he sidled and scraped along the back of the corrugated iron garage, peered into the small window and huffed out a long breath to find it devoid of cars. The owners had to be out.

The hum of an idling engine broke the silence. It crawled along the road less than ten metres away. Another police car or the same one? Rico dared a glance at the edge of the garage. No gaps. Another huff of relief.

A car door clicked shut. Rico shot to the fence gate, reached up, yanked up the kiddie-proof safety catch, winced at the slight squeak as he eased the gate open and swept through. It was torturous to close the gate so slow to minimise noise. The very second the catch caught, he raced across the lawn to the rear of the house and crawled between two stumps, shoving the backpack in front of him. Even though his brain had managed to scramble every cell, he did check to see if footprints led the way in. A handful of soil tossed over his entry seemed to be enough. With the gap less than a metre high, he had to duckwalk to the lowest point he could fit. A pile of dusty camping gear was more than welcome. He eased behind it, lifted a portable gas stove, stood it on end in the gap between the rolled-up tent and what had to be the brick wall of a fireplace in the room above. Hunched on his backside with knees under his chin he could just see over the top of the dark red gas burners. He recalled they'd had a similar one way back but didn't remember if it was used much.

He hoped it was too dark to make him out.

Hushed voices sounded, grew louder. The kookaburras laughed, an extra-long chortle. *Ha, ha, we know where you are. He's under the house - look under the house.*

'He's not here. There's no-where to hide. Come on. We have to go. The sarge called us back to base.' One officer came into view. Dark blue clad legs walked past. Came back, squatted.

Rico's lungs forgot how to work.

'Hudson said to find him.' A different voice, harsher, more insistent.

Damn, Hudson. Had to be under orders from the bastard. Not game to move a muscle, Rico had to ease out the held breath to draw in another. It sounded way too loud. Pity oxygen was essential.

'Why are you taking orders from Hudson? He isn't our boss. The sarge is. Why are you so intent on catching this guy? It's the father we have orders to find.'

'The son is the key.' Another crouched figure peered into the gloom, right at Rico.

With hooded eyes to hide the white, Rico could make out every feature on the man's face. Crooked nose looked as though it had been broken and not set under the care of a plastic surgeon. Tattoo peeked over his collar. Rugged, not handsome.

Muscle bound. Number two cut on ginger hair. Ruddy features to go with the hair. A face he will remember with ease. A name would be appreciated.

'Enrico was last seen in the west. There's been no sign of him here. According to the bank, he's dead so why are you looking for him? There's nothing but junk under there.' The first man stood. 'Come on. We need to get back to the station or our heads will roll.'

'He met his mother.' The second man made another sweep with his eyes, ever so slow, paused on Rico.

'It was a nephew.'

Rico shut his eyes and hauled in a breath as the second man stood.

'Nah, too convenient. Hudson is certain it's Enrico.'

'Hudson wouldn't have a clue. He's an arsehole. If he's so sure, why isn't he here?'

A crackle of a two-way. 'Shaw, where are you? Get back here pronto. We've got a serious prang. Dead victim. Looks to be deliberate. Over.'

'Sorry Sarge, on our way. No sign of our fugitive. False lead. Over.' Shaw sounded aggrieved.

'Why did you lie?' The other voice faded, along with footsteps.

'Shut you face.' The gate squeaked. Banged shut.

When Rico could make out the scrapes along the shed wall, he slumped in relief. Shaw. The name seemed familiar. Could he have read it on the list? Was he an officer he'd met in the past? One way to find out. The very moment he heard the engine roar to life, Rico removed the burners, set them where he'd found them. As he crawled from the small space, he swiped away sticky webs intent on causing his skin to crawl. Little black blobs with a dash of red on the back, centred in his mind. Since it was too soon to return to the street he sat cross-legged under the edge of the house, scanned his body for spiders, brushed off a huntsman. He didn't mind them for they dined on flies and mosquitos. It was the little buggers like red-backs, white tails and the dreaded Sydney trapdoor spiders that speared him with fear.

It took seconds to take out his laptop, boot it up. Five minutes later he had the answer. Michael Shaw worked for Tony. He needed to give the name to James, typed out an email and was about to press the send button when a thought stabbed. If they had traced his calls to James, they sure as hell would search for his email account, which was under his real name. A new phone became a priority. Wish he'd known about this VPN magic.

A nearby rumble spun his head to the right. The garage door. Rico slammed down the lid on the laptop, shoved it in the backpack pocket. He scrambled upright the same time he stumbled across the lawn. Not caring a damn about squeaks, he tugged up the latch, shot through the gate but took the time to not let it bang before he scooted to the rear of the shed where he paused to let his lungs catch up with his body before he crept to the gap next to the fence.

Had to be careful, he thought, to not make a sound. Right at the corner, he honed his ears on the activity in the garage. Two doors opened, closed. Voices murmured too soft to make out. Maybe a woman and child. Quick footsteps. A *click, click* of a remote. A different door, maybe into the house. *Slam.* Silence.

Rico eased around the shed corner; backpack held in front. Pressed against the fence to minimise any echo in the shed, he sidled, squeezed and wriggled to the end. The five metres to the road, seemed like fifty. Five metres where he could be spotted. Five metres to make it obvious he was a trespasser on private property. Just walk, said his gut while every strung-out nerve told him to run for his life.

He walked, slipped his arms in the straps and hoisted the backpack where it belonged. He was sick of carting the damn thing around but where could he leave it? Maybe it was time to take the chance to scout out his own home.

Back on the road, he headed east, towards the water, towards the safety of the bush where he could hide. To his right, Sydney high-rises poked their heads above the horizon. The CBD wasn't far away but too far to make on foot before nightfall. He paused at an intersection, glanced both ways, spied a sign to the left: Library. A grin broke out. Libraries meant computers to send emails and even maybe a taxi. Rico spun around, in search of the other police cars. Had there been more than one? Had they all been called back? Did he dare take the risk?

Twenty Four

*A**ttn: James Ward.***

Many thanks for the help and advice you gave to the young woman I sent your way. To assist in your enquiries re: son-in-law, Tony, question Officer Michael Shaw who works for him. Will contact tomorrow with further details.

Kind regards
Russell Jones.

It was the third attempt to get the message right without saying too much yet relate the essentials. He'd learned to his detriment how James was smart enough to understand the real message, so let him decode this one. Rico added his phone number with a postscript at the end. *Took your advice re: security.* The server in the phone shop had explained in minute detail how to buy and load a VPN and connected the whole system to his laptop. Now all messages would be much safer.

He pressed send and sat back against the wall of his new abode. The on-site van in the nearest caravan park to the CBD was more like an outback donga from a long-vacated mine site. At a guess, everything inside was at least twenty years old and had received basic maintenance from day one. Scratches and dents abounded. The Vinyl on the floor had been scrubbed so many times there was little pattern left but at least the place was clean. There were no balls of dust, no piles of sand or grit. The stainless-steel sink gleamed, the bed was comfortable with no gross stains on the bedhead or linen, which had the aroma of freshness. The soft, fluffy towel was the newest item. Best of all, not a single spider web could be found.

Outside was graced with well-watered mown lawn and so many shady trees it gave the appearance of a little bit of paradise. The beach on the side of a river inlet wasn't far away. A short walk had taken mere minutes once he had settled in and dumped the heavy backpack on the floor. The hamburger and coffee tasted a whole lot better when eaten next to the water, a place where serenity seemed to always ease any angst he held.

Rico jolted upright when his new phone rang. He scrambled to unplug the charger and prayed the new battery had enough charge.

'Hello.'

'Russell, now, are we?'

'James, I thought you were in court all day.'

'Yes, well, when the culprit changes their plea from not guilty to guilty seconds after I've outlined reams of indisputable proof, it shuts things down real quick. Fifty hours of solid preparation and formulated arguments down the drain but the result was worth it. Tell me about this officer.'

'Found his name in the files after he had me cornered. He was more concerned about my whereabouts than my father's. From the conversation I overheard, he had orders from his sarge which he was about to ignore until his offsider egged him on. The conversation set up alarm bells. Discovered he works for Tony. Probably to keep vice away from the brothels or pre-warn when a raid was planned. Had to have been given orders from Tony. He almost found me. Too close.'

'Where are you?'

'Not where I was. I hightailed it from the north shore. Lucky to hail a taxi. Now west of the CBD. Got me an on-site van for the night.'

'Do you have access to a printer?'

'No, why?'

'I'm about to forward you an important document.'

A shudder beset Rico. The old adage of someone *walking over your grave* came to mind. 'Is this good news or bad?'

James laughed. 'You'll have to read it to find out. By the way, your mother wasn't arrested but the joker who threatened her has landed himself in a gaol cell, pending your proof. They need the proof A.S.A.P. They can hold him so many hours, but you know this. If he gets released it could put your mother in danger.'

'In other words, you want all the files.'

'Better to give them to the person named on the document.'

'Give me a minute to look.' Rico's fingers worked so fast to open his email folder, he fumbled and had to start again. Open at last, he clicked on the attachment, waited long seconds for it to open, scanned and gasped. 'Holy Moley, is this for real?'

'Sure is. You have a full pardon in exchange for full disclosure of all files regarding your father's extra-curricular activities.'

'Is this legit? I can't believe it.'

'It's legit. Had a bit of help from the Commissioner of Police here in the west. He chatted to your commissioner along with the feds. Since you've been out of action for the past five years, during which you had almost no contact with your father, according to the visitor log, and your name features no-where on any of the info to date, they believe you are clean. But they do want the hidden computer in exchange to close the deal.'

'I don't know what to say. Thank you. I'm stunned.'

'You're welcome. What you did is huge and bloody dangerous if your father ever finds out.'

'Have they caught him yet?'

'Hadn't last time I spoke with the commissioner. Seems he's found somewhere to lie low.'

'Must have gained some outside help. Has to be one of his cronies.'

'Can't be many left on the loose.'

'The police force must be getting pretty low on numbers.'

'Not so sure. The AFP commissioner gave me the low down. Around half a dozen officers in most states. Seems they left Tasmania alone. One from Darwin. But the number of wealthy entrepreneurs is high. Seems little of their wealth has been obtained by legal means. Quite a few were already on the investigation list. Known bikie gang members are a feature but we already knew how little of their activities are on the right side of the law. Might be a few gang wars when underlings try to muscle in on territory and vie for leadership. Could be an interesting few months. Then there are the government workers. Too damn many.'

'With Dad on the loose he could be going all out to distribute illicit drugs to get rid of his cache. He's sure to have a stockpile somewhere.'

'Would you know where?'

'Never knew. Wasn't interested and it wasn't a topic he ever spoke to me about. Tony would know for sure. All I did was keep the books up to date. Knew about the properties, the accounts and what activities he was involved in but I never carried out any dirty work.'

'What about when you were on the force? Did you ever, shall we say, finagle things for your father?'

'Finagle, I like the word, but no. Much to my father's disgust I applied to work in the traffic branch for this very reason. Never told the old man I applied on purpose. I was never a dirty cop, I promise.'

'Good to know. Now, you need to print off the letter I emailed. Carry it with you at all times. Personally, I'd make several copies in case there is still some rogue officer out there. There's a phone number for you to ring. Your police commissioner trusts this man, a Superintendent, I think. You are to give the details of the whereabouts of the hidden computer to this one man.'

Rico shuddered at the thought of trusting a police officer. 'How sure are you I can trust their word?'

'Now you are asking. Ninety-nine percent. In this business I've learnt to never trust a human one hundred percent, well, apart from my wife and kids.'

'Not Amanda?'

'Amy. She has every reason to lie about many things but I believed every detail she gave me although some of it was hard to swallow. But she had plenty of evidence to back up what she said. Indisputable evidence which has got both you and me into the place we now are. She is one very brave young woman and my estimation of you has gone up a great deal. Despite the danger to yourself, you've done a great service to the entire country.'

'Yeah, but I hadn't planned on living long enough to get caught up in the aftermath. I'm sick of lugging around my clothes, hiding away and living in different, less than salubrious lodgings every night.'

'You're stronger than you thought. If I were you, I'd concentrate on being there for your mother. Her life will be tough and unpleasant for quite a while. She will have to front a lengthy court appearance where some shifty defence lawyer will grill her if any are game enough to act for your father. It won't be easy for her, nor your two sisters. Do you think they were involved?'

'God, I hope not but I don't know since I've had little contact with them for five years. They didn't lower themselves to visit the dregs of society in prison, even though both of their husbands are on a much lower rung than I could ever be, but Mama came every week.' He snorted at the thought of his two brothers-in-law. Would Maria and Lucy make prison visits now? Maybe, like Mama, they would seek a divorce.

'You're close to your mother, aren't you?'

'Yeah.'

'Then be the shoulder she will need.'

'Thanks, James, for your trust and for everything you've done for me. I don't deserve it. I can never be the type of man you are.'

'Sure you can. You've already proved yourself. You have to remember, you came from violence and cruelty, not the loving and supportive environment I grew up in. Jon and I knew right from wrong from an early age. Physical punishment was never a part of our education, not like you where you were always put down by one parent who you never dared disobey through fear. You chose to become a cop, took the oath to serve and protect and from what you've said, never crossed the line in that regard. So give yourself some credit. Oops. Have to go. Seems my colleague has a problem. He looks about to blow a gasket. Keep in touch.'

Rico sighed at the click, leant back, closed his eyes and thought about what James said. It was true how he never crossed the line to dishonour his badge. True, he kept the books full of criminal activity of the worst kind but to him, it was a job he got paid for: a job he was forced into. Every cent of the money he was paid by his father was kept in an offshore account, kept separate from his investments and normal work salary. As for trust, it wasn't a strong word in his vocabulary at the moment. There wasn't a single milligram of trust for the bastard and never would be. Not much for any police officer either, since the only ones he'd come across since release had been of the nasty variety. Mama was the one person he could attach the word to, other than James. And James wanted him to trust a superintendent. It would be a tough call.

After five minutes of brain shutdown, Rico opened his eyes and woke up the computer programme which had been in sync with him and gone into sleep mode. A more thorough read of the document revealed how they had no interest in him, with the skipping of parole no longer an issue. In reality, it was the one reason they would look for him since he'd served his time and hadn't broken any laws since. The superintendent's name and contact details were underlined on the bottom of the email.

Extreme caution had him shove in the memory stick to search the list of names to ensure a certain Super's name wasn't included. It took another five minutes before he ran a hand through his hair, harrumphed and squirmed then finally punched in the attached phone number. For some reason, a shaft of fear stabbed on every six rings of the phone. He'd been scared before, many times, but this time the fear seemed to be of the absolute terror variety.

'Nelson,' a voice barked, which managed to increase the level of terror.

'Superintendent Nelson, I was given this number to ring by James Ward.'

'Rico Giovannazzo? Is that you?' came back so clear and so fast Rico darted a glance around the van in search of the man.

'Yes.' It was the only word he could think of to say.

'Where are you?'

'Where I am isn't important.'

'Sorry, I understand. What I meant was, are you in Sydney?'

'What does it matter?'

'Well, I'm under the impression you have a vital object to hand over to us in return for a certain pardon.'

'Which is the reason for this phone call.'

'Yes, yes, of course. So how do you want to do this? We can meet one-on-one or you can give me the location and I can retrieve it.'

'I'd rather meet but what guarantee have I got that it won't be a set-up.'

'You have my word, and the commissioner's. A message has already gone out to instruct you are no longer a person of interest.'

'Seems your message didn't reach everyone yet.'

'What do you mean?'

'Had a run-in earlier today with a Constable Michael Shaw, who was hell bent on taking me in. He's crooked. Takes money from Tony Lombardo. Lots of money. He's got his fingers in the prostitution pie.'

'Damn, not another one. We've got Hudson in a holding cell but need your evidence. Is there proof of this Shaw included?'

'Yes, every last detail with dates, amounts of payments and for what reason. Checked the list, couldn't find your name.'

'I don't know how to take that?'

'Well, I rang you so take it as I hope to hell I can trust you. James said I could, and he is about the only person I do trust at the moment.'

'Not sure what guarantee I can give you apart from my word. I guess I could say I wouldn't have got to my position if I couldn't be trusted.'

Rico laughed. 'Yet you have a judge who hands down weak sentences to hardened criminals, who frees crooks and runs a huge criminal syndicate. Not much of an assurance.'

'True. Yet I am about to trust you when you are the son of said judge and know every last detail of said syndicate and you did skip parole.'

'*Touche*. I had no choice about the parole bit. A crime gang boss doesn't get his power by being Mr Nice Guy. Especially to his son to the extent he sent an assassin to eradicate me.'

'Heard about your little affray. Johanssen, wasn't it?'

'Yes, he's the one. We'll meet at my mother's house. I need two hours. If I spot any sign of surveillance within cooee of the house, you won't see me.'

'They're there to catch your father.'

'He's too smart to show up at the house. He'll have no doubt the place is under constant surveillance. He has money.'

'How? We froze his accounts.'

'He talked the bank into taking ten grand from my account to pay for my funeral.'

'Bloody hell. Without a death certificate?'

'He's a judge.'

'Not any longer. By the way, I can't see how a meet-up at your mother's house is any help since a team has searched the house, twice now. Found no hidden computer.'

'It's there. I've seen it recently. Read the files. Downloaded them. How do you think I could give you as much info as I have?'

'Couldn't your mother give it to us?'

Rico laughed again. 'Mama has no idea about any of my father's dealings. Well, she has now after all these arrests but I can promise you, she is an innocent victim who has lived under the hard thumb of a physical and emotional abuser. I spoke to her. She stayed in the marriage to protect her children, and herself. If she'd left, he would have hunted her down and the result would not have been pretty.'

'Were you ever involved?'

'Not in any of the crimes, no. I've already admitted how I handled the books so I guess in a way I knew every detail about my father's crimes but not once did I participate.'

'Why didn't you come to us before this?'

This time, Rico's laugh came out as a scoff. 'It's obvious you were brought up in a normal happy family household. Not one where the code is – you talk, you die. Not one where you are constantly told how useless you are. Where a backhander is the norm whenever you dare open your mouth to say anything other than, *Yes, Sir*. Unless you've lived it you wouldn't have a clue. I was about to give him up five years ago but life got in the way. Until I served my time, I couldn't access any proof.'

'So why now?'

'I've had enough. When your own father sends an assassin to murder you and those you love, it has to stop.'

'I'm sorry. Two hours. It'll be dark by then. I'll pull the surveillance back half an hour before. You have my word.'

'Okay. I pray to God I can trust you. Two hours.' Rico hung up and with eyes closed, clunked his head back against the wall and swore.

Twenty Five

Should have done this days ago, Rico thought as he drove towards his childhood home. A common sedan hired in his third pseudonym made more sense than exposing himself to thousands of CCTV cameras. Although now, if he believed the Super, he had nothing to worry about. It didn't mean he wouldn't worry, nor did it mean he was about to roam the city without a care.

He slowed at the corner, searched both ways, caught sight of the papers on the passenger seat and smiled. Six copies of the all-important paper sat folded in half, thanks to the caravan park office girl who allowed him to connect his computer to their printer. A smile broke out. Road clear, he rounded the corner. The smile vanished in a split second as fear wrapped around his neck, tightened its grip to trap his breath in his throat. The avenue of trees had always been a pleasure to drive under but now the dark shadows sent out a sinister message. Almost leafless branches cast shadows like the long fingers of the grim reaper. Too afraid to drift along the road for it would be obvious who he was if hidden surveillance were still there, he maintained a steady speed while eyes darted from side-to-side on the lookout for any suspicious vehicle or lurking surveillance officer.

He passed the house, reached the corner, turned and trawled the streets around the nearby blocks. It appeared the Super had kept his word for Rico couldn't spot any suspicious cars or activity. When he reached the house, he reversed into the drive and drew to a halt with the front bumper in line with the gateway. Illegal to park on the footpath, no cars would be able to block his car in if he needed a quick getaway. Even though the dread hadn't abated, he alighted and peered around. Almost happy he was safe, he reached back into the car and cut the engine. The silence was heavy until the trill of a warbler, out past his bedtime, lightened the atmosphere. A cicada joined in until Rico moved around the other side where he took one copy of the paper, folded it into four, slipped it into his shirt pocket and shoved the rest in the glove box. As soon as he could, he would put them in a safe place.

Even through the dull light of evening, familiar red brick walls and orange tiled roof greeted him as he walked along the paved path towards the front door. It was a shock to see piles of sodden leaves, left over from the recent storm, hunched against garden edges and the base of trees and bushes. The groundsman must have been arrested. Johhny wouldn't dare to not have every leaf vanish almost before it hit the ground.

He knocked, stood with his back to the wall so he could scan the front garden and street, ever alert for treachery. At the snick of the lock, he turned back. The door opened.

'Rico?' Mama's face showed stunned surprise before it broke out into a wide grin. 'Oh, Rico.' She surged forwards, placed both hands on the side of his head and reached up with a kiss on both cheeks. 'Oh, Rico,' she sobbed as a wash of tears spread over her eyes.

It was an amazing sensation to wrap his arms around her and hold her against his chest. Too long. It had been far too long since he'd been free to hold Mama in a tight embrace. 'Mama.' It was almost impossible to fight back his own tears but he managed with a deep sniff and cough to clear away the wodge of emotion.

She stood back and dropped her hands to his upper arms. 'Why are you here?'

'You don't want me here?' he teased.

'Of course I do but what about… you know.'

'It's okay, Mama. Can we go inside? I'll explain inside.'

'Of course, of course. Come on. Let me find you some food. You haven't eaten, have you? What would you like? And a drink?'

Rico laughed. 'Slow down, I'm fine. Come and sit with me so I can explain.' He ushered her into the kitchen, the hub of the house: the one room where he remembered there had been warmth and harmony. It was the room where, as a kid, they would laugh while Mama cooked fabulous meals or sorted dry washing into individual piles before they were ironed and folded. The room where she made them sit to do their homework before they were allowed to relax. To her, education was number one necessity. But only in the hours when his father wasn't there. Whenever the bastard came home, the atmosphere turned on its head. The safest place then, was holed up in his bedroom with the door locked and a wedge underneath.

They both pulled out chairs and sat, him at the end, his mother at right angles with her hands gripped tight to his.

'Tell me,' she said with a fierce squeeze on his hand.

'First, I'm no longer wanted by the police. They have no interest in me. All they are interested in is re-capturing Dad.'

'This is good. Why did they want you in any case? You served your time, paid your dues.'

'I skipped parole when I went to Perth but now all is forgiven because... hell, this is so hard. I don't want to involve you.'

'Enrico Joseph Giovannazzo, you will tell me every last detail. Since I am married to Matteo, I am already involved. Far more than I like. More than I want. So tell me all.'

'I'll tell you what you need to know. Soon, in the next few minutes, a police superintendent will arrive here. I have made a deal to hand over a hidden computer in exchange for my freedom.'

'Computer? They have already taken all the computers from this house.'

'Not all. Dad has a secret hidey hole where he keeps another computer with all the details of his… umm…'

'Family business?'

Rico snorted. 'Yeah, family business.'

'His illegal, nasty family of crooks. Not my family. Why call it a family when none of his family are involved? More like his horrible gang of criminals.' Mama spat the words out.

'Tony and Peter are part of it.'

'Bah, they are not of my family. They are nothing to me now. Criminals they are. I hope they rot in their cells. All they do is bring disrepute to my girls and grandchildren.'

'Dad got them involved. This is all the fault of one man.'

'And I hope he rots in his cell too and when he dies, which I hope will be soon, he can rot in hell. He better not show his face around here.'

Rico couldn't help but smile at his mother's vitriol. It seemed thirty-five years of held-in anger could now be released. The smile vanished at the loud raps on the door. 'That will be Superintendent Nelson.' He hoped. Better not be a trap.

'I will open the door. This is my house. You sit,' said Mama as she rose and shoved him back down. Old traditions had never faded with his mother. It was her duty to welcome guests, to offer them refreshment and make them welcome. Maybe not this particular guest.

Even so, Rico crept to the door to listen for voices and sneaky footsteps. The male voice sounded right, as did the man's words. Rico shot to the window, parted the blind slats and peered into the night. In the few minutes he'd been inside the evening had darkened to night but not enough he couldn't make out shapes. An unmarked car was parked on the verge in line with the street. The driveway was still clear. The lack of movement eased his tension a tad but fear still gripped and tore at his innards. He wondered if it would ever go away. If there could be a time he didn't skulk in shadows, or search faces, or could walk the streets without a sensation of impending doom.

When footsteps neared, he shot back to a different chair: one from where he could reach the back door with ease. Nervous fingers drummed on the table. A man appeared, still in uniform, a hat wedged in the crook of his elbow. Superintendent Nelson was a tall, lean man with wrinkles of age and thick black hair with suave streaks of grey at the sides. Maybe mid-fifties, Rico guessed. A hand shot out in greeting.

'Rico, good to meet you at last.'

'Sir,' he said then winced. Old habits hadn't yet died.

'You're no longer in the force, Mark will do.' They shook with a firm grip.

'Feels kind of awkward to call a superior by their first name.'

'I'm not your superior. I'm just a grateful member of the public who appreciates all you are doing for us.'

'Doing?' Mama asked with fingers pressed hard into Rico's upper arm.

Rico caught Nelson's eye with a quick glance. He patted Mama's hand. 'The computer. It has the details they need to convict everyone involved in the family business.'

'Do not ever use the word family and your father in the same sentence.' Mama stalked to the sink, grabbed the kettle and filled it with the tap on full. Water splashed, Mama muttered, the kettle banged on the bench.

'Speaking of computers,' said Nelson. 'Can we get down to business?'

'Sure, follow me.' After another quick scan outside, Rico turned and led the way through the house, along the passage in the wing at right angles to the sitting room, past four bedrooms to the end. He opened the door to the den. It was a large room at the rear of the house, entered at his father's say-so. If he so much as suspected someone had come in when he wasn't there, retribution would be severe. It was after Rico had become the bookkeeper he was given free rein to enter when he wasn't on duty.

The furniture looked as it had for years except for the lack of electronic gear, although items had been moved to different positions. A large antique desk stood against the side wall. Never before had the top been bare. It usually sat out with a captain's swivel chair between it and the wall. The chair now faced the far corner as though in time-out for bad behaviour. A pool table with a sheet over the top, looked forlorn. It had been shoved against the opposite wall in the search. A large TV screen hung on the wall over the table. Two sofas had been shoved against the curtained French doors.

Rico turned to the corner drink's cabinet, still with its arrangement of whiskeys and glasses although they were an untidy mess. He reached up, felt around and wedged a fingernail under the top of a bolt. Mama hissed in a breath when the bolt lifted. The hiss turned to gasp when Rico swung the cabinet away from the wall.

'*Christos*,' Mama said at the same time Nelson swore.

It was a struggle for Rico to keep a straight face at the contrast of both exclamations but both were swear words for his mother never used God, or Christ in vain. He understood her shock for she never knew the cabinet moved and even more of a shock was the armoury of firearms against the recessed wall. The hidden recess measured a metre both ways from the corner and went from floor to almost the ceiling. Guns and rifles of all descriptions sat on hooks. Mama would never have been shown this secret hideaway.

'Are they all legal?' asked Nelson in such a tone, he was as stunned as his mother.

'I wouldn't have a clue although Dad did have a licence. Not sure how many of these are included in the licence. To be honest, I doubt it.'

'You never asked?'

Rico turned to Nelson and glared. 'Valued my health too much.'

'You never asked, you obeyed,' came a whisper from the other side.

Rico turned to see his mother close to tears. He swung an arm around her shoulder and drew her close. 'Maybe now you get the message,' he said to Nelson.

'I'm beginning to understand. I'm sorry. Wish I knew earlier. Where is this computer?'

Rico pointed to the back of the cabinet. A laptop with cords attached to a power outlet in the wall, sat in a narrow niche. 'Every detail you want is on the hard drive. I might warn you; I have a copy, downloaded the day after I was released from prison. I'll keep the thumb drives in a safe place for my own safety.' He quirked an eyebrow at Nelson.

'I understand. Do you mind if I have forensics collect these firearms? I have feeling we might need to test them against bullets we've found with…' he glanced at Mama.

'The bodies you found,' she finished for him. 'I know. Didn't before. I had no idea about…' she swept a hand up and down towards the wall of firearms of all makes and sizes. They all looked fearsome. She crossed herself as a shudder wove across her shoulders.

'Sure,' Rico answered for her. He turned to Nelson. 'I want to move in here for a few days. To protect Mama in case…'

'Your father turns up. I understand. I'll let the officers know to leave you alone.'

'Thank you. Let's get out of here. It gives me the heebie-jeebies.' He unhooked the laptop, handed it to Nelson and led the way out. They returned to the kitchen where habit formed over the past few weeks, had him glance through the kitchen window again. He spun around, made a grab for Nelson. 'You damn well lied to me.'

'What, no.' Nelson shrugged Rico's hands from the front of his uniform.

'Then why is there a police car parked across the driveway entrance?'

Twenty Six

'I swear…' Nelson leant over the sink. 'What the hell is going on? They had their orders. Who are those kids?'

Rico nudged closer so they were shoulder to shoulder. Next to the open rear door of the car, a female officer stood holding the hands of two youngsters, a boy and a girl. Tears streamed from the eyes of the little ones while the officer stared, grim-faced, up at the window.

'Who are they?' asked Rico.

'What, where?' Mama brushed against Rico's side and stood on tiptoe. 'Oh, my gosh. Maria's two.' She spun around and raced to the door. 'What's happened? Maria… oh, dear God, what's happened to Maria?'

Before Rico could get his brain cells aligned, the front door slammed. A quick glance at Nelson, they both moved at the same time, met at the kitchen doorway. Rico stood back to let Nelson through but beat him to the front door. A wail greeted them when he flung the door open. Mama had already squatted in front of the children with her arms out wide. They both threw their bodies at her so hard, she wobbled and had to shuffle on bent knees to maintain her balance. Loud sobs rent the air and quietened the night life as Rico neared.

'What happened?' He came to a standstill behind Mama who shot up and turned to him, a child wrapped around each of her legs.

'Maria… they arrested Maria.'

'Huh, why?'

'I don't know?'

'Let me handle this.' Nelson placed a hand on Mama's shoulder and gave it a little squeeze before he turned to the constable, a single stripe on her sleeve. 'Give me the details, Constable.'

'We arrested Mrs Rizzo for possession of drugs.' The woman indicated the back seat of the car.

Rico squatted to peer in. His sister sat huddled in the corner of the back seat with her blotchy face awash with tears. She wore blue jeans and a pretty floral blouse. Her long hair was doing its best to escape the confines of a pony tail. 'Maria, what happened?' He hadn't seen her for over five years, had never met her kids although knew of them since Mama had kept him up to date with family matters on each of her visits. She'd shown him photos of Lucy's kids as well but neither sister had bothered to visit him in the den of iniquity. Wouldn't lower themselves. Different story now. Would she expect him to visit? Has she visited Peter? It was a shock to see how Maria looked to be at least ten years older than Mama, yet his youngest sister was still shy of thirty.

'I didn't know,' Maria stuttered.

'Didn't know what?'

'What was in the bags.'

'Excuse me.' The constable moved next to Rico to block his view of Maria. When he stumbled and fell onto his backside, he wondered if it was a deliberate shove. To him, it appeared she was trying to make an impression on her superior but it wasn't the right way to go about it. 'We have to take her in for questioning. Just brought her children to their grandmother since there was no-one else to care for them. We could get child services involved. They'll have to go to foster homes.'

Rico scrambled upright. 'No!' Both Rico and his mother yelled at the same time.

Nelson eased his way between Rico and the constable. 'We can question her here.' He swung around to indicate the house. 'Inside. Less trauma for the young'uns.'

'But this is not…' interrupted the constable.

Nelson held up and hand to stop her. 'We can record it on my phone. We'll have three officers.' He indicated the young probationary officer in the driver's seat, who sat rigid, arms over the top of the steering wheel and with eyes straight ahead. There was a look of resignation on his face.

'I presume you have read her, her rights?' Nelson added.

'Yes, of course.' The constable straightened with chest puffed out as though to tell Nelson she wasn't an idiot.

'As I expected,' Nelson smiled at the constable to ease the tension. It didn't change her fierce face. 'Let's get Mrs Rizzo inside.' He turned to Mama. 'Maybe you could entertain these two while we get to the bottom of things.' He tapped each child on the head.

'Yes, but I need to know what this is all about.' Mama untangled the toddlers from her legs, grasped their hands and turned towards the house with tiny slow steps. Rico wondered if it was to keep pace with the children or to ensure she didn't miss a single word.

'Nelson, can I sit in on the interview? I was a cop. Maria might find it easier with me there. She's has a timid nature. My guess is she'll clam up, too afraid to open her mouth.'

'Okay, we'll give it a go.'

'Sir, this is highly unconventional.' The constable glared at Rico and pointed a finger at his chest. 'He's a criminal, should be in gaol along with the rest of the gang.'

'Constable,' Nelson roared. 'I will not tolerate your insubordination. Rico is no longer a person of interest. You are not *au fait* with all the details and this won't be the first time we have interviewed suspects in places other than a police station. An order has already been issued about this young man here. He is to be left alone. Now, you have two choices. Either do as I say or find yourself in some outback post for the next ten years.'

'Sir.' The red-faced constable stood to attention and saluted.

Rico had to swallow a grin. It wasn't the first time he'd been witness to the grilling of an officer by their superior. When he dared a peek at the constable, she glared at him. His grin escaped. With a scowl, the constable marched around to the other side of the car and ordered Maria out in much the same tone Nelson had used. The driver climbed out at the same time. Rico figured it was because the poor man thought it was to him the order had been given. A sheepish grin crept from the young man's mouth when he realised his error. Both officers stood either side of Maria, each with a hand on her upper arms. Maria's head hung low as she stumbled between them. Rico winced at the sight of the handcuffs when she rounded the car.

It was a weird sensation to follow behind the trail of humans in this out-of-the-world situation. Mama hurried ahead with the two kids, Maria and officers on their tail. Nelson waited until Rico caught up then walked beside him. 'Bring back memories?' he asked.

'I applied for traffic branch, much to my father's disgust. He couldn't use me to influence outcomes.'

Nelson laughed. 'You want to re-kindle your questioning technique?'

Rico glanced at him. 'I've already pissed off your young constable.'

'She needs to learn a little more tact and respect, especially on how to speak to her superiors.'

'Yes, Sir.' Rico gave a tiny mock salute at which Nelson laughed again. A grain of trust had swollen a fraction.

They settled around the kitchen table. Maria sat alone on one side, head almost melded with her chest, manacled hands in her lap. Nelson pulled out a chair opposite. The male constable stood at the back door while the female went to sit next to Nelson. She paused on bent knees when Nelson eyed her with one raised eyebrow.

'I rather think Mrs Rizzo will be more amenable to her brother's questions. Maybe you could stand guard at the other door.'

'Sir,' she muttered as she stood back. A red blush bloomed up her neck and face. Another fierce glare shot pure hatred in Rico's direction. He shrugged and eased into the seat next to Nelson. One pissed-off young officer didn't concern him after the life he'd led.

'Constable, please outline how you came to arrest Mrs Rizzo.' Nelson directed his question to the male constable who jerked when he realised the question was to him and his partner had been overlooked.

Rico bit the inside of his cheek to prevent a smile. The poor guy had no stripes on his sleeve, which indicated he was a probationary constable.

Tonight might be an interesting learning experience for him.

'Sir, we were on surveillance duty outside the Rizzo home.'

'In case Giovannazzo turned up?' asked Nelson.

'Yes, sir. But we had orders to follow the suspect should she leave the house in case they met up elsewhere. When she put the children in their safety seats we figured she might be headed for the shops or to visit family. As instructed, I phoned my Sarge to say we were about to leave the house. We followed her to a storage facility on the outskirts of the suburb. It appeared she wasn't sure where to go for she paused at each corner to read street signs and had to turn back twice. The way she skulked around when she got there, looked suspicious, you know, searching the area, creeping on tiptoes, dodging from shadow to shadow. She had a key to both the gate and a storage shed. I think they were attached to the car keys for she shuffled through the one key ring. We observed her cart a dozen black heavy-duty plastic bags and stow them in the boot of her car. The way the bags were folded over into large, neat rectangles and taped with gaffer tape, well, Sir, we'd both seen it before. Since knew why her husband had been arrested, we figured it was kind of obvious what was in the bags so we moved in.'

Sobs came from Maria. Both hands lifted and she swiped her eyes with her lower arm. Rico, stood, whooped a handful of tissues from the box on the fridge and bunched them into Maria's hand.

'What did Mrs Rizzo have to say?' asked Nelson.

'Said she was ordered to pick up packages from the facility. Stated she didn't know what was in the bags.'

'Is this true Mrs Rizzo?'

With her head still low, Maria nodded.

Nelson nudged Rico. 'See if you can get all the details.'

Rico ignored the female *harrumph* from behind. 'Maria, you need to lift your head.' It took several seconds before Maria raised her head far enough she could peek through swollen red eyes at Rico.

'Who gave the order?' he asked.

'Luke.'

'Speak louder. Superintendent Nelson needs to record your answers. Too soft and he might miss an important fact. It could get misinterpreted – to your detriment.'

Maria sniffed, swiped her eyes and cleared her throat. 'Luke.'

'Who is Luke?' It wasn't a name he knew but sounded familiar.

'Dad's accountant.'

Rico turned to Nelson. 'The name rings a bell but he must be new.'

'Did he visit you or phone?' Rico asked.

'Phone.'

Again, Rico turned to Nelson. 'You didn't have a tap on her phone?'

'We did. The name wasn't known to us. They might have listened for names we knew. Might have thought he was just some friend.'

'Seems they missed something vital.' Rico said to himself.

'So it seems. Go on.' Nelson didn't sound happy.

'Maria, tell me the gist of the phone call, everything you can remember?'

'He said I had to pick up some parcels. It was urgent. Had to be done within the hour. I asked why. He said orders.' Maria stared at Rico. 'You know what that means.'

'Yeah, I know, but there was a police car outside. Why didn't you go to them?'

'I didn't know they were there. Besides, Dad is free. I was too scared to not obey. He could have been there, watching, waiting.'

'Why did you involve your kids?'

'What else was I supposed to do with them? Peter's not there. Rang Lucy. She said no because it's too late and her kids were in bed. Bitch.'

Half of Rico's mind centred on what Maria said while half shot back to the past. The girls had always got on well, like twins almost, answered for each other, never argued. Now it appeared there was a rift between them. Mama had never mentioned any differences.

'What else was said?' he asked.

'Nothing.'

'Nothing? So how did you know where to go?'

'The instructions were on a piece of paper, folded in the door handle of my car.'

A loud gasp came from behind. Rico landed his eyes on Nelson, who twisted to the constable behind. 'How in hell's name did someone get to Mrs Rizzo's car without you spotting them?' growled Nelson.

The woman squirmed then sent a glare across the room to the other officer. Nelson stood so fast, even Rico jolted. It was almost impossible to prevent his face moving a single millimetre when Nelson stormed the few steps to the woman and planted his hands on his hips. 'You are the senior of the two. It was your responsibility to carry out orders and make sure no-one came or went. What the hell were you doing?'

'Watching, Sir. We didn't see.'

'Well that's bloody obvious. You might have been watching something, but it wasn't where your eyes should have been. Better not be your mobile phone or an outback post will be a damn sight closer.' Nelson spun around and plonked back into his chair, which sent up a spine-chilling scrape of legs on the tiles. 'Bloody disaster,' he said under his breath. 'If the phone conversation was as we just heard, why wasn't action taken. It's obvious what it means. Keep going,' he added a little louder with a nudge to Rico's arm.

'Maria,' Rico reached across the table to place one hand on her arm but was shocked when she recoiled at his touch. He withdrew his hand. Was he so odious to his own sister? 'What were the instructions?'

'Directions where to go, how many packages to pick up, where to take them. I had one hour or my kids…' she choked, 'my babies would disappear.' The tears began to fall again.

Rico swore under his breath as he twisted around to the constable. 'Where is the paper?'

The woman blanched, glanced at Nelson who had also turned. The shuffle from foot-to-foot said a lot. She gulped. 'Don't know,' she finally admitted.

'You didn't search her?'

Even Rico jumped at the bellow from beside him.

'No, Sir.'

'Why the hell not?' Nelson leapt from his chair and hovered over the woman.

Rico began to feel sorry for her and figured her next posting would be the toughest, most remote station Nelson could find within the N.S.W. borders. And it might be tomorrow she would have to pack her bags, or even tonight. He glanced at the young male who had gone white with mouth and eyes agog. Poor guy was getting more of an education than he'd anticipated.

'In my pocket,' came from Maria in a husky voice. She recoiled and lifted her shackled hands over the head in protective mode when the male constable grabbed her shoulder.

Stunned at her actions, Rico stood and rounded the table. He indicated for the officer to stand back. When Maria gave every indication of being terrified, he figured he knew why for he'd seen the same fear on his mother's face. With utmost care, he squatted next to her and took his time to reach out for her hand. 'Peter beat you, didn't he?'

Her head landed in the crook of his shoulder. A deluge of tears soaked through the fabric of his shirt. Tremors wove down her body. Now he knew why she had turned into such a timid little mouse. She was too damn scared to do or say anything in case any word or action would be taken the wrong way.

'How long have you been abused?' Rico asked her ear.

'Not long after we married.'

'Did you not tell anyone?'

'Went to Dad. He laughed. Said it was the man's right to keep his wife compliant anyway he wanted.'

'No, it's not. It's not okay.'

'You can't talk.'

No, he couldn't. 'What happened between Amanda and me wasn't because I beat her into submission. It was a one-off severe reaction to the combination of two chemicals. I accepted full responsibility, even though it was Dad who insisted

I take steroids and he supplied them. I paid for my crime and lost the love of my life in the process. I have never and will never use my physical strength to get what I want from a woman. Dad has always been an out-and-out bully.'

'He never beat Mama.' Maria lifted her head, sniffed and wiped her wet face on Rico's shirt.

'Yeah, he did. Mama hid it well.'

'Really? I never knew, never noticed.'

'None of us did. If I'd known, I would have put a stop to it.'

Maria snorted. 'Like you weren't scared of him as well.'

'Always but he didn't dare lash out at me after I grew taller than him. Now,' he stood back a bit to peer into her wretched face. 'Let me have the paper so we can finish this interview and go catch the bastard.'

A weak smile spread from her lips as she tried to put a hand in the pocket of her jeans. 'You'd better get it, I can't.'

'Okay, but please don't recoil when I touch you for I will never harm you. I promise.'

The smile was a little wider as she nodded. Even so, he took care to slide his hand in and draw out a folded piece of paper, which he opened out on the table. It took the briefest of glances before he swore with eyes slammed shut.

'What's wrong?' asked Nelson.

Rico turned to him. 'I recognise the writing. Dad wrote this, which means this Luke character is the man who is helping him. Could be the mastermind behind the escape.' He paused as a memory surged from the recesses of his brain. 'I'm quite sure it's Luke Bianchi, the son of his lawyer. The same man who was instrumental in stealing ten grand from my bank account. Never made the connection until now but it makes sense. I can't recall his name on any of the files I've read. If he was smart, he would ensure his name was left off. If you find this man, you will find my father.' He read the note again. The words addled his brain with what ifs, maybes and probable's. 'Maria's kids will need protection. When the bastard makes a threat, he never backs down. The hour is long past. I doubt either man will be found at the drop off point but it might be worth sending a crew to search the area. Either man could have been watching Maria and seen her get arrested. If I were you, I'd increase surveillance on Lucy as well.'

Rico turned to the female constable. 'What was the quantity of drugs and what were they?'

'I don't know for sure but we estimated about five kilos in each packet. White powder. We left when crime scene gang arrived.'

Rico searched the ceiling as his mind tried to sort itself out. Around sixty kilos. Had to be a normal storage place for Peter to distribute to buyers. He eased Maria back into her chair, plonked the tissue box in front of her and returned to his own seat. 'Might be kind to remove the handcuffs for Maria is no threat. In fact, it wouldn't surprise me if the old man sends an assassin to do away with her the same he did with me. She now knows more than he'd want. Says how desperate he is.'

Maria gasped. 'No way, he wouldn't.'

'He did. I was in hospital in Perth. He sent a man to kill me. If you don't obey, you die and you didn't succeed in carrying out his order. He doesn't give a damn who you are.'

'He wouldn't kill anyone.'

Rico laughed; he couldn't help it.

'She doesn't know?' asked Nelson.

'Obviously not.'

'Know what?' asked Maria.

Rico figured he needed to be brutal or sweet little sister wouldn't believe the truth. 'About the number of bodies the police have dug up on the Forestville property. Amanda's lawyer is one and a federal officer who knew her new identity.'

'Really? I don't believe you.'

'It's all true,' said Nelson. 'He also shot two police officers when he escaped. We know he sent someone to Perth to kill both Rico and Amanda but he didn't succeed.' Nelson turned to Rico. 'Your sisters have no idea, do they?'

'I can't speak for either of them but I doubt it. Mama was suspicious about some incidents but until you arrested Dad and questioned her, she had been kept in the dark. Not women's business. It was a harsh shock when she found out. By the way, she wants to sell her house. It's in her name and she needs the money. Dad kept her on a shoestring and I presume you've frozen all of his accounts since he resorted to stealing from me. Maybe why he set up tonight's little caper. He needs money. I want to sell my place as well. Start over.'

Rico turned to Maria. 'Do you have any idea what Peter was involved in?'

She screwed her eyes. 'I don't know what you mean.'

'What he did for Dad.'

'I don't know what you are talking about. Pete ran a business.'

Rico snorted. 'Yeah, he sure did. Have you any idea what sort of business?'

'Import and export.'

Rico could only stare at Nelson. Both men shook their head.

'She really had no idea,' said Nelson. 'I find this hard to believe.'

'It's the way they operate.' Rico turned to Maria. 'Peter imported drugs by the truckload, sold them to dealers. He worked for Dad who is the mastermind of a huge crime syndicate. Peter is a criminal of the worst kind, kept half of Australia supplied with illicit drugs.'

Maria's mouth dropped open, her eyes rounded as she stared at him for a good five seconds before her head dropped to the table with a thump and long groan. 'And Tony?' she asked with her head still down.

'I guess you need to know the lot. Tony is just as evil. Brought in underage girls for the sex trade, kept them as slaves, ran four brothels, lived off the earnings of prostitution and probably slept with them all.'

Another long, loud groan came from the table. 'Did Lucy know?'

'Not sure. I doubt it unless she became suspicious and did her own investigation. It wouldn't surprise me if she did. Lucy isn't afraid to stand up for herself.'

Maria lifted her head. 'Which is why she got belted more than us as a kid. God, I hate this family.'

'You and me both, little sister.' Rico swept Maria up out of her chair and rocked her from side-to-side as he held her tight while she wept out thirty years of angst and pain.

'We still have to take your sister in to the station.' Nelson placed a hand on Rico's shoulder.

'No,' Maria squealed. 'I didn't know.'

Rico stood back to peer in her face, a hand on each of her shoulders. 'It's important you give a proper statement; one they will write down for you to sign. Make sure you read the final typed statement and agree with every word. If even a single word is incorrect, make sure you have it fixed.'

A tear-stained face begged him. 'Why?'

'Correct process has to be adhered to so there can be no loophole to land you in prison for a long term. You were caught as a drug courier and sixty kilos is a massive amount. Under normal circumstances, your prison term would be for a long, long time.'

'No,' she wailed. 'I had no idea.'

'I understand and I'm quite sure Nelson here will put in a good word for you. You will need a lawyer to sit by you the entire time you are questioned. They will ensure everything is legitimate.'

'Dad had a good lawyer. Can I ring him?'

Stunned, Rico plopped into his chair. 'Hell, no.'

'Why not?'

'Dear, God.' Rico tunnelled frustrated fingers through his hair.

'Your father's lawyer was arrested the same time as your father,' said Nelson as he placed a gentle hand on Maria's lower arm.

'He's in on this as well?' This time it was Maria who plonked down.

'Up to his illegal eyeballs, along with at least a hundred other people and the number is growing.

Maria's head landed on the table again with a loud *kerchunk*.

Twenty Seven

Rico was happy with his position, parked in a layby outside a line of small shops at the side of the local church. If he twisted from side-to-side to peer through thick shrubs, he had a clear view of the front and one side of his property situated on the opposite corner. A stab in his gut told him something wasn't quite right but he couldn't figure out what it was. Even though he been assured he had nothing to worry about, he'd searched the area for surveillance people but hadn't detected any. It didn't mean they weren't there.

In the few days he'd managed to spend at home between prison and being sent west, he had been more interested in rejoicing his freedom than in taking note of any deterioration to the house and garden. Basic maintenance had been done by a man hired to keep the garden tidy and make any urgent outside repairs: a man whose services had since been terminated.

Curious, he ran his eyes across the tiled roof for a more intimate study. The lines were neat with a few leaves and twigs scattered over the expanse. They were to be expected after a string of storm fronts in such a leafy suburb. There didn't appear to be any broken tiles, the gutters were straight and in good repair. He cast his eyes lower. Downpipes were where they should be and didn't hang away from the wall. The windows could do with a good wash but none were broken. Further down, shrubs had filled out and covered most of the lower walls. They all needed a good haircut, something he had intended to get stuck into but now, he wondered if it would ever happen: if he would ever get to live here again. It might be a good idea to hire a landscaper to give the garden a makeover before he put it on the market. First impressions are important.

With all the latest hoo-ha over the past three weeks, his life was now on hold. Who knew how this entire mess would pan out? Despite the message from James and assurance from Nelson, there was still deep-seated doubt the local police didn't have him on the radar for skipping parole, thanks to the old bastard, who didn't give a damn about Rico's welfare, or anyone else's. Certainly not Maria's, who now knew what it was like to spend time ensconced in a tiny gaol cell. As yet, no-one knew how long she would have to stay there. At least until her first appearance in court. Nelson had promised her circumstances would be taken into account but it wasn't Nelson who would make the final judgement. Sixty kilos of dope was a large amount to be caught with. His conscience twigged. She'd asked him to go with her to the station. He still wasn't sure whether he'd stepped away because it was the last place he wanted to show his face or for payback. Not once had she lowered herself to visit him in prison. His excuse had been to stay at home to protect her kids and Mama, which she had accepted given the threat levelled at her but deep in his gut he knew the real reason wasn't anywhere near so solicitous.

Instead, he'd slept well in his old bedroom in the home where he'd been raised. The fact he had secreted a 9mm handgun, along with a box of ammunition, from his father's stash before a team had arrived to confiscate the arsenal, had increased his sense of security. If the bastard showed up, he would have no hesitation in using the gun.

A smile broke out. So good to have a place where he could leave the damn backpack for a while. And he'd met his niece and nephew, even though they were reluctant to give him more than a shy hello. He couldn't blame them. He was as much a stranger to them as they were to him.

What concerned him more was the sadness in his mother's face. For two nights and a day she had tried to hide her worry for the sake of the kids but he could tell she struggled to maintain the joviality a grandma needed to give to such young grandchildren. Her life had been turned upside down and also inside out. To find out your partner is nothing more than a cruel wild animal who had lied to you all of your life, had to be one of the worst things to happen to such an amazing woman.

A thought came – had sending him west been a deliberate ploy to get Rico out of his father's life? Add on the kill order. Realisation hit. He banged a fist on the steering wheel as a sting of regret caused his stomach to tighten. All these little incidents now made more sense and were too damn obvious. The journey to the west on a fool's errand, the ridiculous demands, Zappacosta and Johannsen – they were all attempts to either put him back in prison or under the ground. His head shook of its own accord. He'd been such a fool. Eyes shut; he pressed his head back against the top of the seat while rampant memories flicked through his mind.

Knock, knock. Rico lifted his head and spun it to the side window. A woman with a worried frown indicated for him to wind down the window.

'Are you all right?' she asked when he complied.

'Yes, sure, I… I was sorting things in my mind.'

'You can only park here for half an hour.' She tapped her watch.

It was then he noticed the khaki uniform with a council logo on the shirt pocket. A portable ticket vending machine was gripped in one hand.

'Sorry, I lost track of time. I'll move.'

She smiled. 'As long as you're okay.'

'Yeah, and thanks for caring. I appreciate it.' Rico started the engine, checked for traffic and eased from the bay with a salute and nod to the parking inspector before he wound the window up. After a slow meander around nearby blocks, he pulled onto the verge as near to the rear of his property as he could get without driving into the river but far enough away it appeared he might be a visitor at the neighbour's house.

He scanned the side of the house, noted the plainness of the red brick wall with no garden bed to create verdant shapes of interest. A mistake when the garden had been planned, he now realised. The small window at the end glinted sunlight whereas the others... Hell, all the others had their blinds down. Rico's heart stalled as he shut his eyes to picture how he had left the house.

The first thing he'd done after being delivered home from prison by his father was to roll up every blind and open the windows to let light and air inside to drive out the mustiness. More important, the sight and sensation of his own garden and the water beyond brought him such relief after five years of incarceration. And he sure didn't close the blinds before he flew west. So who did?

Sudden tension simmered in his gut while uncertainty about what to do settled in his mind. Someone had been here. Inside. Maybe they still were. With his eyes trained on the padlocked side gate, he opened the car door and eased out but paused to reach back in to get his sunglasses. He put the over-sized shades in place, clicked the remote and pocketed the keys. 'Act normal, don't skulk,' he said under his breath.

To see if anything else was out of place and double check there was no surveillance, he strolled the block plus the one across from the front of his, where he slowed to an amble to study his own backyard. It was as he'd left it, cleared of outside furniture, garden implements or any items. Mature trees lined up along the rear fence and cast their shadows on the patchy lawn in need of restoration and a good run-over with a mower. A heavy dose of fertilizer would do wonders. Beyond it, reflections shimmered on the river, where once had stood his launch. Now, he couldn't figure why he'd bought the damn thing. Status seemed to be important back then. No longer. At least prison had taught him some lessons about life. It hadn't taken long for his sister to sell the boat and even better, the half a million dollars had sat in his account to gain a modicum of interest.

Like the front, most shrubs needed to be pruned and the back patio would look a damn sight better without the piles of autumn leaves and piles of dirt left by dried puddles.

The lonely, uncurtained window yelled a message to his gut - *beware.* In case eyes behind the glass watched as he passed, he kept his head low, although he doubted any locals would recognise him. Who else would be in his house? Maybe Mama or his sisters had been in to give the place a dust as they had for five years but he doubted it. Why would they when they knew he had been released and none of their cars were here? Although Mama knew he'd been in hospital and wasn't that slip of the tongue a huge error of judgement. It had almost got him killed. She also knew he was back in Sydney so maybe she had called in to see if he was home. She had a key. There hadn't been a chance to tell her he spent each night in a different cheap lodging which made it more possible she had called and it was logical she could have used the bathroom, furled the blind to see properly and forgotten to close it when she left. Happy with the logical thought, he continued to stroll with eyes flicking in all directions to ensure there were no covert watchers.

At the corner he paused to search both ways along the road as if he was about to cross. It took a moment to figure it would be wise to cross to ensure any unwanted attention wasn't honed onto him. The quick glances to the front of the house as he strode past, indicated nothing out of place but still the window stabbed a strong message despite the logical conclusion. After he'd passed his property, he crossed the road again with his eyes on the padlocked gate to the driveway. Here he was pleased to see small piles of leaves and a few weeds had taken up residence in the fine pavement cracks against the gate panels. No car had driven through those gates. But some human had been inside in the past three weeks. There was one way to find out who and why.

Rico spun around on one heel and headed for the personal front gate. The pebbled concrete pathway from gate to door wore swirls of orange leaves to show the world their glorious autumn colours even though they were still weighted down with moisture. At the slight squeak as he opened the gate, he paused and ran his eyes over the front windows. There was no movement at any of the blinds, no shadows from inside.

He crossed the lawn to peer through the garage window. Empty. Good. No stranger's car or even a familiar one. As he returned to the path, he kept close to the front wall to make it less likely any one upstairs could spy him. At the front door, he cast an uneasy glance along both sides of the house even though he was certain there was no-one else on the property. Hell, he'd spent the last hour scouting out the place.

He tried to ignore the queasiness in the pit of his stomach. Nothing to worry about his brain kept telling him but for some reason his gut said different. Determined to get this over with, he removed the key from his wallet, shoved it in the lock and twisted. The snick echoed as the barrel released. Ever so slow, he eased the door open a fraction.

A shiver ran down his spine when the landline inside rang. He screwed his face in question. The phone hadn't been reconnected when he left for Perth even though he'd rung to have it done. He scoffed at his own question. It had been over three weeks. Of course, it had been reconnected. He pressed his shoulder against the wall to listen.

Brrng. No footsteps.

Brrng. No squeak of a chair to indicate somebody rose to answer.

Brrng. A click and there was his own voice. 'I am unable to take your call at the moment, please leave a message.'

Click. The caller hung up before leaving a message. With a shake of his head for stupidity, Rico shoved the door wider but stood behind the jamb in case an intruder barged out or fired a shot. Although it was unlikely a gun would be used in a residential area, or at least, not a legal one, although with his family it was a strong possibility.

Silence. Not even a hushed footstep, sweep of curtain or the huff of a caught breath.

After a slow count to ten, he flicked his head around the door frame. As it should be, the spacious entry was devoid of life. A soft snort escaped. Why he was so uptight about his own empty house, he had no idea. It was ridiculous the way he was so damn cautious. The same picture given to him as a house-warming present, sat centred on the wall opposite the door. The same narrow hall table of polished teak sat under the picture. A thin layer of undisturbed dust coated the top. A dish for keys, mail and knick-knacks stood empty. All as he'd left them three weeks ago.

Less cautious, he stepped inside where eyes flicked from side-to-side. So far, nothing was out of place. He stood behind the wall of the archway that led into the main open plan living area, waited several seconds before he dared a quick glance into the main room.

The black leather L-shaped settee sat in the centre of the living room as it always had. Straight ahead, the wall of picture windows had the dark blue drapes drawn. The neat folds blocked out the river scene: the reason he'd built here. The corner drink's cabinet showed a full rack of wine bottles on top and closed doors to the cupboards under the bench, which was clear, apart from dust.

A shaft of sunlight reached through a small gap in the window, pointed out the large flatscreen which took up much of the end wall. It had never seen much use as he'd had it installed a week before his marriage: a week before his life spiralled out of control. Next to it hung two small oil paintings he'd bought from the artist. Both depicted different views of his favourite beach on the south coast. A stab of remorse hit. Amanda had designed a beach house for the block he owned there. It would never get built. He wasn't even sure he wanted to keep the block.

This room was the one feature he'd re-designed several times before he was happy with the layout. A small table and four dining chairs separated the lounge from the ultra-modern kitchen at the far end. The table had been adequate for his needs at the time – pre-Amanda. He'd planned to replace it with a bigger, family size suite but it never happened.

Eyes scanned along the wall, paused on the low table in front of the settee. A tremor wove itself across his shoulders as his gut tightened. It should have been clear but the top wore an untidy pile of books to one side, a haphazard heap of papers in the centre. Next to it lay a small plate with a half-eaten muffin, a mug of coffee and a remote control. These were the only items out of place plus the whiff of an unpleasant odour.

The discomfort in his stomach didn't ease at the overwhelming silence. He rounded the settee and placed the back of his hand against the mug even though the sludge on top of the coffee told him the brew was neither fresh nor hot. Stone cold. A squeeze on the muffin. Not stale so it couldn't have been there long, maybe since the night before. He lifted the plate and sniffed. Chocolate chip but not the source of the less pleasant stench. As he replaced the plate, he searched the room for any other anomalies.

When he could spy no other food or out of place object, he crept to the first door on the left, the guest bedroom suite but the one he'd used as his own because it was on the ground floor, close to the kitchen. He paused, studied the other doors. The end one led to the laundry and side entry, the other to a largish den he'd set up as a study. All the doors were shut – the same way he'd left them.

Which should he open first? He swore under his breath, took one step, twisted the bedroom doorknob, shoved and reeled back. A man's body lay sprawled at an awkward angle, face down on his bed and with a bullet wound to the back of the head. Dark, dried blood trails ran from the wound onto the quilt, the dark maroon hiding most of the evidence. As he moved closer, he noticed a pistol gripped in the man's right hand.

Uncertain what to do, he paused before turning the body over but thought better of it. He damn well knew to never interfere with the evidence but he had to know. This was his house. Someone had been squatting in his home for at least part of the past three weeks. And they sure weren't model citizens. He couldn't call the police for he would be arrested and what would he tell them? There's a dead man on my bed? Oh, sure and who would be number one suspect? Besides, few people knew he was here and it was imperative no-one else found out.

James Ward. He understood Rico's situation, maybe he could suggest what the hell to do about this.

He took phone number three from his shirt pocket, bought up the one number he'd put into the address book and pressed the call button.

A toilet flushed; the sound so close it had to come from the ensuite. In a flash, he spun around, grabbed the gun and aimed head high at the door. A split second later the door opened. A man emerged.

Rico almost dropped the weapon in shock. 'What the hell are you doing in my house?'

The man paused, took a step back, his face stunned as he lifted his eyes. 'Uh, Rico, you're de... how did you... put the gun down.'

'I'm what, old man - dead? Via Johansson?'

'I don't know what you're talking about.' A red flush raced up Matteo's neck and bloomed on his face so fast it was obvious he lied.

'Sure you do. Johansson admitted it, before he ran like a scared rabbit.' He leant forwards a fraction. 'Before he was arrested.' He indicated with his head towards the bed. 'Who's that?'

'A traitor.'

'Traitor? What did he do?'

'Ratted to the cops.'

'Did he confess and who is he?'

'Of course he didn't – too scared. Whimpered like the coward he is. Begged. Cried. What real man cries?'

'Maybe he told you the truth.'

'No way. It had to have been him. No-one else knew.'

'Knew what?'

'Every damn thing. He printed off every detail, squealed to the cops.'

'Are you sure? I mean, it could have been me.'

'Don't be so damn stupid. You don't have a clue about any events of the last five years.' He waved a hand in the air. 'Put the damn gun down.'

Rico shook his head. 'Uh, uh, not going to happen. Who is he?'

'Luke.'

'Bianchi, your lawyer's son?' Rico already knew these details but he wanted a confession. If he was lucky, James Ward had the nous to listen in. He'd heard the hello. 'Maybe you can explain what the hell you are doing in my house.'

'Had to hide out somewhere. Can't go home. Cops have it under surveillance, same with the girls. Now you're here, you can run messages for me.'

Rico laughed but ceased in an instant when Matteo took a step towards him with one fist clenched and the other with a taser held out, ready to fire.

'Don't move,' Rico snarled as he steadied his arm, peered along the barrel. 'One step closer and I fire.'

'You don't have the guts, wouldn't know how to shoot.' The taser wavered.

'I trained as a cop, shot many times, but never at a human. I'm not a murderer like you.'

Matteo aimed, eyed along the top as though taking aim with a gun.

'I wouldn't if I were you. I will shoot you.'

'You wouldn't dare. I'm your father.'

'And I'm your son but you didn't care about the relationship when you gave the kill order for me. So don't imagine for one second I give a damn about you. You sent Zappacosta to murder Amanda. Guess what? I foiled the attempt, had him arrested.

She never did anything wrong, didn't deserve any of the pain you meted out to her.'

A roar preceded Matteo's surge forwards. In a flash, Rico spun sideways, lowered his hand, aimed for the knee, pulled the trigger.

Bang. The echoing blast rattled his ear drums.

Matteo stopped in his tracks, eyes wide, mouth dropped open. Ever so slow, he folded to the ground with a long, high-pitched yowl. His shoulders shook in accompaniment to several gasps.

'I'll kill you,' Matteo growled as he wrapped both hands around his shattered knee. Blood flowed between his fingers.

Rico kicked the dropped taser out of reach and realised it had already been used. The cartridge was spent. 'I have the gun, you don't.' He studied the firearm. 'Police issue. Where did you get it?'

'None of your damn business,' Matteo gasped in obvious pain. 'Help me here,' he whimpered with screwed eyes.

'Probably from the police officer you shot to escape.' Rico removed the bullets, counted them. 'Four bullets missing.' He put the phone to his mouth. 'Did you get all those details, James?'

'What the…?' came from his father at the same time James answered. 'Recorded it. Did you kill him?'

'No, just let him feel what it was like to be knee-capped, his favourite way of inflicting pain to get people to confess. Self-defence. He had a taser aimed at me as he lurched towards me. Also police issue. I'm in my house. Luke Bianchi is dead, on my bed. Been dead for a while, maybe the night before last or sometime between. I'll dispose of the other bullets so the bastard can't do any more harm. Do what you have to do.'

'Call the police?'

'Yes, give me ten to collect a couple of items.' He hung up, took his time to slip the phone in his shirt pocket, his eyes honed on his snivelling excuse for a father, who wriggled like a worm towards the taser.

Rico laughed when the electrodes jiggled from the end as though they had been stuffed back in. 'You do realise once that model taser has been used the cartridge has run out of gas and it won't fire again.'

It was so damn good to see the man in pain. It was even better to see him fight back tears without success. Bullies are nothing more than glorified cowards when their power is taken away. A lesson he should have learned years ago.

Matteo began to crawl towards him, a trail of blood left on the polished wood floor. 'Who were you talking to?'

'None of your business,' With the edge of his shirt, Rico took utmost care to wipe the gun clean and kept it held with the fabric. 'You've got twenty-four hours to get yourself and him,' he nodded towards the body, 'out of here and have my home spotless. Twenty-four hours before I call the police.' He placed the gun on the end of the bed, stepped closer, put one foot on his father's back and pressed down until the bastard lay flat. Rico bent over, pulled out the wallet from the back pocket of his own chinos. Lord, the bastard had even raided Rico's wardrobe. As he stepped back, the kick to his father's injured knee was deliberate. The scream gave him inordinate pleasure as he opened the wallet and removed the wad of one-hundred-dollar notes.

He wiped the wallet clean, flung it on the ground, squatted and waved the money in front of his father's eyes. 'My money. Money you stole from my account. Such a wonderful father and husband. No qualms about beating up your wife, cheating on her or ensuring she has no funds of her own. No qualms about stealing from your own flesh and blood. Not even a flicker of remorse about sending an assassin to murder your own child or to coerce your daughter into being a drug courier. You are nothing but a scumbag – the lowest of the low and that's giving you credit.'

He stood, stepped back, took care to pick up the gun with the hem of his shirt. 'Catch,' he called. He flung the gun towards Matteo. Pure reaction had the man catch the weapon. It now held only Matteo's fingerprints but by the way the gun was cuddled as though it was a treasure, the bastard hadn't realised.

'Rico,' echoed through the house as he went to get what he came for. In the study, he ran his fingers along the ledge under the desk, wriggled out the key from the slot he'd filed out five years previous. Scuffles sounded, several groans with a whimper between each one. Out the doorway, Rico paused at a thump. Leant against the wall for support, his father stood on one leg, blood poured down the other and dripped onto the floor.

'You can't leave me. You have to help me. I'm your father.'

Rico sneered at the plea. 'Sure I can leave you. I don't owe you a damn thing.' He glanced at his watch. 'Twenty-three hours, fifty-five minutes.'

Without another glance, he shoved at the scumbag, smiled at the thump and scream when the bastard hit the ground. Small payback for the number of backhanders he'd received as a child. With a wide grin spread across his face, he crossed the main room, spun into the entry, yanked the door open but didn't let it snick shut after he'd exited. Might as well make it easy for the police. They won't have to wreck his front door.

'Get back here and do your duty to your father.'

With a shrug, he ran to the rear of the garage, eased out the pseudo post and inserted the key into the small safe set into the high foundations. All the items were still where he'd hidden them before being incarcerated. Hidden where none of his family knew. Three passports and all the important documents everybody keeps in a safe place, including the Title Deed to this house. As an afterthought, he dropped the bullets in so they wouldn't be found. Safe closed, he replaced the post and ran back to the car he'd hired. He made a three-point turn and burst out in laughter at the sound of sirens. Two marked cars, lights flashing, passed him. More sirens came from different directions, a cacophony of urgency guaranteed to bring neighbours out to witness the big man being cowed to his rightful size.

Twenty Eight

'Rico, get back here. Don't you dare... I'll kill you,' Matteo yelled while he crawled along the floor, dragging his right leg. He reached the coffee table, levered his body far enough up he could kneel on one knee. He managed to swing his right leg out to the side with a held breath to prevent the escape of a scream. The damn leg refused to work.

'Rico,' he yelled again. A groan followed at the stab of agony when the muscles in his leg tensed as he pressed both hands down hard on the table. Elbows straight, it took too much time to push himself up far enough he could wriggle his backside onto the table. Bit by bit he eased the leg around in front of him with an unbidden scream he couldn't hold back.

A metallic clang sounded like the front gate.

'Rico, get back here.'

An engine hummed to life. Tyres squealed.

Matteo cursed until the screech of sirens silenced him. 'The little bastard lied,' Matteo whispered as scrambled brain cells figured out what the hell he could do. He had to get out. Get to Luke's car. He swore. The bloody car was parked two blocks over. Gut clenched tight, he heaved his body upright, hobbled, gasped and managed to get both feet under him. A red hot poker speared upwards, seared the muscles in his thigh, ground together the shattered bone fragments in his knee. 'Bastard, bastard, bastard,' he cursed in time with each limp towards the front door. When the pain became too much he slumped against the wall, unable to make it to the archway, unable to reach the front door. Eyes squeezed tight; his breath rasped until the stillness eased the agony a little. Desperation clawed at his mind. Have to get out, have to get out. With gritted teeth he forced his body upright, swallowed the scream, rounded the corner and lurched towards the front door. Have to get out. Have to get out.

The door swung open, banged against the wall, swung back. 'Police. Put your hands behind your head.'

Too stunned to move, Matteo stared at the door. It opened again, much slower. A gun appeared, followed by a fierce face. One Matteo recognised. The bloody Pommy sergeant from Sydney Central. Navy clad legs stepped in. The sergeant straightened his body with arms out in front, gun aimed at Matteo's chest.

'Hands behind your head,' the sergeant growled as two other officers rushed in and stood each side of him, one with a taser, the other with gun aimed.

'Get down on the floor, arms spread out to the side.'

'Can't, injured,' Matteo managed to get out a split second before all three men rushed forward, manhandled him to the floor, ripped his hands behind his back and cuffs clicked into place. The pain was so intense he couldn't catch his breath to squeal - or gasp - or speak. Eyes shut to ride out the stabs of agony, he managed to blow out his cheeks before fingers gripped the back of his shirt. His scream echoed around the room as he was hauled over, dragged across the floor and shoved against the wall with his legs splayed out in front of him. Hands searched pockets; ran up and down his arms, his legs. Fingers probed his sides and chest and withdrew the gun he'd slipped into the waistband of Rico's trousers. A much younger constable, one he'd never seen before, held the gun up with thumb and forefinger looped around the trigger. He dropped it into a plastic bag he took from his back pocket.

'He's unarmed, search the house.' The sergeant perched his backside on the coffee table and leered. 'What happened?' He nodded towards Matteo's knee.

'I was shot. What does it look like?'

'Who shot you?'

'My son.'

'Rico?'

'Only got one son.'

'Where is he?'

'Gone, drove off.'

'Search for Rico, fellas,' the sergeant yelled. 'Even though I don't believe you since you reported him dead to the bank.' He studied the gun. 'Police issue. I gather this is the one you stole after you shot Phil Roberts.'

'No, Rico left it here.'

An evil laugh came from the sergeant. 'Why lie when it will take mere hours to test it for fingerprints and a match to bullets retrieved from two police officers? Sure the serial number will match the one for the missing gun.'

'Dead man in here. Luke Bianchi,' came a voice from the room next door.

The sergeant raised his eyebrows. 'I assume Rico shot him as well.'

'Yes, he did.'

'When?'

'Just now.'

The man laughed. 'Really? Why lie? We know you shot him. When we retrieve the bullet it will be tested the same as the others and the coroner will know how long the man has been dead. Most fathers will defend their children with their lives but not you. You're such a coward. You blame your poor son for every misdemeanour and crime you have committed, even those crimes when he was tucked away in a prison cell and now, crimes he's supposed to have committed after his death. When was it you reported his death? Let me think. Days ago.'

'He was here, I tell you. You think I would shoot myself?'

'You want to know what I think? I think you are capable of any damn fool thing, especially if you can lay blame on some other poor sucker.'

'Bed's been slept in upstairs. Take-away crap spread all over the room. Forensics will have a field day. Plenty of evidence. Other bedrooms are clear. No-one else upstairs.' The voice arrived before the officer appeared.

The third officer joined them. 'Bianchi's been dead for a while, maybe a day.'

'Call the coroner and forensics,' said the sergeant as he lifted an eyebrow to Matteo.

'Already done, they're on their way.' He inclined his head towards Matteo. 'Looks like he received some of his own medicine. Who shot him?'

'Self-inflicted to lay blame on the son.' The sergeant grinned at Matteo.

'Rico? Isn't he dead?'

'Our friend here reckons Rico was here yet he also swore to the bank his son was dead. Beats me how a dead man can fire a gun. Seems a ghost shot him.'

'Do we need an ambulance?' asked the young constable.

'Nah, the injury isn't life threatening. Bleeding has slowed so no main vein has been compromised.'

'This is illegal,' Matteo butted in. 'I need urgent medical treatment. I'm bleeding to death here.' He swept one hand towards his knee and winced at the dribble of blood to make out it was worse than it appeared. 'I know the law.'

When all three officers laughed Matteo sent them a scowl. 'I'll sue you bastards.'

'Look forward to it. You're such a hypocrite,' scoffed the sergeant. 'I've ploughed my way through the reams of evidence. The one man who has broken every law ever enacted says he knows the law. Must be the joke of the century.'

'I tell you Rico was here. He shot me. You should know this since it was him who rang you.'

'Rang me? When?'

'Just now. How else did you know to come here?'

'I can assure you it wasn't your son who called us.' The sergeant leant forwards, prodded Matteo in the chest. 'It was my superintendent who called to give me the head's up.'

'No way. Had to be Rico pretending to be your super. He damn well shot me. Left not fifteen minutes ago.'

'You think I don't know the voice of my own super? You think I don't recognise the super's number on my mobile phone? Get real. And how can Rico call if he's a dead man as you swore to the bank?'

'I thought he was dead but now I know better. He was here, damn you.'

'Wasn't it Rico who…'

The sergeant held up one hand to silence the constable. 'Is there a paddy wagon here yet? Go check.'

'Rico who, what?' asked Matteo. The thoughts shooting through his mind were not in the least pleasant. But no way, Rico couldn't have known half of the details. The one person who knew so much now lay dead in the room next door. Luke got what he deserved, more so after he stuffed up the coke pick-up two nights ago. You talk, you die. You fail your task, you die. Stupid idiot failed at both. Pity the death couldn't have been longer and more painful.

'Wasn't it Rico who jumped parole.' The sergeant's answer interrupted Matteo's thoughts. 'But we don't have to worry about such a minor indiscretion now, do we? We're not interested in your son. Apart from what landed him in prison to start with, we have not a single indication he has broken any law, so there's no need to search for him. You are the only person we have any interest in. Well, you and your cronies and hell, we've almost run out of gaol cells with the number of squealers we've locked away. And man, haven't they all squealed like starving rats who can smell a fresh wodge of cheese? Your name has been said so often it echoes through every room where we've taken statements. Matteo ordered this, Matteo did that, Matteo, Matteo, Matteo.'

'Paddy wagon is here.' The youngest officer returned.

'Okay, get this bastard in it. It will give me great pleasure to have him back in Sydney Central where I will personally keep an eye on him. Where he will be chained to his bed.'

'I need urgent medical attention.' As Matteo straightened his back against the wall, he sent a fierce scowl to the pompous sergeant.

'I'll think about it but first...'

Matteo was swung away from the wall so fast he didn't have time to catch his breath at the shaft of agony.

'Shove him in the wagon.'

Both upper arms were grasped at the same time, a man on each side of him. It was impossible to hold back the screams as he was dragged across the floor, through the doorway, along the path to the gate. Two more constables stood, one each side of the open door to the wagon.

'Grab the top of his legs. He won't be able to climb in of his own accord.'

'No,' Matteo screamed. The two new men gripped his thighs tight while the other two put one hand behind his shoulders and tightened their hold on his upper arms. They hoisted him high and fed him into the back of the van.

Everything became blurry and dark.

Twenty Nine

It was a different room, scrubbed clean with disinfectant strong enough to hide other odours. The sharp scent burnt his sinuses, shocked him to full awareness. The sneeze woke up every pain molecule in his body. Each one shuddered a path through his nervous system and seemed to settle in his right knee. A surge of memory hit. Rico. The gun. Got shot. Police. Paddy wagon. The agony of the drive. The surprise to find himself wheeled into a hospital and not Sydney Central Police Station. An even bigger shock when he realised he had arrived at Section Two of the hospital at Long Bay Prison. The last place he wanted to ever be. A memory surfaced of being wheeled into surgery, a mask over his face, a prick in his hand and fuzziness.

A deep groan rumbled up as brain cells aligned. He was in a prisoner ward, well-guarded. A place he knew about but had never visited. He twisted his still fuzzy head to the right. Cream walls with a dark grey dado strip a third of the way up and window trim the same colour. A barred window, the dark grey grille ominous. Couldn't be pale, could it. Had to stand out. Matteo swore as he flipped his head to the other side and swore again. The door was heavy metal, the dark grey bars even more imposing than the window grille. Next to the bed stood a monitor attached to him via a blood pressure cuff, a pulse recorder on his index finger and a drip line feeding into the back of his hand. Regular beeps from the monitor echoed. It was difficult to lift his head which seemed to be weighted down with lead. A quick glance towards his feet. His leg was bandaged from halfway down his thigh to an equal distance down his shin. It was then he noticed the ankle restraint on his left leg. He tugged. It rattled, metal against the metal of the bed.

He tried to turn over but couldn't when a similar loud rattle came from his right side along with a tug on his right wrist. Shit. He was more secure than he'd been in the prison van. Now stretched out on a narrow steel bed, manacled left and right and with a non-functioning leg that thrummed until he tried to move a muscle when a red-hot poker stabbed into it. The only limb capable of moving more than a few centimetres was his left arm.

Footsteps neared: heavy footsteps. A jangle of keys, a rattle of wheels followed. An armed guard appeared behind the bars of the doorway. A big man with broad shoulders, buzz cut hair and a serious face. A wide weapon belt was prominent, more so when the man's hands settled on the butt of both a taser and a pistol in a silent message.

A man in scrubs moved next to him, lifted a file from the trolley he'd been pushing. The door opened. Both men entered. The nurse eyed him, smiled, ran his eyes over the monitor, jotted notes on a file, unhooked the bag of fluid.

The guard stood tall with little room for the nurse to move. One of the guard's hands remained hovered over his holstered weapon, the other over the handle of a taser. Unmoving eyes dared Matteo to do anything other than breathe.

'I'm thirsty,' said Matteo. He was but it was more of a way to break the silence and get rid of the stare.

'Here.' The nurse lifted a paper cup from the metal bench, bent the top of a plastic straw over the rim and held the cup close to Matteo's lips with one hand while the other wriggled behind his shoulders to lift his head a little higher. He sucked. The cool water washed over an arid tongue. So damn good. He swished and swallowed, drank some more until a slurp told him the cup was empty.

'How's my knee?' he asked as the empty cup went back on the ledge and the nurse refilled it from a plastic jug kept out of Matteo's reach.

'Bullet was removed, along with bone fragments. The doctor will explain more.'

'Will I be able to walk?' He knew what could happen when a person had been shot in the knee. It depended on the damage whether or not there would be much movement. He always made sure the damage was considerable and the pain at the maximum. He'd never expected to be on the receiving end. Bloody Rico would pay.

'The doctor will explain.'

'When?'

'When he makes his rounds.'

'When will that be?'

'Enough,' growled the guard. He straightened and tightened the grip on both weapons. 'He'll come when he has time.' The guard nodded to the nurse. 'You done?'

'I need to remove the canula. Patient is in no danger. No more fluids are needed. His vital signs are normal.' As the nurse bent towards the back of Matteo's hand, the guard shuffled sideways to keep an eye on proceedings. Seemed he wasn't about to take any chances.

A sticky patch tore the few dark hairs from the back of Matteo's hand as it was peeled away. Even though the canula was taken out from his flesh slowly it still stung. A tiny wad of cotton wool was immediately pressed over the small wound and taped into place. The gadget was removed from his finger and the pressure cuff unwrapped with a ripping noise. The nurse wrapped, coiled and folded all the bits and pieces, balanced them on a small metal shelf on the machine and moved the monitor next to the still open door.

'I need to piss,' said Matteo. They would have to unshackle him, help him to the bathroom. If there was one. He searched the room, noticed a normal wooden door in the opposite corner. Had to be a private bathroom. They sure wouldn't let him mingle with other patients even though they would all be prisoners. One of his men would have to be close by. Had any been injured when they'd been arrested?

The nurse sent a questioning glance to the guard. 'I'll get a bottle.'

'Hell no,' Matteo said at the same time the guard nodded. 'I'm not pissing in some bottle. Take me to the bathroom.'

'Not going to happen.' Just out of reach, the guard puffed out his chest, settled his feet shoulder-width apart while hands twitched on his weapons. 'Go,' he said to the nurse. 'Come straight back.'

Discretion meant Matteo kept his mouth shut and eyes closed until he heard the steps of the nurse return. Despite his determination to show bravado, embarrassment caused a rush of heat to his neck and cheeks while the nurse bunched up the surgical gown and held the plastic torture chamber in place until he was done. He didn't miss the smirk on the guard's face. Arsehole. Within seconds, all machinery was wheeled from the room, the men left and the metal door clicked shut with an ominous twist of a key.

With nothing to do, he closed his eyes and begged for sleep.

His eyes jolted open to stare at the stark white ceiling. He listened. Dead silence. But some sound woke him. He turned his head to the right. A sharp shock of fear beset him. A man stood at the window; his eyes honed on some object outside. It was hard to make out against the glare but it looked like he was in a police uniform.

'Good to see you are awake.'

Matteo shot his head the other way. A man in blue scrubs stood next to him, a file in one hand, a pen in the other.

The man nodded towards the window. 'The officer wants to get a statement about the injury to your knee. Since he's an armed officer we don't need a security guard. How are you feeling?'

'Not sure. Okay. Sore. Tired. Who are you?'

'I operated on your knee which makes me your surgeon. You made a mess of it.'

'You think I would shoot myself?'

A snort came from the right. Matteo shot the officer a quick glance. He hadn't moved.

'I understand the fingerprints on the weapon are yours. There was gunpowder residue on the clothes you wore. The bullet was fired from the gun you held. The officer here will tell you more but first – your injury. It might be possible to do a knee replacement in the future.'

'Replacement? What the hell?'

'It will be hell when you first try to walk, which will be when you have your first physiotherapy session. The knee cap was damaged. You managed to blast large chips off both the femur and tibia ends of the knee. I removed the fragments, did my best to file off the sharp edges but when you put any weight on the joint it will hurt. A lot. You have neurovascular damage. Not a lot I can do about it until the injury heals. You will always have a limp but on the bright side, you won't have to undergo an amputation.'

'Amputation! Bloody hell. I'll kill Rico for this.'

'Excuse me?' With wide eyes and a slack jaw the doctor took a step back.

'My son, Rico. He was the one who shot me.'

'Oh, the report says otherwise. Maybe the officer here can tell you more. Apart from the knee injury, you are fine. I'll leave you to speak with the officer.'

While his brain tried to digest the information he'd been given, Mateo watched the doctor leave. He turned back to the window to see the police officer take his time to turn. Again, the glare from the light outside made it difficult to see any features. The man took one step forward. Mateo blinked to clear his eyes for a better view. Another step. Facial features became more distinct. Another step.

Mateo frowned. He had to be hallucinating. He shook his head in disbelief, certain he was seeing things. When the man stepped closer, a muzzle pointed at Mateo's head.

'What the…' Mateo stuttered. 'Phil? How did you…' In an instant he realised he needed to change tack. He smiled. 'Phil, glad to see you. You can help me get out of here.'

The muzzled wavered, came closer. 'Sure, I'll help you. The same way you helped me when I put

328

my job and my life on the line for you. How did you repay me? Eh? Like this?'

He fired. Before Matteo could move, prongs shot out. They punctured the flesh on his face and neck. Sharp bolts of electricity sped through his nervous system. He shuddered, jolted, jerked. Lights flashed in the back of his eyes. Followed by immediate blackness. Light, dark, light, dark as his brain shuddered like crystals in a salt shaker. Muscles flexed. Seized up. Acute pain.

He stilled. Pain echoed. Anxiety hovered. Brain cells fogged over. He couldn't think, couldn't process. He forced his eyes to open. A man hovered over him. Eyes hooded, thin lips curved in a snarl. Matteo stared at the face, incredulous. He tried to open his mouth but it was taped shut. When did that happen?

The man reached over, tugged, tore at the skin under Matteo's eye. Another yank, from his neck this time. He winced at the sharp pain.

'You weren't satisfied with a taser shot, were you?' Spittle hit Matteo's face. 'I did everything to help you escape – succeeded, but you… you slimy, ungrateful bastard. You had no compunction in doing this.' A gun, silencer attached, wavered in front of Matteo's face.

A hard, cold muzzle pressed into the space between his eyes. Paused. It moved down, pressed into one eye. Hot moisture flooded between his legs. The circle of steel scraped down one cheek, pushed hard against the jaw bone. 'One, two, three,' was counted out aloud. Matteo froze, too scared to breathe.

The muzzle scoured along his jaw. Underneath. Jabbed up in the curve. 'One, two, three.'

It ran down his throat, screwed into his voice box. His breath hitched, eyes stared, too afraid to move, too petrified to breathe. His hands clenched until he remembered one arm was free. He swung, aimed for the head.

Barely a noise. The sudden sting sent the message. Hot fire filled his chest. Blood spurted past his eyes.

'Karma is a bitch,' hissed in his ear followed by a glob of spit. On silent feet, the man strode to the door, pulled it shut and vanished.

'Mmm, mmm, mmm,' Matteo tried to yell against the tape. He attempted to tug it away but his hands didn't seem to work. The room went fuzzy. Greyness descended.

Thirty

In one sense it was a shock to see how fast Mama had begun to sort items into three piles: to keep - for charity - the bin. Said bin already sat in the front yard, the biggest skip bin she had been able to order. In another sense, he understood, for he was keen to pack up his own life and start over, but when your own home had become a murder scene with police tape wrapped around it, it made it difficult. Instead, he carted gear for Mama. His father's wardrobe had been the first thing to be emptied. Every item now resided in the bottom of the skip bin. He'd questioned Mama why she didn't send expensive suits, shirts and jackets to the charity shops. *Nobody deserves to wear the clothes of such an evil person.* The words had been spat, so unlike Mama, but he agreed.

With a grin, he dumped a box of almost new, Italian leather shoes in the bin, turned and returned inside, desperate for a coffee. Mama sat at the kitchen table, a small box of loose photographs in front of her. There was a definite trace of tears as she stared at a single photo.

'Mama, are you okay?' Rico rounded the table, placed one hand on her shoulder, settled in the chair next to her and leant over to study the photo.

The picture had faded, the colours washed out. Even so, every detail of the scene could be made out. Drawn up on dull white sand, the wooden boat

331

sat upside down. Painted white with a blue stripe on the third plank from the top, the boat had nestled itself in the sand with a few scraggy weeds rested against bowed planks. Patches of dried seaweed showed the path towards the water. Almost out of sight, the Mediterranean Sea lay calm, yet a glint of reflected sunlight still sparkled on low ripples. In the background, stone buildings hunched together as though each was needed to support its neighbour. The colour of each seemed to be varied but the age of the photograph had diminished the brightness. It was obvious the beachside town had sat there for many years. Without asking, Rico knew the photo had been taken in Cefalu, Mama's home town, not far from Palermo in Sicily.

He tapped the photo. 'Cefalu?'

When Mama nodded he noticed she had to fight back a new bout of tears, her lips drawn tight together and with a bright wash across her eyes. 'Who's the guy?' A young man, no more than a teenager, stood on the boat's keel, one hand high in a wave, a wide grin on his face. Thick dark hair, in need of a trim, hung almost into his eyes. The thick sweater indicated it was winter. Rico had the impression the man's skin was dark, the same as his.

'I went to school with him. We were good friends.' Mama's voice broke his study of the picture. He lifted his face to see sadness in her eyes.

'At fourteen, I worked for his family. A small restaurant on the beach. Only in summer when many people visited the beach. Lots of tourists and people from the city and the mainland. The family made good money then but not in winter when the crowds vanished. In winter, it was difficult to find work.' Mama reached over, ran a finger along the boat. 'Before the sun rose each morning, he rowed out into the ocean to catch the fish they cooked and sold in the restaurant. He rowed back to shore in time to attend school then spent the evenings with his family in the restaurant, mainly to clean and serve. They were poor, as were we.'

At the hitch in her voice, Rico leant towards Mama. 'You were fond of him, weren't you?'

'*Si*, very much so.' Her voice cracked.

'How fond?'

She shrugged, turned away. Rico suspected it was to hide tears. It was rare – too rare, for her to let tears fall in front of him. Now, he realised, she had kept a deep pain hidden for his entire life. He swept an arm around her shoulders, drew her close. The sniff told him the answer. 'You were in love with him.'

'*Si*. We wanted to marry.'

'What happened?' He leant back so he could see her face but kept anchored with a hand on each of her upper arms. A weird sensation in his gut told him there was an untold story here, especially since she had been engrossed in this photo in particular. His heart twisted at her upturned face, a plea in her teary eyes.

'As you know, my papa started out as a labourer. It was not well paid but he insisted my brother and I get an education because he never had one. He wanted us to have more opportunity, to find good jobs, maybe go to the mainland and work for a big company. To help out, Antonio and I worked after school and on the weekends to pay for the fees and books. We were happy.' She paused, gulped and wiped away the few tears that had managed to escape her strong will. 'Then Antonio fell ill when he was eighteen, not long before he was due to leave for the university. You know about this – I've told it many times.'

Rico grasped his mother's twitchy hands, wrapped his fingers around to still them and ease her distress. 'Yes, cancer, I know. He died.'

'Yes, but not before much money was needed to pay for the treatment. Not that it did any good. Today, I think they may have been able to save him.'

'Probably. Tell me more.'

'Papa worked as a labourer for Matteo's papa who owned the building company. They were rich – very rich. He loaned us the money, said Papa could pay it off week by week as he could afford it. Antonio died. Papa borrowed more money to pay for the funeral.'

Rico swore under his breath for, what he now knew about the so called *family*, the end of this story wasn't of the happy ever after kind. Even though he didn't want to hear any more, he needed the details. 'Where does Dad fit into this story and what happened to this other guy – the one you wanted to marry?'

'Matteo was already in Australia, at university, to study law. His older brother was there in some business. I never knew what sort of business. Anyhow, by the time Antonio died, I had turned eighteen. Papa wanted me to marry. I was too young but told him who I wanted to marry when I was a bit older.'

'This man.' Rico tapped the photo.

'Yes. Papa agreed. He also agreed to let me find full-time work so I could save money to marry but then there was an accident on the work site. Matteo's father was injured so bad he couldn't walk. Since they were the oldest of six children, Matteo and his brother came home to sort out the company. After a couple of weeks, they came around, spoke with Papa. There was a great deal of shouting. They demanded repayment of the loan within seven days. Even if we had sold every item we owned, including our little home, it was impossible to find enough money. Papa couldn't pay. Matteo and his brother came around a week later to collect. The threats could be heard down the street. Neither man was pleasant, in fact they were so nasty, so mean... oh, God.' Mama buried her face in her hands and began to weep.

The loud sobs wrenched Rico's innards as he squatted next to her and drew her into his arms. 'Mama, please don't cry. Here...' He stood, whipped a handful of tissues from the box on the refrigerator and scrunched them into his mother's fingers. It took a good five minutes before the sobs ceased and Mama fought back the tears.

'I need to tell you the rest.'

'Okay but stop if it gets too much.'

A weak smile crept out but he bet it was forced, the same way he now knew she had forced smiles all of his life. 'In the end a deal was made. They would forgive the loan for my hand in marriage.'

The words were rushed out so fast, he almost didn't make them out. 'And your father agreed?'

Mama shrugged. 'He didn't have any choice.'

'Of course he did. You did.' Anger surged upwards from deep in his gut.

'You don't understand. Arranged marriages were common. They still are back home. I had no choice but I insisted on six months to sort my life.'

'This wasn't an arranged marriage. You were bought, damn it. Coerced. Blackmailed.'

'Do not swear.' She swatted his hand.

Rico couldn't help a smile. 'Damn is mild compared to what I said in my head.'

'Rico!'

'You went ahead with the marriage.'

'Not before I ran away.'

Rico reeled back in surprise. 'You ran away? Where?'

She pointed to the picture. 'He got me on a fishing trawler. I went to the mainland. We were going to elope. But he had to stay in Cefalu to prove he didn't know where I was and to sort things while he saved so we could marry. It took four weeks before Matteo's family found me, dragged me in front of a priest. We were married that night and flew here to Australia the next day.'

'How, without a passport?'

'I had a passport. Back then everyone needed one, even to get to nearby countries. There was no European Union at the time. It was difficult when I arrived here, my English was not good, I hated Matteo and was desperate to return home. I hadn't even been allowed to see my parents to say goodbye. After the… first time… when he forced himself on me, I lost all hope. It was like I was in a far-off world. In bed, I pretended I was dead.' She stared up at Rico, her cheeks a pretty shade of pink. Even though the embarrassment was obvious, so was the deep-seated pain in her eyes.

'Six months later I caught him in bed with another woman. I was so angry. Never before had I felt such anger, disappointment and the pain… it hurt so much. The next night I stole money from his wallet and when he left for work the morning after, I stole more money from a safe he had in the office. It was lucky my passport was in there as well but it took a week of hiding near the airport before I could find a way to fly back to Italy. Not a direct flight for he would have searched those. I flew to Darwin first. Next, I went to Perth and Singapore. From there I flew to Athens and caught a train to Italy. I was too scared to face my parents for I knew they would be furious and there was the issue of the loan. Also it would be the first place his family would look for me.'

'Where did you go?'

A beautiful smile broke out as she pointed to the picture. 'I contacted him. He came. We hid on the other side of the island. The best four weeks of my life. I loved him then. I still love him now. He's the only man I've ever loved, well, apart from you but a mother's love is different from the true love between a man and a woman.' She rubbed his hand, ran her fingers up his arm, gripped tight.

'What happened?' He placed one hand over hers, gave it a squeeze.

She scowled. 'What do you think? Matteo came, with a mob of cruel men. Family, he said. But they weren't blood family. They caught me in the street, bundled me into a car, drove off. I was imprisoned in their family home for two weeks, always with an armed bully as guard. We argued a lot. Matteo demanded I return with him to Australia but I refused on account of his infidelity. After another two weeks, I had no choice but to agree.'

'How come? What happened?'

'If I didn't, Papa would be hurt in a work accident. Mama would commit suicide in grief. Well, that's what they said but I knew, deep inside here,' she thumped her chest, 'there would be no accident and both would be murdered. So I came back to Australia.'

Rico groaned as he stood, drew his mother up from the chair and wrapped his arms around her. When her head dropped to his shoulder he rocked her gently from side-to-side as the tears flowed again. This time they didn't want to stop, so he let her cry. 'You lived with this monster to save your parents. *Greater love has no man than to…* dear God, Mama, you are a saint.'

They stood for a long time, huddled together until the tears ran dry. Everything inside him hollowed out and left a lump of lead instead. At the same time an incredible warmth flooded inside, at the knowledge of how his mother had given up any chance of happiness for her parent's lives.

'I'm sorry,' Mama said between a sniff and a stutter as she pulled away.

'You have nothing to be sorry for. Let's sit.' He settled her back into a chair, dragged his around to keep close. 'What about this guy? What happened to him?' Ghastly pictures tumbled through Rico's mind as he lifted the photo and studied the man, intrigued. He damn well knew what happened to any person who crossed *the family.*

'He wasn't with me when I was caught. He was at work. They never knew. No-one knew – ever, well, except for him and me.'

'Is he still alive?'

Mama smiled. 'Yes.'

The intrigue grew. 'How do you know?'

'I write to him every year. He writes back.'

'Surely not to the house.' His father opened all the mail. He would have read all private mail addressed to his mother. She wouldn't have survived.

'I'm not stupid, Rico. Of course not. I give him Gina's address. She understands, knows what Matteo is like. Her husband was the same but lucky for her, he died. I wasn't so lucky – until now. Now he is back in gaol and is out of my life. At last I am free or will be when the divorce is granted.'

'Tell me more about him.' Rico ran his finger over the man. 'Does he still wait for you or did he give up and find another love?'

'He married. Had two sons and a daughter with his wife but he's now a widower.'

'What's his name?'

Silence. Rico glanced at his mother. Her eyes were shut. The hint of a smile turned the corners of her mouth upwards. 'Joseph.'

'Huh? My middle name.'

'Yes, because he is your father.'

'Huh? Excuse me?' Rico released his hold, shot from the seat, reeled around, leant over the sink with straight arms. Fingers gripped the edge. Disbelief robbed him of breath. He turned back to see a worried frown crease his mother's forehead. 'He's my father? Not Matteo?'

'Yes.' The single word came out in fear.

'Why... how... are you sure? Why didn't I know?'

'Why do you think? To keep you safe. If Matteo knew he would have killed you and me. I could never tell a soul other than Joseph. He knew. Every year on your birthday I sent him a photograph, told how you were, what you were doing. You look like him and have his temperament: kind, loving. Nothing like Matteo.'

'Holy sh...'

'Rico!'

'Sorry, but this is a shock – a huge shock.' He smiled, regained his seat for his legs had lost the ability to hold him upright. 'But at the same time, the relief is profound. To think I don't have the bastard's DNA.'

'Rico! Language.'

'Sorry, but he is a bastard, of the worst kind. There are no decent words to describe him other than an out-and-out bastard.' He slumped forwards, across the table. 'This is so unbelievable. I'm lost for words, don't know what to say.' He gripped his face with both hands, shut his eyes, forced air into his lungs. When his breath evened out, he straightened. 'Are you certain? I mean, how can you be sure?'

'I wasn't pregnant when I left Australia for it was… umm…'

'That time of the month,' Rico finished for her when her cheeks went bright red. It was difficult to prevent a smile at her embarrassment.

'Yes. After four weeks with Joseph, I knew I had conceived for I didn't sleep with Matteo again for two weeks after I'd been caught. He raped me. You could only be Joseph's child and you look like him.'

'I always wondered why my second name was Joseph and not the Italian version of the name. Now I know.' He shook his head in amazement. 'Matteo never suspected?' he added as he looked at Mama again.

'No. He never knew I slept with another man. You think I would be stupid enough to tell him?'

At three loud pounds on the front door, Mama jerked and stared at him with wide eyes.

'You want me to see who's there?' Rico asked.

'No, this is my house.' She rose, shook herself and rubbed a hand down the front of her clothes. 'I'll answer. Might be the police again. Can't be Matteo so there's nothing to worry about.'

Rico was in two minds whether or not to accompany her, but this was one thing she was particular about. Her house. Her responsibility to greet guests. Now he knew why his second name was the anglicised version of Joseph and not,

Guiseppe, like his maternal grandfather. Mama had always said she called him Joseph because he was born in Australia.

At her loud shriek, he ran.

Thirty One

Superintendent Nelson stood in the open doorway, his uniform hat under his elbow, his face grim with lips drawn into a thin line, frown lines between his brow and sadness in his eyes.

'What is it, what's wrong?' Rico asked.

'Matteo,' said his mother at the same time Nelson stepped forward.

'Someone got to your father,' Nelson said.

'Huh? How and he's not my father?'

Nelson scowled. 'What do you mean? I'm talking about Matteo, your father.'

Rico smiled. 'Who, I've just found out, isn't my real father. So whatever you say, I don't give a damn.'

'Oh, well...' Nelson looked flustered. He stepped forward, took the hat out, twisted it around and put it under his other elbow. 'This is a shock.'

'No where near as big a shock as it has been for me. But that aside, you said someone got to him. What happened? I thought he was in a secure hospital cell.'

'He was - is. A police officer turned up. Told the staff he needed a statement about the shot to his knee. The surgeon was about to check on your...err... Matteo so it was decided the officer could act as guard instead of the regular hospital guard. They are privately hired, not prison guards.

The idiot wasn't sure of protocol and left them alone.' His head shook as he shuffled his feet. 'God, now I'm rambling. Anyway, the surgeon did what he had to do and left the officer with Matteo. From the report I received, Matteo was tasered and then shot. Silencer, for no-one heard a gunshot.'

'Bloody hell, is he dead?' Rico grubbed a hand through his hair. Scrambled thoughts went through his mind. This was everything he wanted yet at the same time he had to see the old bastard go through a trial, suffer the indignity, get sent to prison for life.

'Not quite. It appears a jacketed hollow point was fired. As you know, Rico, they expand and create a large wound channel in soft tissue. It made a mess. Your… umm… Matteo isn't expected to live. I've come to offer you a ride to say your goodbyes.'

'Not likely.' Rico stared at his mother after her vehement outburst. 'Good riddance,' she added with a fierce face. 'Glad he's received some of his own medicine. I hope he dies in agony.'

'Mama.'

She turned to him. 'What? Tell me you don't feel the same.'

'Well, yes. I guess I'm more surprised at you, my forever peace-making mama who never raises her voice or says anything bad about a person.' He grinned. 'I'm proud of you for making a stand. So, you don't want to see him, say goodbye and good riddance?'

'No. I have no wish to ever lay eyes on him again. Even dead. And I won't organise or attend a funeral for him. In fact, make sure they burn his body for that's what he deserves – to burn in hell.'

Rico glanced at Nelson, whose eyes had gone round with shock. 'Not much I can add. But. Hang on a second, I might come.'

'Rico, no,' said Mama with a firm grip on his arm.

'I thought of a way to add a bit more misery to the bastard. Give me a second.' He raced back to the kitchen, picked up the photo. Man, he would enjoy this. When he returned to Mama, he showed her the photo and grinned. Mama smiled and nodded.

'Okay, let's go. I hope we make it in time,' he said to Nelson after he placed a peck on Mama's cheek and pocketed the photo.

'What's the photo of?' Nelson asked as they sped south, the police siren clearing the way whenever the route became clogged. It was no more than a ten kilometre journey but heavy Sydney traffic never made a short distance short in time.

'I'll show you when we get there. How sure are you he won't make it?'

'Very sure. Too much tissue damage to repair. Liver was hit and a lung as the bullet passed through. Gut contents leaked into the cavities. Officer knew where to aim. I'll be surprised if he's still alive when we get there,' said Nelson as they rounded a corner. The speed increased, siren gave a

346

blast, traffic slowed and parted to give them a clear passage.

'Do you know who shot him?' Rico asked as they shot through red lights at another intersection.

'We do. Topped himself in the carpark.'

'What? Why?'

'Hospital guards chased him down.'

'Who was it?'

'The officer Matteo shot when he escaped.'

'Do you have a name?'

'Phil Roberts. His name is on the computer files I spent most of the night reading. Seems he was in debt for quite a large gambling loss. Took us a while to figure it out but we're certain he was the one who organised the escape. His gun was used to kill the other officer. We couldn't figure out how one officer was shot miles before the other. At the time, Roberts made up some story which we believed. Said it was outsiders who forced him to drive to where we found the prison van. Said he was tasered and shot by a third party. We now believe it was Matteo who downed Roberts. What happened today must be payback for Matteo was also tasered first. In the face from close range. The barbs tore his skin. Roberts must have organised the escape with the idea he would be forgiven the debt.'

'Instead he was shot to make sure he didn't talk,' Rico finished for Nelson. 'It doesn't surprise me. Dead men can't talk and the bastard would make sure there was no chance Roberts could be broken while he was questioned. Guess my… hell, I don't know what to call him now, other than the bastard. It's obvious he didn't check the man was dead.'

'Maybe he was too keen to get away.'

'More than likely. Self-preservation would have been strong as would zero empathy for anyone other than himself. About time someone stood up to him.'

'You have.'

'Would have done it five years ago if I hadn't stuffed up with Amanda.'

'Why didn't you while you were serving time?'

'You have to be kidding if you think he wouldn't have got to me in prison. Hell, half the inmates have some sort of connection to him. I wouldn't have lasted more than twenty-four hours. Plus, I didn't know if he had access to Amanda. Couldn't take the chance. She has been the major victim in all of this.'

'You're probably right. Do you know where she is?'

'No. She was in Perth. Saw her briefly. Zappacosta was sent to eliminate her. I set the local police onto him. Got him arrested. The lawyer, James Ward, assures me she is safe. It's all I care about. Amanda and Mama.'

'Not your sisters?'

'Not as much. By the way, what happened with Maria?'

'She has a court hearing later today. I've recommended she be released. With her husband unlikely to see freedom for many years, she's the sole carer for two youngsters. There might be a good behaviour bond attached. Where are her kids? I didn't notice them at your place.'

'At their cousins. Where they can play with kids their own age. My other sister came this morning to collect them. Took them to her home. Easier for them if they have someone they know to play with.'

They pulled to a halt at the prison barrier. Nelson flashed his I.D. The barrier lifted. To get in, their bodies were scanned with more thoroughness than Rico had ever experienced before. Pockets were emptied and turned inside out. Two sniffer dogs sniffed, turned away uninterested. Two armed guards led them through the security gates. Amusement at the over-the-top measures caused the corners of Rico's mouth to quiver. It was apparent harsh words had been rumbled about the lack of diligence that had resulted in this emergency.

Flanked by the two officious guards, Rico and Nelson were shoulder-to-shoulder as they strode along a passage with individual cell doors making it look more like a prison than a hospital ward. They drew to a sudden stop at an open door.

'In here.' One guard stood next to the open door and indicated with an open arm. Nelson stood back to let Rico in first. The guards remained at attention in the doorway.

There was blood everywhere. A spray up the wall behind the bedhead of a hospital gurney, on the sheets and drips on the floor. There had been no attempt to clean it away. A pallid face was almost hidden by an oxygen mask. Flaccid naked flesh peaked from swathes of bandages, pressure packs and tape. Eyes were shut. Regular beeps came from a raft of machinery with tubes going and coming every-which-way. One tube gurgled blood from the chest cavity, which rose and fell with each rush of oxygen. A male nurse, or was it a doctor, stood by the bed, his eyes on the monitor. It was hard to tell which he was for he wore scrubs and had a stethoscope around his neck. Not that it mattered.

Rico moved closer, peered at the face which was almost the same colour as the sheet tucked under the armpits. It was obvious the bastard had lost a lot of blood.

'How is he?' Rico asked.

The medico glanced his way. 'Not good. Fading fast.'

'Is he awake? Can he be roused?'

'You could try.'

Even though the thought of touching the evil man sent a shiver of distaste through his gut, Rico leant over and shook a pale arm.

Matteo groaned. His eyelids flickered.

'Old man.' Rico nudged him again.

'Ugh,' came from the mask. It was obvious an effort but the eyes opened. Eyeballs seemed to roll as though they sought a way to focus. They stilled and stared: not at Rico but into him. Even close to death, hatred spilled from the old bastard. 'Save me,

Son.' The mumbled plea through the mask was distinct enough to be heard.

Unable to believe the nerve of the bastard, Rico leant over. 'I'm not your son, old man.' He withdrew the photograph, held it front of still staring eyes, 'See this? Do you recognise the man?'

The eyes widened a fraction. It seemed impossible but Rico was certain more blood drained from the already ghost-like face. 'You do know who he is, don't you?' Rico leant closer, almost nose to nose. 'My father. Not you. You cheated on Mama. You have always cheated on her. Don't think I never knew. Well, guess what you slimy old bastard? She repaid you and cheated on you. I am the result. This man's son. Not your son. Never your son. I gave up believing in God years ago but right now I thank the good Lord there is none of your blood in my body, not even a single gene belongs to you. I come from goodness, not the barbarity and evil of your genes. Go rot in hell. And guess what, you old bastard, you shot an innocent man. Luke Bianchi told you the truth. He wasn't the man who snitched to the police.'

He sprang back when the bastard roared and flailed his hands up in an attempt to grab the photo. Blood oozed from the mouth, dribbled down the crease. Matteo flopped back on the pillow. His eyes shivered shut. Hard, stuttered breaths misted on the mask, coated it in pink specks.

'Move back.' The medico shoved Rico out of the way and busied himself with checks on a pulse, a dab at the blood, a hand on the brow, a quick glance at the monitor where the beeps had become less insistent. Green lines wavered, slowed, quickened, jerked and then flat-lined. A rasp-like groan was followed by a huff.

Silence descended. The only sound in the room was a continuous hum of a machine no longer able to beep.

When there was no doubt, Rico turned and walked away. The further he went, the wider his grin, the lighter the weight that had pressed down on him all of his life.